# The Perception of Gabriella

Jennifer Walters

This book is dedicated to my best friend
And childhood cancer survivor of ASPS,
Raquel.
Your positive attitude and love for life
Continues to inspire me.

# Acknowledgements

I got the idea to write this novel from my best friend, Raquel. She spent many hours telling me about her story surviving cancer at the tender age of ten.

I followed the story of a good friend of mine whose son, Zeke, is currently fighting Embroynal Rhabdomyosarcoma of the prostate/bladder at just three years old. With his ongoing battle, I have decided to donate 25% of the proceeds of this book to help pay for his medical costs and travel expenses.

This story is fiction and the names, characters, places, and incidents are the product of my imagination or are used fictitiously. Any resemblance to actual events, locations, or people that are living or dead, are coincidental.

I want to thank my friends and family, along with my amazing editor, Shirley Fedorak, and my proofreader, Allison Goddard, for all their hard work on my novel. I'd also like to thank my accountability buddy, Shama Jawaid. She helped to keep me on task and to stay focused.

I want to thank my team of amazing beta readers, The Perception of Gabriella Launch Team. Thank you for all your hard work and dedication, helping me to perfect this novel. You are such a talented group of amazing ladies.

Also, I'd like to thank my husband, Owen, and two daughters, Sidney and Alexis. I love you so much and I'm so blessed to have you all in my life.

# Contents

# I NEVER

"It's my turn to pick the movie."

Phillip poured the bag of popcorn into a big plastic bowl. "No, you picked Pretty Woman last Thursday."

I covered my lap with the purple and gold afghan my mother crocheted for me a few years back.

"Oh, no, you picked Star Wars, remember?"

"Fine, you win. What chick flick are we watching tonight?"

He put a pillow on my lap and placed the popcorn on top of it. "Something Borrowed."

"Definitely a chick flick."

"Oh, come on, I know you secretly love them. You say you don't, but I see those tears in your eyes every time," I said, squeezing his cheeks and scrunching his face together.

He pulled his head away. "Don't touch the face." He put his hand underneath his chin and batted his eyelashes.

I took the pillow out from behind my back and hit him upside the head with it. He pulled the pillow away from me, his eyes wide and mouth open.

"Oh, it's on."

He grabbed a handful of popcorn as he jumped up off the couch and began throwing it at me.

I grabbed the whole bowl and held it up in the air.

"Oh, you wouldn't dare. That's the last bag of popcorn. Would you really waste it on me?"

I looked at the bowl. Would it be worth it?

Before I could decide, he snatched the bowl from me and tipped it right over my head. I sat there, staring at him in surprise.

"I can't believe you just did that."

He laughed. "I can't believe you hesitated." He reached on top of my head, pulled off a couple pieces of popcorn and put it right in his mouth. "What a waste. It's delicious."

"Oh, no, you didn't." I jumped on top of him and tackled him to the couch. His soft, rustic brown eyes stared back at me with defiance and determination glowing in them.

Phillip and I met two years ago working at the crisis shelter for abused and neglected children. It is safe place where children are placed when they are taken from their homes due to safety concerns. They stay there until it's safe to go home or they are placed in the foster care system if they don't have any stable relatives.

After Phillip finished the electrical program at Hibbing Community College, he got a job working for the mines, but he still worked at the shelter once a week. He couldn't handle watching children come into the shelter after being subjected to such terrible abuse, but he felt it was his duty to be there for them. We both saw and heard things we didn't want to believe happened to children every day.

The pay wasn't spectacular, and the chaos was not easy to succumb to, but I felt like I could help make a difference for these children that were dealt a bad hand in life. Some days it would really wear on me, and Phillip understood it all like no one else could. I loved getting to know the children and be a small light in their darkness. I wanted to make an impact, wanted to do so much more to help them.

Phillip's dad left his family when he was seven, so he understood what it was like to have an absentee father. He considered his father dead, and we bonded over our losses together. We made Caribou Coffee not only our place to study, but also where we would sit for hours and people watch. I told him things I didn't even tell my own mother or my best friends. I'll admit I had a small crush on him at first, but it quickly vanished as he became more like a brother and best friend to me.

No matter where we went, people gravitated toward Phillip. He was outgoing, friendly, and everyone he met wanted to be his friend. He was the life of the party, and when he danced, space formed around him because everyone wanted to see what he would do next. Quite honestly, at times his dancing was embarrassing, but people liked it. They laughed and mimicked his moves.

I don't remember Phillip ever paying for his own drinks. Girls and guys would swoop in, and he would always pull me into the center of the crowd. He knew how to make me laugh and how to make me feel special.

We moved in together as friends soon after we both graduated from college and planned our strategies for finding our perfect mates. Shortly after, he found Lucy. What can I say about Lucy? She's not a bad person; she's just the girl you hope your brother doesn't end up with. She is clingy and jealous of our relationship, but I continue to try to support him because he loves her. I understood what he sees in her. She is beautiful, smart, and charismatic, but bluntly hates me.

I smiled and pushed him onto his side of the couch. "You're a poor loser. It's so my turn."

"Fine, you win."

Placing a pillow in between us, I pointed at the popcorn on the floor. "Now clean it up. You made the mess; you can clean it up, too."

He didn't argue as he pulled the vacuum out of the closet, and I turned the movie on.

"Now what are we going to eat?"

"Pizza." He grabbed his phone while trying to wrap up the vacuum cord with one hand. Before I had a chance to agree, his phone rang.

"Hang on, it's Lucy." He walked into the other room, and I pushed play again, trying not to let her call distract me.

Halfway through the movie he came in with a pizza, fresh out of the oven. "It's not Sammy's, but it'll do."

I paused the movie. "What did Lucy have to say?"

"She was on break. I guess there was a big brawl at the bar. She sounded pretty shook up."

"I thought you didn't wanna see her anymore. I thought you said she was too clingy."

"And I thought you said you were going to stop giving your opinion when it came to her."

Holding the remote out in front of me, I turned the movie back on and crossed my arms. He sat down next to me, but I pretended not to notice him until he put his arm around me and pulled me in. I tried to resist, but it was hard to stay mad at him.

"You never listen to me about her anyway."

"I always listen to you. You just decided it was for the best to quit putting in your two cents about her, remember?"

The concern in his eyes sparkled in the light, reflecting from the forty-seven-inch television that hung on the wall. Our eyes locked, lingering just a little too long before I nodded back at him and pushed play.

As I rested my head on his shoulder, I realized I kind of idolized Rachel from the movie. She pushed her way past her fears to get the man she loved, even though Kate Hudson's stunning character took everything from her. Rachel all but gave everything away to her, then fought to get it all back. The writer, Emily Giffin, was my favorite author. I dreamed one day I'd become a great author like her.

I jumped up at the pounding on my front door.

"Are you expecting Lucy?"

He checked his phone. "Nope, she's still working."

I peeked through the window. "I wonder who it is then."

Matthew.

I opened the door and he wrapped his drunken arms around me. "Hey, sis."

His hair smelled like vomit and stale cigarettes. I steadied him when he lost his balance. As he walked around me, I noticed he wasn't alone.

The good-looking man behind him smiled from one side of his mouth, warming my body all over. There was something so familiar about him.

He stepped inside the house. "Gabriella?"

I scrunched my eyebrows at him, trying to figure out where I knew him from. Few people called me by my full name.

He unbuttoned his jacket, and I couldn't help but imagine what was beneath the layers. If I met him before, surely I'd remember him.

I extended my hand to see if he'd introduce himself. The curiosity was killing me as I wracked my brain for where I'd seen those eyes. He had a strong jawline and tan skin. He reminded me a lot of Phillip. "Do I know you?"

"I can't believe you don't remember me. I'm crushed. Travis."

I scrunched up my eyebrows again and nodded my head. "Travis who?"

"You don't remember me? Travis, as in Casey and Olivia's son."

My mouth dropped open. I turned around and headed into the living room.

I felt someone following behind me. "Did I say something wrong?"

"No. Why are you here?" I couldn't control the anger I felt.

"I came with Matthew, remember?"

I stopped mid-stride and turned around. "Yeah, I remember, but what the hell are you doing here? You may be able to fool everyone else, but you don't fool me."

"I was thirteen years old. What did I do that upset you this much?"

"Listen to me. You may fool my mom and my brother, but I'm not falling for it. You are just as bad as they are."

Matthew stumbled from behind Travis. "Give it a rest, will ya? Travis isn't his parents. He's a good guy, and we need a place to crash." He put his hand on my shoulder and tapped it as he made his way to the couch.

"Well, I've got it from here. I think you should leave now."

Travis shook his head. "You okay if I leave, Matt?"

"No, no, stay. It must be Gabby's time of the month. Travis is staying or I'll be driving home drunk and you can answer to my wife when I get a D-dub."

I let out a moan and turned to Travis, careful not to get lost in his eyes. "Fine, you can sleep on the floor."

"Did I tell you Gabby is single and has no kids? Pretty sure she doesn't have any friends either."

Phillip walked into the living room. "Is everything all right here?"

"You know Gabby, holding a grudge for the rest of her life on someone who has never done a thing to her," Matthew said.

I turned and glared at him.

"Excuse me? Hi, I'm Phillip," Phillip said, stepping forward to shake Travis's hand. "Have we met before?"

"You may have heard of me. My parents are Casey and Olivia. Are you going to hit me?"

Phillip started laughing. "No, I'm not going to hit you. Don't mind Gabby. She seems to have forgotten her manners. You hungry?"

"I'm good, thanks."

"A drink?" He lifted the bottle of Jack Daniels.

"Please. And what did you say your name was?"

Phillip brought the glass of straight whisky to him, and Travis grabbed it with his left hand so he could shake with his right. "Phillip, but you never said yours."

"Travis."

I stood by the counter, my arms crossed.

"And would you like some whisky?"

"I can get it myself," I said, getting a glass and pouring myself a double.

"Thirsty?" Phillip teased.

I rolled my eyes. "Very."

They both watched me as I drank the whole glass and poured another.

"So, when was the last time you saw Gabby?"

I watched him scrunch up his forehead, "I was about thirteen years old, however long ago that was."

"Wow, Gabbs, you can really hold a grudge."

I turned around forcefully, staring out the windows, my hands in fists.

"You married, kids?"

"Nah, you?"

"Nope. I live here with Gabby. She takes a little while to warm up to you, but she's not too bad to live with."

"Not all of us are as lucky as Matt," Travis said.

"Isn't that the truth. I take it Emily ended up leaving for Duluth tonight?"

"Yes, she did."

"She met us for dinner before she took off for Duluth. She said something about the Greysolon Ballroom."

"Yeah, her and Gabby are putting on a charity event for children. It's their second year."

"Okay, she mentioned raising money for North Star Children's Project. I didn't really get a chance to ask her about it because she mentioned it as she was getting ready to head out the door."

"I'll tell you about it. Unless you want to, Gabby."

"It's really none of his business," I said, turning back around.

"It's an organization they created to raise money for the children in need. Mainly for the children in the foster care system. From Duluth all the way to International Falls. They raise money for the shelters, like the one her and I work for."

Travis nodded his head. "I had no idea Gabriella was such a benevolent contributor to such a great cause, and she works in a shelter, huh? A true Mother Theresa."

I stepped closer to him. "You don't need to talk as if I'm not in the room. Why are you still here? Stop acting like you care."

Phillip continued without looking at me once. "The money is raised so they can go on outings while at the shelter or while they are in foster care. It helps so they can go to the movie theater, got to the YMCA, and other fun things."

"Wow, that's quite impressive."

"These children are going through so much. They've been torn away from their families and the chaos that brought them there. The foundation helps to take their mind off what is going on for even just a couple of hours."

"So many of them are abused and neglected, but a rich man like you wouldn't understand that," I said, clenching my teeth.

"Tell me more," he said, standing up and brushing the hair behind my ear, his hand lingering a little too long. I stood there frozen, unable to move. Finally I snapped out of it and continued.

"One time they got Dora the Explorer and Boots to come to Olcott

Park in Virginia and meet with all the children from the shelter. You should have seen the way their faces lit up with joy that day."

Travis stared at me, his head tilted as if seeing right through me to my soul.

"I can't imagine," he said, his cool whisper giving me the chills right down the back of my spine as I tried to steady myself.

"I better go check on Matthew," Phillip said with a grin as he left the kitchen.

Travis put his hand on mine and I felt the current from his touch run throughout my body, leaving me with goosebumps. I moved my hand onto my hip.

"Well, you got my attention, Travis. What do you want from me?"

"You are beautiful when you're mad, you know that?"

"Why do you care?" I asked, looking anywhere but directly at him.

"Is it sold out?"

"What?"

"The fundraiser."

"Probably."

"That's too bad. I'd love to donate, and it's right in my backyard."

"Your backyard?" What was wrong with me? It was almost as if he had me under a spell. I'm stronger than this.

"I'm living in Duluth."

"You can call Emily and find out. I'm sure she would still be open to taking your money anyway."

"When is it?"

I looked at the calendar behind me, even though I knew the date by heart. "Saturday, August Twenty-Second."

"Wow, that's still quite a few months away. Why did she go tonight then?"

I took a step back. Too close. "She's going for the whole weekend. Tonight she's going to listen to a band, and then Saturday and Sunday she's talking to the philanthropists, meeting with the caterers, and finishing up organizing everything before she sends out the official invites for the dinner."

"That sounds like a big job."

"Get to the point, Travis. What do you want from me?"

"Why do you hate me so much?" He took off his jacket and hung it up on the back of the kitchen chair. As he turned around to grab his glass, I took in his tight jeans and perfect, firm butt. I wanted to hate him; I did hate him.

"So, Matt tells me you are going to school for creative writing."

I poured myself a glass of Merlot and tried to appear casual.

"Actually I'm double majoring in social work too."

"That's quite impressive."

"Some people work hard."

Phillip walked back into the kitchen. "I don't think I've seen Matthew this drunk, ever."

"That's what happens when he goes out with someone who only cares about himself," I said.

"Ouch. I didn't feed him the drinks. He did that all on his own," Travis said.

"So, where do you live, Travis?" Phillip asked, sitting across the table from him.

"In Duluth."

"What do you do there?" he asked, raising his eyebrows at me.

"I'm a financial planner. I came up to meet with some clients and figured I'd meet up with Matthew and Emily while I was here. He seems to be doing really well, other than having a little bit too much to drink tonight."

"Yeah, he tends to do that when Emily is gone," Phillip said.

"Why is that?"

"Emily keeps him in check."

"You know I won't bite. You can come sit down, Gabriella," Travis said. For the first time I noticed his prominent dimples and perfect teeth.

The last time I saw him I must have been five. He was quite a bit older than me, and I had the biggest crush on him. He and his dad came boating with my parents and me a lot that summer up in Side Lake where we had a cabin on Big Sturgeon. Our lake was on a chain of lakes, so we could go boating all day and not get bored with seeing the same area. We would park our boats at Bimbo's restaurant right off Side Lake. Despite the name, it was a very family-friendly bar in the shape of an octagon. They were well known for having the best wings around and one-of-a-kind pizza. After my father passed, my mom and Matt spent some time with Travis's family while I was at camp in the summers.

Matt wasn't even born yet when my dad died. I refused to go to the lake without my dad. It hurt too much. My mom respected my decision when I was just a child, and I haven't been up there since. I wanted to, it was just too painful. Too many memories.

"How's your mom?" Travis asked me.

"Fine."

"More than fine. She is still running marathons," Phillip said.

"Still?" Travis asked. "I haven't talked to her in quite a while."

"Let's play a game to lighten the mood a little," Phillip said, grabbing three shot glasses out of the cupboard.

"I'm going to bed," I said.

Phillip ran in front of me, stopping me from leaving the kitchen.

"I'm not in the mood, Phillip."

"Come on, it'll be fun. I'll do the chores for a week if you play."

"Fine, what game?"

"Sit," he said, pulling out a chair from the table.

I did as I was told, arms crossed as I sat down.

"And it involves drinking," he said, putting a shot glass in front of each of us, along with the bottle of Jack.

"What game is this? Do I have a choice?" Travis asked as he locked eyes with me.

"No choice. Have you ever heard of, I Never?"

"Really?" I said. "Aren't we too old for this game?"

"No, you're never too old for this game. Oh, lighten up. I know you are dying to put Travis on the spot."

"This could be fun," I said, staring back at Travis, but to my surprise he didn't look away, as if challenging me.

I found out Travis's mom tried to break my parents apart a few years ago when mom confessed one night after a few drinks. I always thought her relationship with my dad was perfect, and the news was painful. I didn't hold it against her. I knew how much he meant to her and that she didn't want to think about the rough times in their marriage when he was no longer alive. I loved that their love for each other couldn't be broken.

I knew my mom still kept up with Travis and Casey, but I never asked her any questions about them. Olivia was a pretty horrible woman, but of course mom forgave her for trying to ruin her marriage. My mom was the most forgiving person I knew. She believed forgiveness was the key to happiness, and I believed forgiveness was the key to getting walked all over.

Phillip looked at me, then Travis, and laughed. "Okay, I'll start. I never had a crush on anyone in this room."

We all took a drink.

"When did you have a crush on me?" I said to Travis.

"How do you know I didn't have a crush on Phillip?" he said.

I shook my head and rolled my eyes. "I guess that makes a lot of sense now."

"Your turn," Phillip said to me.

"I never was a rich selfish asshole."

No one drank.

"Whatever," I mumbled under my breath. To my surprise, Travis took a shot.

"Okay, I deserve that one. I never thought I'd be so happy to see Travis walk in the door tonight."

We sat in silence until Phillip took a shot. "You need to be honest, Gabby," Phillip said.

"I never was so excited for Travis to leave," I said, taking a shot. It burned my throat and I began to cough. My stomach was on fire and I could feel the acid in my throat. I got up to run to the bathroom, but it was too late. I threw up all over the kitchen floor. I felt Phillip behind me, holding my hair as my dinner splattered all over the floor. I turned around to find Travis was the one holding my hair. It sent chills down my spine. I wanted to yell at him. I turned around and my knees collapsed, sending me falling into his thick arms. I was so dizzy. I tried to stand up, but failed.

"Bring her to her room. Upstairs, second door on the left. I will clean this up," Phillip said.

I tried to fight it and say no, but the room was spinning and I couldn't stand on my own. Travis's strong arms picked me up like a bride being swept away by her groom, and I gave up trying to fight it. He carried me up the stairs and into my bedroom. He carefully laid me down on my bed and took off my socks. He disappeared and came back with a wet washcloth. I was too weak to yell at him to get away, closing my eyes instead as he wiped my face softly. He laid down next to me, rubbing my head.

"I'm so sorry you hate me. I'm not sure what I've done, but I promise to gain your trust." My head felt so good as his fingers ran through my hair so gently. I turned on my side, and he began to rub my back.

"Thank you. If it wasn't for your parents, my dad would still be alive, but I know it's not your fault," I mumbled, forcing myself to get the words out before I passed out.

# MONEY TROUBLES

My alarm went off at six in the morning. I opened my eyes to find myself drooling on his bare chest. I lifted my head and couldn't help but run the back of my hand over his scruffy whiskers after I wiped the drool off my chin and his chest. He looked so perfect as he slept. How did that young boy turn into this strong, handsome man? I wanted to hate him, but the memories from last night made it difficult.

I couldn't help but smile as he stirred and snored loudly. I carefully pulled his arm off of me and got up slowly, careful not to wake him. I stared at his perfect face and strong jawline and then tip-toed to the shower.

The water burned my skin, but felt good. I was embarrassed that I puked all over the kitchen floor and hoped Phillip cleaned it up. I had to steady myself in the shower a few times as the queasiness continued from the night before. What would I say to him? Why would he take care of me after the way I treated him last night?

I turned off the water and grabbed a towel, praying he was still asleep when I walked in. I wrapped the towel around me after I dried myself off. I opened my bedroom door and saw him laying down, his eyes shut. I held my towel with one hand and tried to open the drawer with the other, but it wouldn't budge. I turned around to make sure he was still sleeping and his eyes were still shut. I bent over again, removing my hand and securing my towel between my breasts. I pulled on the drawer as I felt my towel slipping. I tried to catch it, but it continued to fall. I moved my hand quickly, but only caught one side. I turned to look at him; his eyes

13

were open and a grin spread across his face.

"Good morning, Gabriella."

I grabbed the towel and wrapped myself up. Pretty sure my face was as red as the towel that was wrapped around me.

"I can't believe you weren't sleeping."

"I can't believe you are finally talking to me."

I grabbed my clothes and headed back into the bathroom to change. When I went back into my room, he was making my bed.

"I'm sorry for the way I treated you last night," I said, biting my lip.

He shook his head, sitting on the edge of my bed. "I'm sorry for what my parents did to your family. I'm not like them, you know."

"I know. That was obvious last night. I'm very protective of my dad."

"I can imagine," he said, getting up and walking toward me. "I would really like another chance."

"Chance?"

"Yes, go on a date with me tonight."

"A date? You want me to go on a date with you? I just stopped hating you."

"Yes, this is how you can make it up to me, for me holding your hair while you puked."

I laughed. "I'm not interested in a relationship, but I'll go as friends."

"That's a big leap. I'll take what I can get."

He was quite a womanizer.

"I'll pick you up at six."

"Six it is. You better bring my brother home. I'm sure he's awake."

He nodded his head and walked out the door, shutting it behind him. I sprawled out on my bed, staring at the white ceiling. Did that just happen? Am I really going to dinner with him? It felt so good to let go of the anger, even if he was obviously a womanizer.

"Wow, don't you look hot," Phillip said, staring at me as I made my way down the stairs in my tight black dress and bright red lipstick.

"You don't think I'm too fancy for the bar? I really need to do laundry."

He tightened his lips into a thin line. "I just did it yesterday and I didn't see any of your clothes down there."

"Maybe I just wanted to look nice."

"I see. Are you trying to impress me?" He winked and I rolled my eyes at him.

"Your mom called while you were in the shower, by the way."

I slipped into black leather boots my mom got me last Christmas. "What, what did she say?"

"That she wants us to come over for dinner tomorrow. She invited Matt and Emily, too."

I balanced on one foot and nearly fell over. "Emily is in Duluth. Is Matt going?"

"I'm not sure. She didn't say."

"Hmm."

"Am I supposed to be getting ready? Are we going out tonight?"

Before I could answer him, the doorbell rang.

"It's Travis."

I pushed my way past him to get the door.

"I thought you hated Travis."

"I did, but I'm willing to push past my stubbornness and be friends with him."

"Friends, huh? You sure nothing happened between the two of you last night?"

"Nothing happened," I said, opening up the door.

Travis stood there in his black leather jacket and black button-up spread collar shirt. "Hello, beautiful."

I watched as his eyes explored my every curve.

I squirmed under his scrutiny, grabbing my coat off the hook and pushed him out the door.

"Don't have too much fun," Phillip said.

Travis opened up the door for me, and I thanked him. Was he really this genuine?

Dave's Bar and Grill was packed from wall to wall with people. I was a little overdressed, but Travis didn't seem to notice. We sat down at a high table in the bar area. Lucy was by our side within seconds to take our order.

"Gabby, hey, where's Phillip tonight? Who's this?" She extended her hand.

"Travis," he said.

"I'm Lucy."

"Nice to meet you."

I ordered a glass of Moscato, and Travis ordered a whisky and water. Lucy walked away to get our drinks.

A smirk spread across Travis's face.

"What?"

"You don't like whisky?"

"Not after last night," I said, shivering at the thought. "I'm really sorry I judged you last night when you showed up."

"No need to apologize," he said, grabbing my hand on the table.

"Tell me about your job. I know you live in Duluth. What do you do there?" I asked, releasing my hand from his grip.

"I own my own business in Duluth, and I plan on possibly moving to The Cities to expand my company or buying a second home there for when I see clients."

"And what kind of a business is it. You said finance, right?"

"Yes. I'm a financial planner."

"Oh, so I was right. You make the big bucks."

"I do well, I guess."

"You are a good-looking guy and make tons of money, so how is it you don't have a girlfriend?"

He looked down and I could tell something was bothering him. He took his time before answering. "Well, I had a girlfriend for two years. I actually made a trip up here, not only to see clients, but also to get away from her for a couple of days."

"It's that bad?"

"I'm giving her time to move out. We have been on the out for months, but it's been a struggle to get her out. She is horrible with money, and I always had to pay her bills. I can't get her to work, and one day I came home to find her smoking meth in my bedroom, postcoital, with some guy in my bed. I can't believe I didn't see it. How do you not know your girlfriend is on meth?"

"That's horrible," I said, wondering how he could have missed that. Didn't he ever care about her enough to notice?

"She promised it was just a one-time thing and that she was sorry. She said she did it because I was gone too much and she was lonely. The funny thing is she started throwing dishes at my head and I'm the one who caught her in my bed with some druggy."

"Yikes, you just can't make this shit up."

"You're telling me. Now tell me, why are you single?"

I felt butterflies in my stomach. "I just don't have time to meet anyone. I spend most of my time working and trying to help kids. I want to find someone who cares about them as much as I do."

He ran his fingers through the small amount of hair on top of his head. "I don't think there is a man that can compare to your big heart."

"That's why I don't date," I said, laughing.

"You are amazing, you know that?"

"Well, thank you. I used to live in Duluth when I first started college and Matthew actually graduated from Denfield."

"I faintly remember that."

"Yeah, we all moved back up north when Matthew decided to go to school at the community college and mom stopped working for the paper in Duluth. Mom decided to continue making birthday cakes and make it into a business."

"Wow, that's great."

"I want to be an author but I also want to be a social worker for hospice." I grabbed his arm. "It's Matthew. He's here. Let's go sit with him, Travis."

"Let's go." I gave him no choice as I picked up my glass and set it down in front of the stool right next to Matthew at the bar. "Miss me?"

He looked at me and I backed away. His eyes were swollen and red, and a mixture of puke and cigarettes lingered on his breath as he said hello back. He looked quite annoyed with my presence.

17

"So, Mom tried calling you. She wants us to go to her house tomorrow night for dinner. What do you have going on?"

He put his wrist up in the air, pretending to look at his nonexistent watch. He gulped down his drink and slammed the glass on the bar. "I can't tomorrow."

"What's going on with you? Is everything okay?"

"No, not really."

"What is it? You know you can tell me anything. Is it Emily?"

"No...yes."

Travis took the hint and excused himself to go to the bathroom while I patiently waited for Matt to explain.

"I lost my job."

"What? How? What happened?"

"I don't wanna talk about it."

I put my hand on his arm. "Tell me you told Emily."

He glared at me and then sighed. "No, I haven't told her yet. How can I tell her? We're having a baby in a little over a month. It will devastate her."

"You need to tell her. You need to get through this together. That's what marriage is about."

"I'm a loser."

"You aren't a loser, Matt. What happened?"

He rubbed his eyes with the back of his hand. "I had the lowest sales in the area for three months running."

"You need a new job. You don't wanna work for that stupid company anymore anyway. I always thought you were too good for that corporate job. You have a degree; it's time to use it anyway."

"I know, but the money was so good. I can't believe you are here with Travis. I thought you hated him."

"I do, but..."

He looked behind me as Travis sat back down next to me on the bar stool.

"Emily will understand. It'll be okay."

"I got fired three weeks ago."

I was taking a big gulp of my wine and it came spewing out of my nose and mouth. I coughed. "Three weeks? Oh, Matt. Why haven't you told her? Why didn't you tell me sooner?"

"She's going to be so disappointed, and Mom, too."

"Mom is pretty understanding. She'll be there for you."

"I guess. Can you guys possibly give me a ride home? I really need some sleep. I'm exhausted."

I looked at Travis with a hopeful expression on my face.

"I can give you a ride home. It's no problem. Gabby and I haven't even ordered yet, and to tell you the truth, I'm not really hungry anyway," Travis said, holding his breath and stepping away from the foul smell of vomit and cigarettes surrounding Matt.

"Ok, I just need to let Eric know," Matt said. Eric was a good friend of Matt's, but he was a drunk and Matt always got drunk when he was with him. Emily wasn't a fan of his.

He stood up and landed on the floor next to his bar stool.

He started laughing, a creepy fake laugh I had never heard before. Travis pulled him up and helped him walk out the door. He said goodbye to Eric as he stumbled out the door with us. Eric waved and went back to talking with a girl with a low-cut shirt.

I followed them out into the chilly wind and wished I hadn't worn a short dress on a cold night like tonight.

Matt laughed as if reading my mind. "What's up with the tiny dress, Gabbs?"

Travis nudged him, but he didn't seem to notice.

We dropped him off at home, and I thanked Travis over and over again for helping with my brother.

"It's not a problem. Is everything okay with him? He doesn't look so good."

"Yeah, he's just going through a lot right now."

"So, where do you want to go since we missed our dinner? You must be starving. I know I am."

"I thought you weren't hungry."

"That was so Matt wouldn't argue with me driving him home. I know how he gets."

"That was very kind of you. How about my house and we'll just order in? I'm exhausted and not really feeling much like going out again, especially in this tiny dress."

He appraised my curvaceous figure and a hot flash crept up my neck. I stared out the window and wished the blush away.

At home we sat on the couch and shared a bowl of popcorn.

"The last time I tried to eat popcorn with Phillip he ended up dumping it over my head. Actually, that was last night when you and Matt showed up here."

"Really?"

"Yeah. That was quite a night," I said, stepping closer to him.

"Missy called me today."

"Missy?"

"My ex."

"Oh," I said, hoping he didn't catch the jealousy in my voice. "What did she have to say?"

"She took all of her crap out of my house. I'm hoping she didn't take any of my stuff."

I tried to read his expression to see if this was hard for him, but he had a poker face, or I wasn't good at reading him.

"I'm sure it's not easy for you. When are you planning on going back to Duluth?"

"I'm going back tomorrow night, earlier than expected. I need to go see some clients early Monday morning."

He put his hand on mine, his face softening. "I can come back Friday night if you'd like me to. Or you could come visit me."

I took a moment to take in his invitation. "I'd love to see where you live. I bet Phillip would take my shift on Sunday if you really want me to come visit you." I stepped closer, buttoning his top button.

"Are you kidding? There is nothing I'd like more."

Phillip walked in the door, tripping over my shoes in the hallway. "Travis," he said. "Lucy, this is Travis. The guy I've been telling you about."

Lucy forced a smile. "Actually, we met tonight. They came into the bar earlier."

"Oh, that's where you went to dinner. How was it?"

"We didn't end up staying. We decided to come home early and order in," I said. "I was tired."

Phillip took Lucy's hand and pulled her upstairs. "Well, you kids don't stay up too late. Goodnight."

Travis and I exchanged glances.

He threaded his fingers through my long black hair. "Where were we?"

I desired his lips on mine, and I let out a whimper to draw him in.

This made him smile as his warm breath lingered just above my swollen lips, teasing me.

"Hey," I said, frowning at him.

His hand slid down my face as he took control of my jaw with his big, strong hands and pulled me in. His kiss was hard and passionate, wet and full of need. His tongue dipped between the seam of my lips, separating them and my legs at the same time.

Our bodies fell back onto the couch as one. My only thought was why it took me so long to warm up to him. I wondered what my mom would say. I pulled off his shirt, my palms skimming his satin-smooth shoulders.

He stared into my eyes, and I stared right back.

"One second, there is something I need to tell you."

He stared back at me, blankly this time.

"Is everything okay, Gabbs?"

"Yes, I mean, once we go here, there's no turning back to just friends."

Travis raised an eyebrow. "I can't imagine us just being friends."

"Travis, I'm not looking for anything serious."

"I know." He stood up and paced the room, running his fingers nervously through his hair.

I lifted my black dress over my head and he just stared at me. "It's nothing you haven't seen before," I said, thinking about the incident this morning.

21

"Are you going to help me take off my bra or just stand there with your mouth open?" I said, biting on my finger, my arms crossed.

He walked toward me, taking in every inch of my body as he wrapped his hands around my back to unbuckle the clasp. "I'll go slow. I'll be..."

I placed my pointer finger over his mouth. "Stop talking and show me how it's done."

⌒⌒⌒

I opened my eyes to find Travis nowhere around. I slipped on my robe and went downstairs to see if he left. I smiled when I found him in just his underwear in the kitchen, drinking orange juice out of the carton.

"Go get some clothes on. Phillip or Lucy could wake up any minute," I said, whispering.

I tried not to stare at the indents in his lower back, his broad shoulders and bulging muscles as I followed him up the stairs. I gave in and slapped his firm butt, wanting to squeeze it, but I stopped myself.

He groaned and turned around on the stairs to smile at me. I waved him up the stairs, looking over both of my shoulders in case an audience was watching.

He took off running, diving into my bed headfirst.

I shut the door and shook my head.

He motioned for me to come to him.

"I think you need to remove your robe."

I opened it up, my back to him.

He sat up in bed. "Come and remind me how good you are again." I turned my head as I slipped on a shirt, smirking at him.

"You're a tease."

I walked over to the side of the bed with a pouty lip, mocking him.

He grabbed my hand and pulled me onto the bed. For the first time, I noticed his Sport 7000 series yellow-gold iWatch. I pulled on his wrist so I could stare at the watch I'd only seen on the internet and complained about anyone paying a couple thousand dollars for a watch. I was slightly impressed he bought it, slightly annoyed that he was that showy.

"What, do you have to be somewhere?"

"Yes, but no. Is this a 7000?"

He stopped to think. "Yeah, I guess so. What does yes but no mean?"

I ignored his question. "Quite a bit of money to spend on a watch."

"I had no idea you cared so much about a little watch. You have one," he said, pointing to my wrist.

"This is just a normal iWatchwatch, the original, not even waterproof. I saved up for months for this watch."

He stared at me with a confused look on his face. "Here I am half naked, and you want to talk about watches?"

"I'm sorry, I just thought you were different."

"Different? Wait, you no longer want to get to know me better because I own an expensive watch? Sounds a little judgmental, if you ask me." He sat up and grabbed his pants off the floor.

"I'm sorry. I don't mean to judge. I just thought we had more in common than that."

He shook his head. "Let's enjoy this moment before we start talking money, okay? We are both off the clock."

I closed my eyes and felt his hand cupping my chin and then move up the side of my face. My entire body was on fire with each brush of his hands on my skin. I closed my eyes to enjoy it, thinking about last night.

He dropped his pants and pulled me on top of him.

I slipped my hands beneath his back, and my nails dug in while he began kissing my neck.

All I could think about was his stupid watch. I could see it out of the corner of my eye as his fingers cupped my breasts. I jumped up. "I can't. I just can't."

He shook his head and exhaled. "What is it? Are you afraid this is getting too serious?"

I looked at him sideways and he rubbed his thumb over my cheek.

Goosebumps broke out all over my body from his gentle touch.

"I have to work this morning. Let's talk later."

"What time do you work until?"

"Eight."

"Ok. Should I come over then or do you want to go out?"

"Crap, my mom's dinner. I'll call you."

He found his jeans and jumped into them one leg at a time. "You'll call me, huh?"

I forced myself to look away.

He kissed me on the forehead and walked out of my bedroom, then peeked his head back in. "Thank you for the amazing night. It's crazy to think you are no longer that little snot-nosed girl I remember from my childhood. If I leave my watch at home will you see me again?"

I rolled my eyes and threw my pillow at him, but it stopped halfway and fell to the floor. "I'll...call...you."

He laughed, shook his head, and disappeared down the hall.

# A GLIMMER OF HOPE

I made it to the shelter by eight, exhausted from staying up late with Travis. As I walked in the big brown house with two giant windows and a fenced-in playground in the back, I tried to clear my mind of the image of his beautiful, firm body. The office was centered right in the middle of the shelter house. Huge windows covered two sides of walls, so we could see the living room and kitchen from the office, and they could see in, too. The room was barren, only one desk and two chairs, and no computer because we did all the paperwork by hand. The walls were covered in white paint and not a picture covered the wall. Down the hall, the director had a computer and a fax machine, but we didn't. I think they were afraid we'd spend too much time on the computer instead of working.

I entered the office to meet with Denise for a full report of the day.

Denise squinted at me. "How ya doin? You look a little exhausted this morning."

"Oh, do I? I went out to dinner with an old friend from my childhood I haven't seen since I was like five. We had a good time." I was excited to tell someone about my night.

She winked at me. "And how did Phillip feel about that?"

"Stop, we are just friends."

"You aren't going to see this friend again?"

"Well, I didn't say that."

A smile lit up her face. "Mmm hmm. You're right. Sounds like nothing, nothing at all."

I needed to change the subject. "I see Melanie and Ben are back, huh?" I said, waving at them through the glass window, and they waved back. Denise shot me a look to show me she picked up on me changing the subject, but she didn't challenge me.

"Yes, remember how their mom and dad were in a meth explosion a couple months ago and in prison? Well their aunt and uncle took them in and they are now placed here again because their uncle was abusing them. We have three kids here right now. Melanie, Ben, and Bobby."

My stomach churned. "That is so terrible. Those kids have been through so much."

Gloria came in the door and joined us. "Sorry I'm late. What is so terrible?"

Denise repeated the bad news, and Gloria's eyes were big in disbelief.

"That sweet little girl must be Melanie, but where's Ben?"

Gloria was used to working midnight shifts and finally switched over to day shifts within the last week, so she didn't know Ben and Melanie like the rest of us.

"Yes, that's her," Denise said. "I think Ben went back into his room. He was just here. They were taken from Dad and placed in Mom's sister's house when this all happened. It was supposed to be a safe place, but social services found out they were being abused."

"Wow, those poor kids," I said. "They've been here what, like three times now?"

"Four. Oh, you haven't heard the worst of it, Gloria. I was just telling Gabby their aunt's husband was abusing Melanie physically and verbally. Possibly Ben, too. Social services took them from the home and brought them here early this morning."

"You didn't say that exactly, wow," I said, letting out a deep exhale.

"That is so horrible. It pisses me off just thinking about it. Those poor little kids," Gloria said, putting her purse in the closet. "Could things get any worse for them?"

Denise handed me a set of keys and then turned to Gloria. "Just wait until you hear that little Melanie speak. Her beautiful long blonde hair, and those big blue eyes almost bring you to tears, thinking of what she must be going through. Sometimes I hate my job," she sighed and covered her eyes.

I stared at the beautiful little girl through the glass. "Just remember, we are sometimes the only glimmer of hope they have in their lives. We need to be strong for them."

Denise put her hands down and smiled at me. "You know, you are right. I know how much you donate to the shelter with your foundation and it's quite inspiring. It's not like we make a lot of money, but you are always making sure these kids have a good Christmas, Halloween costumes, or even just toys to play with. Maybe one day you will consider stepping into my role so I can retire."

I patted her shoulder as I walked past her. "I definitely don't have the time to run a shelter, and you do such a great job, you can't retire. Sometimes I feel like I could do more. It's not their fault they were dealt a bad hand. I love this place. Don't get me wrong, but when I'm done with college I want to start writing novels and work for hospice."

She took a step in my direction, raising her voice. "I'd hate to see you leave, but I understand you want to go in another direction."

I smiled and nodded. "It won't be for a long time and who knows, I may end up staying one day a week. I don't know how I'd be able to stop helping these children."

She smiled in my direction before heading into her office. Gloria and I made our way into the living room.

Ben was a ball of fire when he came out of his bedroom. He made a huge mess in the living room with all the toys the shelter had to offer. His excitement rubbed off on me as I helped set up the train tracks and turn on Thomas the Tank Engine and a few other trains.

His eyes lit up as the train sped around the track. For just a moment, the stress erased from his face and happiness radiated as he forgot his troubles and just played like a "normal" little boy.

What exactly was normal anyway?

At dinnertime, Melanie was shoving the chicken nuggets in her pockets when she thought I wasn't looking and asking for more. I pretended not to see her, unsure of how to handle it. When we finished dinner, I told the children to put their dishes in the sink. Melanie began grabbing nuggets out of the pan and stuffing as many as she could into her mouth. Bobby quickly finished and went to his bedroom like most teens did when they were here.

I knelt down so I was closer to her height. "Melanie, slow down. You're going to choke."

Gloria came out of the office and handed me a napkin.

Melanie shook her head and tried to run away. I held on to her arms. "Melanie, you need to spit those out. You are going to choke."

She pursed her lips and turned away.

"Melanie, I promise you can eat more if you just spit those out. I won't let you go hungry, I promise." I focused on keeping my voice calm and not yelling at her. I was scared she was going to choke, but didn't want to frighten her.

She leaned over and spit them into my hand as big crocodile tears streamed down her face. "Please don't be mad. I'm sorry, so sorry."

I hugged her. "Hey, hey, it's okay. I'm not mad at you, sweetheart. I was just scared you were going to choke. You can talk to me. I won't let you starve, I promise."

"So sorry," she repeated.

"Now, come sit down next to me in this chair. We can eat together."

Although I don't like to eat kid-friendly food, I knew she would feel much better if I were to eat with her, so I did. She took huge bites and didn't chew enough before swallowing, so I had to keep redirecting her and reassuring her that I wouldn't take away her food until she was done.

"Honey, why did you put chicken nuggets in your pockets? I'd hate for you to have food stuck inside your pockets, yuck."

She shrugged her shoulders and looked away from me.

"I promise you will get plenty of food here, okay?" I couldn't say it enough; she didn't seem to believe me. What has this little girl been through?

Her bottom lip quivered and the tears welled up in her eyes again. She put her fork down on the table and crossed her arms, then bowed her head.

Gloria and I exchanged worried glances as she began to break down.

"How about a bubble bath?" I said, trying to cheer her up in an exciting tone.

Her lip still quivered, but she nodded in agreement. I took her hand and led her to the back bedroom. We picked out pajamas and put them in her room since she came with few clothes.

She snatched the warm pajamas out of my hands and hugged them under her chin. "Elsa!"

"I take it you are a Frozen fan, huh?"

She nodded.

I took her hand and led her down the hall to the bathroom. "Melanie, how old are you?"

She held up all her fingers on one hand and her face lit up.

"Five?"

She nodded, switching from walking to skipping down the hall.

"Slow down. I don't want you to trip."

Once she got into the bath, she couldn't stop talking. A big change from the little girl crying and going mute at the kitchen table. We talked about Frozen, and I found out she loved all the Disney princesses.

"I miss my mommy," she said.

"I know you do, honey. Have you ever been on a vacation before?"

Her eyes lit up. "Like Disney World?"

"Have you been to Disney World?"

"No, but Mommy and Daddy said one day they will bring us."

"Wow, that would be a lot of fun, huh? Well, this is like a vacation; maybe not as good as Disney World though. To be honest, I've always wanted to go to Disney World, but never had the chance. Who is your favorite princess?"

"Elsa."

"I like Elsa, too. My favorite princess is Cinderella. Right now you get to hang out here with all of us and we get to do fun stuff, like color pictures and draw, and sometimes we even get to go swimming. Doesn't that sound like fun?"

"I guess, but I want my mommy and daddy. Why can't they be here, too?"

"Your mommy and daddy are really busy right now and they can't be here, but I know they miss you and your brother very, very much. For now, we will have to settle for playing Barbies, and maybe even going to a movie at the theater. How does that sound?"

The thought of her broken family made my heart hurt.

"I think I'm going to really like it here this time; don't tell Ben," she said in a loud whisper. "He's seven and he says you are going to take us away from Mommy and Daddy, but you're not, are you?"

I felt the blood drain from my face and my hands clammed up. A line of dirt at the water level got my attention. When was the last time these poor kids even got a bath? "Your parents love you very much."

I turned my back to her as I pulled out the chicken nuggets from the pockets of her jeans. I picked up her shirt and found three in there. I felt something mush in my hand and looked down at the sock I was holding, where I found the remains of another one. I threw them in the garbage and covered them with toilet paper while Melanie was lying down in the bath after I washed her hair.

After her bath, Melanie dressed, and I set up the bath for Ben. He left a line of dirt around the bathtub, too. He smelled like urine and stale cigarette smoke, which left me almost gagging. I wasn't sure if he wanted me in there since he was seven, but he told me it was okay as long as he got to have a washcloth over his "thingy." Kids.

After he got out of the bath, I went to check on Melanie in the living room. She was on the floor, cradling a doll in her arms. When she saw me sit down, she climbed on my lap in the big brown rocking chair and snuggled in. I spent the next half-hour running my fingers through her hair and saying a silent prayer for their family.

When we finally put the children to bed, Melanie came out crying for her mom. I laid down in bed with her and sang to her until she finally fell asleep. I knew I was going to be late for my mom's dinner, but I didn't want to leave her.

I kissed my two fingers and placed them on her forehead. "Goodnight, sweetheart. Goodnight," I whispered.

# SCARS

"You had sex with him?"

I couldn't believe how angry he was. "It's none of your business."

"I'm glad to hear you didn't just hop into bed with the first guy to show up at your door." He threw open the refrigerator door and grabbed the milk.

"Travis isn't exactly a stranger. This is my life, not yours. I can sleep with whoever I want."

"Gabbs, he's like, what, ten years older than you?"

"Not even, more like seven or eight, and it's none of your damn business."

"Sorry, but I'm going to call you out when I think you are being an idiot. A couple days ago you couldn't stand the guy."

I looked at him sideways, hoping to burn a hole right through him. "An idiot, huh? I never said that to you about your girlfriend even though that was exactly what I was thinking."

"Ouch."

Hands on my hips, I glared at him. "I'm not a teenager, Phillip, and what I do is my business, not yours."

Phillip shook his head. "I'm sorry. It just seems soon, that's all."

"Well, I really like him, and I'm going to Duluth to stay with him this weekend."

"Is he still in town?"

"No, I ended up having to work late last night so I didn't get to see him before he left."

"Having withdrawals already?"

I turned my back on him, grabbed my running shoes, and quickly tied them up. I needed to get away from him before I said something I didn't mean or he said something he couldn't take back.

"Well, hopefully he didn't give you herpes."

"Seriously, Phillip? We had fun and I told him I wasn't ready for a serious relationship. What, are you jealous? You are my friend, not my boyfriend."

"I'm concerned. What is your mom going to say when she finds out you're seeing Travis?"

I was definitely going to see Travis in Duluth this weekend just to get away from Phillip.

"Just stop talking. We are done having this conversation."

"It's your life. Did you get the message that the dinner is rescheduled because your mom had to make a last-minute cake for a little boy's birthday? But she is planning on rescheduling it for another day when everyone can be there."

"Yeah, I got the message."

"I'm sorry. I'm just worried about you. I know you don't have any trust for men and Travis comes off as being popular with the ladies and you know...saying all the right things. I'm glad you are finally seeing someone. I just don't want a guy like that to scare you away."

"Don't worry so much," I said, turning away.

"I do worry. You've been through a lot. Your dad was murdered, Gabby."

I snapped around. "I don't want to talk about my dad's murder. Just let it go, okay?"

He lowered his head.

"I'm sorry I snapped. Just let me be happy, okay?"

"I do want you to be happy."

"Then take my shift on Sunday so I can go see Travis."

"Fine, well played. How can I say no now?"

My frown was instantly turned upside down when Melanie screamed out my name and came running to me. She wrapped her tiny body around my leg.

"You're here, you're here. I missed you so much."

I dropped to my knees and hugged her. "Why hello, Melanie. I missed you, too. How are you?"

Her big blue eyes glowed with excitement as she jumped up and down. "Will you play dolls with me, Gabby, please?"

I stood up, picking up my purse off the ground. "I have a quick meeting and then I'd love to."

Her lip puffed downward, and she gave me puppy dog eyes. "Okay."

"Don't be sad. I won't be long."

"Promise?"

"Are you kidding me? I can't wait to play with you. I love dolls."

"So, the day was okay. I guess Melanie and Ben's dad was sentenced today for selling meth. He's going to be in jail for a few years," Denise said.

"What about their mom?" I asked.

"She's in jail and then going to treatment. I guess she told the police she knew their dad was making and selling meth with her sister's boyfriend when she wasn't around, but she still didn't stop it. I guess the kids were around when it happened. They don't really tell us anything, so what we hear is just secondhand," she said, while filling out some more paperwork.

"So where do they go now?"

"Doesn't sound like they have much family, so I'm not sure who will be taking them in. Those poor kids. Who knows how long it will be."

"That's so terrible," I said, grabbing the shelter keys from the closet. "I'm not sure if it's better that the kids go with their parents or not."

I watched Melanie through the glass window as she combed Malibu Barbie's hair.

She caught my glance and waved at me. I waved back.

"That's for social services to figure out."

Gloria tossed her pen on the desk and shook her head. "We all knew this was going to happen, but those poor kids. Social services better not put them back with that aunt and uncle after what they did to them."

"I can't imagine they would place them with the aunt and uncle again," Denise said. "They have the best interest of the children in mind."

"I just wanna take them home," I whispered.

"They will probably be placed in the foster care system. Right now there aren't many openings, so they will be here until they find them a place to live," Denise said.

"How long can they stay here?" I asked.

"As long as we can keep them. We will file an extended emergency order if needed."

"Is there anything we can do?"

"You can keep doing what you are doing and be there for those kids. This is going to be the hardest time in their life, and they will never forget us; hopefully it's in a good way." Denise grinned. "Or you can take them home."

"Is that really something we can do? Be their foster parents, that easy?"

Denise looked up at me with a shocked expression. "Yes, you can really do that. Gabby, if you are seriously interested, give them a call. With kids in this kind of situation, I always worry where they will end up. Just make sure you think about it. It isn't as easy as it sounds. It's a big decision to make."

I nodded my head.

"You can always call social services and find out what the process is. I know it can be a lot."

I nodded, crossing my arms as I watched Ben come into the living room and sit in the chair, a box of Legos on his lap. He looked so sad, so broken. I just wanted to take all of his pain away.

"We have two new teenagers today. One is a sixteen-year-old boy, the other, a fifteen-year-old girl. We need to make sure we know where they are at all times, because we know what can happen when teenagers are left unsupervised with raging hormones."

I nodded.

"You are both familiar with the sixteen-year-old boy, John. He comes in at least twice a year. His father tends to get physical a couple times a year and John takes off, the cops are called, and his dad insists he comes to the shelter as a runaway. The girl was brought in from the hospital. She was under suicide watch for taking some pills and calling the helpline."

"Did she get her stomach pumped?" I said.

"No, she threatened to take them, but she didn't. She admitted to being molested by her father growing up. She's really a sweet girl, just lost."

"Sad. It's a cruel world," Gloria said.

"On the flip side, if they do their chores and earn enough points, one of you can take the older ones to a movie. We have a gift card to the movie theater."

"That would be nice," I said.

"I'll take them to a movie, if it's okay with you, Gabby."

"Yeah, no problem. I wouldn't mind spending the day with Melanie and Ben."

"Great, I'll go talk to them."

I followed Gloria out of the room and heard Melanie giggling. I turned the corner to find her hanging upside down on the couch, her head nearly touching the ground.

"Why are you upside down, Gabby?"

She giggled and her face turned red. "Quit walking on the ceiling."

"Be careful, all the blood is rushing to your head, you silly girl." I laughed and helped her back on the couch.

She giggled and tried to tickle me. "No, you're silly."

I tapped her belly with my pointer finger. "No, you're silly."

Ben jumped on the couch and yelled, "What about me?"

"I could never forget about you, Ben. Come here."

Instead of hugging me like I expected him to, he started jumping on the couch, and sticking his tongue out at me. "No, I don't wanna. Come make me."

I pointed to the floor. "Ben, stop jumping on the couch, before you get hurt."

He shook his head and jumped harder and higher. "No."

I stood up to guide him to the floor, but it was too late and he flew off, landing face down into the carpet. His nose began to bleed profusely, leaving him in tears.

"Come and sit at the kitchen table. I'll get you a towel. Pinch your nose," I directed.

He pinched his nose and walked into the kitchen, leaving a trail of blood from the couch to the chair he sat down at. I had a feeling I would be scrubbing the carpet later, but I didn't care as long as he was okay.

Melanie was crying as she followed us into the kitchen. "No, Ben, no!" Her crying became more hysterical.

Gloria wrapped her up in a big hug. "Melanie, Melanie, calm down."

She was breathing hard, unable to catch her breath. She fell to her knees and cried into Gloria's lap.

Gloria shot me a nervous look as she patted Melanie's back.

"It's going to be okay. He had an accident," Gloria said.

I put on a pair of rubber gloves and found a towel in the kitchen drawer. "Here, hold this on your nose and squeeze, Ben. Don't tilt your head back. Just hold this tight, okay?"

He nodded at me, tears streaming down his face and mixing with the blood.

"It's going to be okay, Ben. I'll be right back. I'm going to get a washcloth to clean your face, okay?"

He nodded back, his big eyes following me.

Gloria escorted Melanie back into the living room, holding on to her waist so she wouldn't step in the blood as she walked.

"It's just a little nose bleed, okay? Ben is going to be fine."

"She's just upset because the last time my uncle hit me, he broke my nose," Ben said.

I couldn't breathe at the image in my head of someone hitting the kids. I knew I needed to report this as soon as everything settled down. These poor kids. I couldn't imagine their life and what they must be going through.

"Don't worry, I'm tough," he said. "It didn't hurt too bad."

After his nose stopped bleeding, I gave him a bath. This time I noticed scars on his body as he climbed in. I silently scolded myself for not seeing them before. The bathroom lighting was dark, but that was no excuse. I was probably too busy thinking about what I was going to do when I got home, or how many miles I needed to run the next day. How did I miss this?

I pointed to a small scar on his shoulder. "Ouch, what happened there?"

"Oh, that. I wasn't listening to Uncle Frank when he told me to stop teasing Melanie, so he stopped me with his cigarette."

"And that one?" I pointed to a long scar on his belly, not sure how to prepare for his answer.

"Uncle Frank and Dad were cutting up fish and I was in the garage after they told me I couldn't go in there, and Uncle Frank tried to push me outta there, but pushed me with his hand that had the knife. He didn't mean to. It was an accident."

He looked down at the bath water and frowned. "I'm tough."

"Do they still hurt?"

He looked up at me with his big eyes. "It's my fault. I'm a screw up."

I picked my words carefully before I said anything. "It's not your fault, Ben. None of this is your fault. You know that, right?"

He tilted his head and crossed his arms, his expression distant and shut down.

I sprayed pink shampoo into my hands and rubbed them together, lathering it into his hair. My whole body felt tingly as I imagined a man putting out his cigarette into this small child's arm. I got the chills, my body feeling weak at the thought. I wiped away the sweat dripping from my forehead with the back of my hand.

My stomach churned as my fingers brushed over a big knob on the top of his head. "What happened here, Ben? You really got quite a knob."

He stared blankly at me, frozen. No direct eye contact as he hesitated before answering. "That's from when I stopped him from hurting Melanie."

Acid rose in my stomach. I knew what was to come.

I used a cup to wash the shampoo out of his hair. "How did he hurt Melanie, buddy?"

"Promise you won't tell?"

I avoided making a promise I couldn't keep. "I am here to help."

He stared deep into my eyes, and I could tell that was not the answer he wanted to hear.

"Never mind, it's none of your business. Stop asking me questions. I wanna go home. I wanna go home!"

I stood up and back away from the bathtub, my hands held up in surrender. "I won't ask any more questions, I promise. Okay? I'm sorry I upset you. You don't have to tell me anything you don't want to."

He wiped his tears and put his head under the water. I took a step forward to make sure he was okay. He was under there for too long, and just as I was getting ready to pull him up, he sat up and splashed me.

"Hey, you scared me."

"I wanna get out. I wanna get out now."

I smiled warmly and held up a towel, ready to wrap it around him. "No problem, buddy."

"Don't touch me! I can do it myself."

"Okay, buddy, I'll be right outside the bathroom door if you need me. Your pajamas are right here by the sink, okay?"

He didn't acknowledge my words at all. I turned around and stepped out the door. I leaned my back against it and silently scolded myself for messing up the trust I built with him.

# IF IT'S MEANT TO BE, IT'LL BE

"A brother and sister, huh?" Emily said early Thursday morning. "Yeah, I think I'm ready. How did you and Matt know you were ready to become parents?"

"I dunno. I think the idea of trying to make a baby was exciting, then the reality of actually being a parent sinks in when you find out it's for sure. It's exciting and terrifying. I keep thinking, what if I'm a terrible mother, or what if my baby cries every time I hold it? Should I nurse, and am I a bad mother if I don't? Should I find out what the sex is or is that bad luck? Should I have my shower before the baby is born or after? Who should be the godparents? Uh, I have so many questions and I haven't even had the baby yet."

"Oh, Em, you are going to be a great mama. Heck, probably the best mother I know."

"Well thank you, Gabby. Luckily I have a lot of help and support, except that brother of yours. I think he's getting nervous about the baby being born and he's pulling away."

"I'm sure he's just having new dad jitters. Maybe he has some other things going on."

"I'm sure you're right. Well, if you foster older kids and decide to adopt them, maybe you can give me some pointers as this baby grows up," she said, rubbing her expanding belly.

"I'm focusing on foster care right now, don't get me more nervous. Is it horrible that I want to do this with Phillip? I mean, he's my best friend. I just worry what Travis is going to say."

"It may be hard for him to hear at first, but he'll understand. If he doesn't, then you don't need him in your life, right?"

"Yeah, that's true."

"Do you have to work today?"

"No, I don't work again until tomorrow afternoon, so I think I'll call social services and find out what my options are."

"Wow, that's quick. Are you sure this is what you want to do? You don't think you wanna give it a little more time?"

"I'm ready, Em."

"Okay, just making sure. Please, if there is anything I can do to help, you know I'm always here."

"Thanks, Emily. I don't mean to be snappy. I just know this is what I need to do."

That was putting it mildly. I knew what it was like to grow up without a parent, and I still had a mom who was amazing. I couldn't let these kids get thrown into another foster home and have them come back to the shelter abused again. Enough was enough.

"Everything will work out. You're doing the right thing. You know it's not going to be easy, but it never is. Well, I better go. Your brother and I are meeting for lunch. There is something going on with him and I am going to find out before this baby is born."

I said goodbye and shook my head at my brother for not telling her yet.

I spent the rest of the day cleaning. Travis called to tell me he missed me and that he had a surprise for me at his house. He said he was busy in Minneapolis all week meeting clients and looking at houses, but he promised he would be back in Duluth tomorrow before I got to his house.

⤫

"How was your day?" Phillip said as I walked in the door.

"Well, I talked to a social worker today about adopting Melanie and Ben."

He took the grocery bags from me. "You want to foster them? Wow, that was quick. What did they say?"

"They asked me if the kids were Native American and told me if they don't have any other relatives willing to take them, I had a good chance since I am a caretaker for them at the shelter. They told me that what I was doing was admirable and that there just weren't enough foster homes for these children. They asked me if I had extra space in my house and I said yes. They asked if I had support and I told them our long line of support."

"Are you sure this is what you want to do?"

"I was hoping you'd like to help me with them."

"Maybe, I haven't even met them yet. Are they good kids? I don't even know."

"Yes, they're good kids. I wouldn't ask you to do this unless I thought you'd like them," I said, sarcastically.

"Can you give me some time to think about this and meet them first? Being a foster parent isn't something I can just decide on a whim."

"I understand. I guess I'm just really excited about this."

"I get that, but this is the first I've heard of them," he said, placing his hands on the table and leaning over it, in deep thought.

"I'm all in and if you decide to take this on with me, it would make me feel much better."

"Fine, if you feel like this is what you need to do, I'll do it."

"Seriously? You don't need time to think about it after all?"

"If it's meant to be, it'll be."

"Well, she told me to take some time to think about it and if we decide to go ahead with this, I need to fill out the online application. They would also need to conduct a background check, of course, and that we had a huge packet to fill out before it could be official. Then, she said, if everything is cleared, they would come to our house and make sure the living environment is up to code and make sure we are licensable."

Phillip looked a little pale. "Wow, that sounds like a lot of steps," he said, wiping his brow.

"She assured me the process was pretty painless and that she would look into the children I inquired about. She wants me to take another day or two to make sure to discuss it with friends and family, and with you. I already filled out the application and plan on filling out the packet tonight."

"I think that's a good idea. Once we take them in, we can't change our minds."

"What do you mean?"

Phillip put a hand on my shoulder. "This isn't going to be easy. They have been hurt, really hurt."

I blinked and shook my head. "I know." I leaned my head on his shoulder. "I'm sorry. I just can't watch them get hurt anymore."

"I know, but you need to remember that social services won't just let them back with the terrible uncle again. There are going to be so many children that come through the shelter, and we can't take them all in."

"We can't?"

Phillip laughed. "I wish we could."

"I know. Me, too."

I kissed him on the cheek out of excitement, and he turned and stared at me, his eyebrows wrinkled up.

"What was that for?" he said. "It's this father role that has you hot and heavy," he teased.

I slapped him on the shoulder, and he winced in pain.

"Oh, stop. I didn't hit you that hard." I got up and went to my bedroom to call Travis.

We talked on the phone for close to two hours that night. He told me how much he missed me and how he hated that we lived so far apart. He told me he was very productive in The Cities this week, and he was leaning toward joining a big company in downtown Minneapolis instead of working for himself, but he still hadn't decided for sure yet.

"Would you ever move?"

I thought about Melanie and Ben. "I'm not sure, maybe someday."

"Someday, huh?"

"I'm not planning on moving in with you. You know I'm not ready for anything serious."

"I know," he said.

"The truth is I'm thinking about becoming a foster parent."

Travis chuckled. "You are really selfless, you know that? I love that about you."

Love?

"Well, it's not like you are planning on doing it tomorrow."

"Well, actually I am. Not tomorrow, but...you see, there is a brother and sister at the shelter right now and--"

"Right now? You want to do this right now?"

"Well, not right now right now, but sooner than later."

"Gabby, I wanted to wait, but I was really hoping you'd consider moving in with me. I know you may think it is too soon, but you and Phillip do it and I know we can make it wor--"

"You want me to move in with you? You aren't listening to me. I'm not ready for a serious relationship. I thought I was clear."

"Don't get all nervous. Just promise you'll wait to make this call until we talk. Gabby, please, for me."

I sat there, frozen, unable to talk.

"Gabby, please, answer me."

"Okay, I promise."

∽

On Friday night, I drove to Duluth to meet Travis. I was so excited, I could hardly believe it as I spent an hour getting ready. At the same time, I was trying so hard to put my feelings aside because I wanted to be a foster parent more than anything for Ben and Melanie. I knew I needed to let it go until the conversation came up.

I walked into Red Lobster in Canal Park and there he was, sitting at the table right next to the bar. He stood up when he saw me come in and pulled out my chair for me. Our eyes locked.

I pulled off my jacket and hung it over the chair.

"You look amazing," he said.

I sat down and sipped the glass of red wine in front of me.

"How was the drive down?"

His confidence made me relax a bit. "It wasn't too bad. The hill on the way here was pretty slick though."

"Maybe you need new tires."

I grinned. "Or four-wheel drive."

He nodded. "Do you like lobster?"

"I love lobster."

I looked for menus on the table. "Where are the menus?"

He placed his hand on mine. "I already ordered for us."

Red flag.

"What did you order?"

"The Ultimate Feast. It is a wide variety of their best seafood. I figured you'd like something on the plate."

"You could have waited for me."

Travis shrugged. "I thought I'd order before the dinner rush."

The restaurant was quickly filling up. Yes, definitely a kind gesture.

"Well, thank you. How was The Cities?"

"It went really well. I'm definitely buying a place down there. I haven't decided if I'm going to keep my home in Duluth and commute."

"So you may sell your company in Duluth and work for that company?"

"I'm not sure. I may just expand my company to Minneapolis and St. Paul."

"Wow, that sounds risky."

"Risky? Risky would be you taking a leap with me."

I kept a deadpan face. "A leap, huh? What if you're actually a serial killer? You totally fit the stereotype for a serial killer. Has anyone ever told you that you resemble Ted Bundy?"

Travis raised an eyebrow. "Ted Bundy, huh? He may have been a heartless, evil sociopath, but he was handsome and charismatic."

I laughed and threw my napkin at him. "You're right. That's how he lured in his victims. You're a horrible person, and I don't think taking a leap is the best decision for me."

He grunted, and his eyes twinkled. "Me? You're the one eating dinner with Ted Bundy."

"I guess you have a point there."

"Why do you always throw things at me? First the pillow, now your napkin. What if you get mad at me in the kitchen? Will it be a knife and dishes if there is nothing else around?"

"It's bound to happen eventually. It happened with your last girlfriend, right?"

He laughed. "Eventually, huh? Sounds like you are making plans for the future for us."

"You never know."

He nodded his head. "I love to see you opening up."

I shook my head. "Maybe I'm afraid I'm going to be your next victim."

He stared at my chest and then his eyes slowly scrolled up to my eyes. "I hope so."

I stared down at my drink, trying to act as though I didn't hear him coming on to me.

The waitress brought us our food, and although the platter of food was huge, I ate every bite. The lobster, dipped in butter, had me moaning quietly at each bite. Travis made fun of me by moaning louder and I kicked him under the table.

He replied, "I can't help myself. We have to go to Joe's Crab Shack sometime if you think Red Lobster is good. Have you ever been there?"

"No."

"You'd be amazed. Do you like to travel?"

I took my time chewing. "I love to travel. I just never make the time."

I went with Emily to Florida a couple years ago. Emily used to live in Florida, but her mom was an alcoholic, so she moved to Minnesota as soon as she graduated from college. Although her mom was still an alcoholic, she still liked to keep in touch and visit her once every year or two, and lucky for me, Matthew couldn't get the time off of work, so I got to go with her. Florida was the only state I'd ever been to other than Minnesota. The bright sun, rain showers, and warm weather had me dreaming of another vacation.

"Well, you should definitely travel more. It's always an adventure."

"Are you planning on going anywhere soon?" I asked, eating my last bite of shrimp, as I scanned the room for our waitress to get me another drink.

"Yeah, a work trip, and I'd like to go to Seattle next year."

"I've always wanted to run the Rock 'n' Roll Marathon in Seattle."

"Then you should come."

"Maybe I will."

He smiled, reached across the table, and grabbed my hand in his. His thumb caressed my hand and I felt mine sweating inside his, but I liked it. He was grabbing my heart right out of my chest, and I knew I was falling for him no matter how hard I fought it.

We lingered at Red Lobster, lost in conversation, not returning to his house until close to midnight. The three-story house had the look of a castle from what I could see in the dark. It was as if we were lost in the shadow of the enormous home.

We walked up the stairs and the light outside turned on, putting a spotlight on us and revealing that the house was made of red brick and huge white support pillars that were about two stories high with what looked like Roman Doric capitals, but it was hard to tell with how dark it was and how high they were.

Travis opened up the front door and let me go in first. The soaring ceilings and walls of windows made it very hard for me to hide my awe. "This is a beautiful place. I'm sure it won't be hard to sell."

"Yeah, selling it isn't the problem. It's in a great location overlooking Lake Superior, but you can't see that in the dark."

I was pretty sure that was not the only reason it would sell so easily. The vast foyer showcased a wooden staircase to the third floor loft, and to the right, I saw the kitchen with a huge butcher block and miles of cupboards. The walls were red and brown, which made me wonder if he hired an interior decorator or did it on his own. He must have hired a professional; this was too beautiful for a man to do on his own.

"How many rooms are there in this place?"

"Three bedrooms and four bathrooms. I want to show you something."

I followed him up the stairs to the third level and into a large bedroom. We walked through the bedroom to another staircase that took us to the rooftop deck. I looked around me, awestricken that he lived in this home.

It was so elegant, I felt a little uncomfortable being there. He was in a different world than I was. I'd never even been in a home this nice.

The brisk wind made its way off the lake, and I shivered in the chill air.

He pulled out a chair beside a small glass table. "Have a seat."

I sat down and he joined me. He turned on a small portable heater under the table and I put my hands in front of it. I looked at the white rails that surrounded the roof. Even the roof was nicer than my home.

"This is so beautiful."

"Well, don't get attached. I may end up selling it. I found a house in Bloomington and a place in downtown Minneapolis that isn't too shabby either."

I shook my head. "You really were productive down there this week, weren't you?"

He winked. "I may just buy both."

"You are really spoiled, you know that? Most people don't buy on impulse; we have to save our money."

"I'll buy a trailer house if that is what it takes to get you to understand that it's just money and things."

"I know, but all this money makes me uncomfortable."

"Why?"

"Because it's beyond anything I could ever afford and that just makes me uncomfortable."

"Don't let it. Let me see your hands."

"What?"

"Let me see your hands."

I pulled them away from the heater and put them on the table. He took them in between his hands and began to rub them, using friction and blowing on them.

"You know, they were warm when I had them in front of the heater."

He ignored my comment. "Should we go inside? I'd love to show you my room."

"I bet you would," I said under my breath, but if he heard me he didn't show it.

I followed him into the master suite on the second floor. Huge windows lined the wall from floor to ceiling. A white recliner faced the window and a king-size bed with a red comforter was pushed up against the wall. I touched the bed and the many pillows that lined the headboard. A gigantic hot tub took up the far corner.

"This house probably cost more than I'll make in my lifetime." His money and house intimidated me. I'd never be good enough for him. He could have any woman he wanted, so why me?

"It's just a house. Stop thinking about the money and just relax. You are being judgmental."

"I'm sorry," I said as I watched him fall backward on the bed and turn on his side to look at me.

"Now, come have a seat," he said, patting the comforter in front of him.

"How about we go downstairs?"

He got up. "You are impossible, you know that?"

# SILVER SPOON

I woke up when the light from the east shined through the window and into my eyes. I found Travis sleeping in a recliner, and I realized I must have fallen asleep on the couch. He looked so peaceful, so handsome all curled up under his Minnesota Wild quilt.

I thought back to the morning at my house when he was only in his underwear, snuggled in between my sheets, and a shiver shot through my body. I smiled at the memory of his perfect body and the way it felt against mine.

My phone rang in my jacket, hanging on the table. I hurried to answer it before it woke him.

"Hello," I said in the softest whisper. I made my way to the sliding glass door and stepped out onto the deck. I was in awe at the beautiful view of the lake, but chilled in just my socks and pajamas.

"Why are you whispering?"

I looked over my shoulder to see if he was still sleeping on the chair.

"Because I didn't want to wake Travis."

"He's still sleeping? It's close to noon," Emily said.

"I guess we were up a little late last night." I looked over the deck and into the trees that surrounded the back side of the house. The deck was huge and seemed to wrap around his house. I could hear the waves in the distance and remembered it was Lake Superior. The snow stuck to the trees around me, as if they were painted to perfection.

She giggled. "Doing what? I want to hear all about it."

"I'll fill you in when we go dress shopping, okay?"

"But that's not until two. I can't wait that long."

"I'm not talking about it right now. You'll have to wait."

"Fine, but I want details. You have to give me something."

I thought about it. "Okay, his house looks like a castle, and it's three stories high. I seriously keep thinking Rapunzel is locked up in the highest window."

She laughed. "He really is loaded, isn't he? Gabbs, you found a good one."

"Why, because he's rich?"

"No, because he is a great guy that happens to have a lot of money. There is nothing wrong with a man that's rich."

"I can take care of myself. We lead different lives, worry about different things. I don't deserve this man, nor need him to be happy."

"I know you don't, and you're doing a great job I must add, but you deserve happiness. Even if it does come with a huge house and other bonuses. He is the lucky one."

"He's selling it."

"What? I don't think I heard you right."

"You heard me right He is thinking about selling the house. He's buying a house that he mentioned is even bigger than this one. Em, this house has to be close to four-thousand square feet."

"All the way to The Cities? Holy crap. You better not throw him away just because he has money. That's some sort of backward discrimination, you know."

I laughed while looking over my shoulder. Travis was sliding the door open, his hair a mess.

"I gotta go. I'll see you in a couple hours, okay?"

"Wait...I--"

I hung up the phone and turned around again.

"Who was that?"

"Emily."

He looked at his watch and rubbed his eyes. "Emily? She didn't call to cancel your shopping plans, did she?"

"Actually she wanted to make sure I wasn't taken by a sociopath serial killer from the seventies, and no, she called to confirm our plans."

He just shook his head at me and stepped closer.

"That's too bad. I was hoping she'd cancel and I'd get to spend the rest of the day with you."

"Nope, sorry."

"It's just not my lucky day."

He took another step closer and stared deeply into my eyes, challenging me to come closer. "You look cold. Why aren't you coming in?"

"Because you're blocking the door."

"Not me," he said, clearly blocking the door.

I pushed on his chest to make him get out of my way.

He grabbed my wrists and held them with just one hand. The other hand pulled on my chin so my eyes met his gaze. He stroked my hair behind my ear with two fingers.

I tilted my head to the side as I studied the expression on his face.

"If I promise not to kill you, would you come inside with me so I can make you breakfast?"

I broke away from his loose grip. "You don't need to bribe me. I'm starving."

"I'm one hell of a cook. You will be impressed."

"You better be."

He pushed me against the wall and kissed me like I've never been kissed before. I pulled away, breathlessly trying to escape, even though every bit of my being was telling me to continue.

He sighed as I grabbed my overnight bag and carried it up to his bedroom to change.

"I'll call you when it's ready."

I peeked over the railing and flashed him a smile, but he was busy grabbing a pan from the bottom of the stove. I watched him for a moment as he began cooking. He looked so happy as he cracked the eggs and began beating them in the bowl. He glanced my way and I stepped back immediately, sure my cover was blown.

"Are you spying on me?"

"I don't know what you are talking about."

I made my way into his bedroom and slammed the door loudly

enough that he would know I was no longer lingering.

My red sweater hung low and I smiled as I noticed how well the color brought out my jet black hair. I did my makeup a little heavy and put on my brightest red lipstick, which was sure to keep his attention. I took one last look at the way my butt looked in my tight jeans and smiled. All the running and swimming was really paying off.

The smell of bacon made my stomach growl and lured me to the kitchen.

He finished making breakfast and dished up our plates. As his eyes met mine, he stood frozen in place for a second, then shook his head as if to shake away his thoughts.

"I had a really good time talking to you all night again," he said.

My face grew warm. "I had a really good time, too."

"I must tell you, I've been worrying that you regret us sleeping together the other night."

"Really? I thought girls always just throw themselves in your bed when you meet them."

"Well, in my defense, I didn't just meet you, but I'm serious. I really like you, Gabriella."

"I like you, too."

He winked at me and a cocky smile spread across his face; I snorted my annoyance.

"What was that for?"

"You are good-looking, but a little too cocky for my taste."

"I like to call it confident. You make me nervous; that's my nerves speaking."

I shook my head at him. "You, nervous?"

"Yes, you make me nervous. Can't you tell?"

"Oh, I'm sure you say that to all the girls."

He took a bite of his omelet. "How many girls do you think there are exactly?"

"I don't think I want to know the answer to that question. I'm not sure you and I are much alike."

His sad eyes stared at me. "Why do you say that?"

"You're a little too much man for me."

"Too much man?" he repeated, emphasizing the word man.

"That's what I said."

"How do you mean?"

I swept my arms around the room. "You live here, for one. I live a different life. I work with children who have nothing and you, you have so much, probably too much..."

"I do well and I work hard. There's nothing wrong with that, is there?"

I chewed on my lip. "I work hard, too, but I'm not in it for the money."

"Gabriella, I'm not in it for the money. That just happens to be a bonus with my job."

"You were born with a silver spoon in your mouth. C'mon, I know who your dad is."

Travis snorted. "My dad isn't a good person or a good lawyer. He was sued for embezzlement when I was eighteen, and I had to pay for college out of my pocket, working two jobs and going to school full-time. Trust me, I have earned every bit of my money on my own."

"I'm sorry. I didn't know."

He shrugged. "How could you? I don't tell everyone I see. It's not like I see him very often, and my mom cares more about plastic surgery and her husband's kids than she does me. I'm proud of everything I've done and I love helping people make money. I'm very good at what I do."

"I didn't realize you were so passionate."

He held out his hands and bowed. "What you see is what you get. I'm not a rich snob. I just love spending my money. I hope you can look beyond the money and see me for who I really am."

"And who is that, exactly?"

"I'll tell you something you don't know about me. It's easy to judge, but I'm also an RN."

"What? You are?"

"I am. I have thought about leaving finance for a long time and going back to nursing, but I guess I felt like I had something to prove to my mom and my dad, you know."

I put my hand on his. I was so glad to see there was more to him than just money. "All of this doesn't mean anything to me. Follow your heart," I said, pointing to the house around me.

"That's the thing. I love what I do. I mean, yeah, at first I was in it for the money. I had no idea how happy I'd be in my career. And I don't have to work midnights like I would as an RN."

"I can see that. I'm sorry I judged you."

I ate my plate clean as I tried to imagine him in scrubs. Maybe I was the jerk for judging him without knowing who he really was. Would I feel differently if he made less money and had a smaller house?

We finished up our breakfast, then he walked me out to my car.

"I hope you consider my offer and come back tonight after your shopping date."

"Hmm, it's a possibility."

"That's all I ask. Have fun with Emily. Tell her I said hello."

He leaned in to kiss me, but I put my finger up to his lips. "Later."

"So, tell me more about your night. You know I'm a married woman, so I have to live the single life vicariously through you, right?"

I laughed. "It was a lot of fun. He's sweet."

"Sweet? How was the sex?"

"Tell me how you really feel, Em."

"Oh, c'mon. I'm dying to find out more, and you are giving me nothing."

"As long as you never share your love life between you and my brother with me. There are some things that should never be shared."

"Deal."

"Well, he's moving a little too fast for me. I just don't feel like I'll ever be good enough for him, you know."

"I can understand that. What you're forgetting is you deserve him. Money is just money, and look at his childhood, who his parents are. I hate to break it to you, but he's not too good for you. He's lucky to have you. Like I told you on the phone."

Emily pulled a blue dress off the rack.

"That's gorgeous. It would really bring out your blue eyes."

"I think you should give him a shot."

"Give him a shot? He asked me to move in with him."

"I know. That's sweet."

"Sweet?"

She grabbed another blue dress and swung it over her arm. "It's really sweet. I'm not saying you have to move in with him. Just do the long distance thing until you figure it out. It doesn't have to be a game, you know."

"We'll see. Today is about the fundraiser and finding the perfect dress. How do you know which dress you are going to fit into after the baby is born?"

"I'm not worried about it. Oh, look at this one." She pulled a beautiful long red silk dress from the rack. "You will look absolutely amazing in this one. You know how phenomenal you look in red."

"I'll try it on, but the back is so bare. I'm just not sure I'll feel comfortable in it."

"Get out of your comfort zone for once. You are going to look hot."

We found a couple more dresses, and Emily's eyes popped out of her head at the sight of me in the red silk dress she picked out. "That's the one!"

"You don't think it's a little too fancy? It sure doesn't leave much to the imagination."

"Are you kidding me? It's perfect. No dress is too fancy for the Greysolon. You'll blow his socks off."

"I'm not even sure if he's going."

"He called me about tickets already. He's definitely going."

She headed for the fitting room with the last dress, which was by far the most beautiful dress on her. It was snug, but it would definitely fit her after she had the baby.

She insisted on buying both the dresses, claiming it was a tax write-off, and I didn't argue.

"Would you like to spend some time with Travis instead of going out to eat? I don't mind getting home to Matthew anyway."

Emily and myself were the only people, other than my mom, that could get away with calling him by his full name. He hated it, but Emily thought it was cute. My brother worshiped her and let her get away with it.

"How did it go with Matthew? Did you find out what is bothering him?"

"He lost his job and hid it from me."

"Oh, no."

"Yeah, but after a lot of tears he picked himself up, and he's been applying for jobs ever since."

"That's great."

"I hope so. He just hid it for so long. It scares me because if you don't have trust, there is no marriage."

"I'm sorry."

"Don't worry about me. Go see Travis," she said, forcing a smile at me.

"I guess I can go see him if you aren't hungry."

"You go. I'll see you at Jill's tomorrow night."

"Jill's?"

"The dinner was rescheduled and is at Jill's now, didn't she tell you?"

"No, she didn't mention it."

"Well, if you can't make it, don't worry about it. You just go have fun with Travis. Do you work Monday?"

"Yep, bright and early. I'll let you know."

"And Gab, give him a chance before you shoot him down, okay?"

I hugged her goodbye. "Yeah, yeah."

"No one is ever too good for you. Don't forget that."

# A SURPRISE VISITOR

I pulled up at his castle and rang the doorbell, then tried the knob when no one answered. Open. I peeked my head in.

"Hello?"

I took off my shoes and went looking for him. My feet led me into the basement after hearing a noise from downstairs, possibly a grunt? The television was blasting and Travis was doing pull-ups while P90X blared. His shirt was off and his muscles bulged as I watched him do at least ten.

I shouted over the noise. "Is that all you got?"

Travis grinned and turned off the television. "Well, look who came back," he said, sweat dripping from his forehead.

"Don't turn it off on my account. I don't mind watching."

He grabbed a towel and mopped up the sweat on his bare chest and face and flexed his pecs. I looked away, pretending not to notice.

"Does that mean you're taking me up on my offer and staying another night?"

His flushed cheeks and the glow of his wet torso had me weak in the knees.

"If the offer still stands."

"How about a little walk by the lake?"

"I'd love that."

He pulled a sweatshirt over his bare, wet chest. It was just too hard to think with all those muscles bulging.

The lake went on for miles. I shivered from the cold. He noticed and pulled me in close, wrapping his arm around me, and I felt him kiss the top of my head.

"Your hair smells so good. Like flowers mixed with Tide."

"Well, that doesn't sound like a great combination. I haven't used Tide in years."

"Really? Why not?"

"I like to stick with organic and non-toxic."

"I'm impressed."

I followed Travis down the back stairs where pine trees and thick snow blocked the lake view. We walked through a path in the woods until we reached the rocky cliff that overlooked the water.

"Do you ever swim in there?"

"Nah, the water is too cold all year. I go to smaller lakes up north when I want to swim. The view is beautiful, but the water is too deep and the lake is too big and cold. Have you ever been swimming in Lake Superior?"

"Mom and Jill used to take us to Canal Park where we would walk the bike path and get ice cream. We'd walk out to the lighthouse, and sometimes if we were lucky enough, we'd get pooped on by the seagulls passing by."

He shook his head and laughed. "The lake is beautiful over there. That's not too far from my house, you know. The bike path is just a couple miles down the road that goes to Canal Park."

I put my hand on his. "I know. I run Grandma's Marathon every year with my mom. Well, not every year. Sometimes we just do the half."

He put a strand of my hair that was blowing in the wind behind my ear. "You continue to impress me."

"You're impressed that I run Grandma's? You know I run."

"I'm impressed you run with your mom."

"Are you kidding me? She's been running Grandma's for years. Her and my father even ran it together, you know, before he died."

I turned my face away from him and stared back at the lake. Mentioning my dad to him choked me up. I did not want to break down, not now.

"I don't remember much about your dad, but I do remember the day he came over and talked some sense into my mom. I'm pretty sure he was the only guy she ever listened to."

The fact that he put my dad and his mom in the same sentence made my body heat up.

"Is it hard not talking to your parents anymore?"

He bent down to pick up a stick in front of him that was blocking the path. "Sometimes. They are my family, but it's hard to forgive them for what they did, not just to your parents, but they have done some terrible things to me and many others."

"I'm sorry," I said, with more meaning than I expected.

He turned to me, putting his hand behind my neck, our mouths just a whisper away. "I'm so glad you came back."

A noise from behind Travis had us both jump as we turned around to see what was making the commotion. We watched as two squirrels chased each other through the trees and then one stopping to face the other squirrel. We both broke out in laughter that they could scare us so much, which startled the squirrels as they ran deeper into the woods.

"That scared the crap out of me," he said, hunched over. He stood back up. "Let's go this way."

"Why do you want to leave Duluth? It's so beautiful here."

"I wanted to extend my clientele. Try something new."

"Can we go inside now? I'm freezing," I said.

He nodded and took my hand in his as we made our way back.

"More than anything, I wanted a change, I guess. I've lived here most of my life."

Hibbing made me feel that way. I dreamed about living somewhere else, being closer to a real mall that actually had more than just two clothing stores in it and being able to go rock climbing without having to drive an hour. On the flip side, I wasn't sure I wanted to move away from the place I'd called home most of my life. I couldn't imagine being far away from Mom and Jill, even Matt and Emily, and especially Phillip. My family was nowhere near perfect, but it was my family.

"Do you like living in Hibbing?"

"It has its ups and downs."

I followed him as he made his way around the house. We entered through the front door and headed right to the fireplace to warm up.

"Like?"

"Well, it's a small town. We all kind of take care of each other, you know. Everyone knows everyone, and the traffic is light. We have the Mesabi Trail that I'm pretty sure I can't live without."

"Can't live without, huh? What kind of a trail is it?"

He pulled a wool blanket off his couch and wrapped it around me.

"Before you answer that, want a cup of hot tea?"

"Do you have any green tea?"

He flashed me a grin. "Do I have green tea?"

"Then I'd love a cup. You don't know what the Mesabi Trail is? It's a bike path that goes across The Range. It's like seventy-five miles long and is supposed to be damn near one hundred and fifty miles long or so by the time it's finished. We run it and bike it all summer long. It overlooks the mines in places, and it's just so peaceful. We'll have to take a ride down it this summer. I've seen so many animals on the path, like squirrels, skunks, deer, and even bears."

"Bears? That doesn't sound exciting to me."

"Oh, they're harmless, and more scared of you than you are of them, unless you get in between them and their cubs. You really have to give it a try. It's nothing like Duluth. Don't get me wrong, the path here is great, but there aren't as many people on the Mesabi Trail, and it is so much longer."

"Are there ice cream shops on the path?"

I punched his shoulder. "No, there's no ice cream shops, but you don't need one, its breathtaking views are one-of-a-kind. Sometimes I wear my triathlon suit and stop and swim in the Buhl Pit. It's so clear, and the cliffs on the trail are great for cliff jumping."

"I wouldn't have thought of you as a cliff jumper. You really are a rebel, aren't you?"

We both moved to sit on the floor in front of the fire. He reached over to grab a blanket and I pushed him over. This time he came back at me and pinned my wrists to the floor above my head as he straddled my torso.

"I've had enough of your abuse young lady. Are you ticklish at all?"

"No," I lied.

"Hmm, I guess I'm going to have to try anyway."

He held my wrists with one hand above my head as he tickled me under my arms and sides. I began laughing, begging him to get off me, doing my best to wiggle myself out of his grasp and failing.

"What did you say? I know you aren't ticklish."

He dug his fingers deeper into my skin.

I cried out. "Stop, you're hurting me!"

Finally he gave in and let me go. "I'm an old man. Stop abusing me."

"Old man, huh? When did thirties get old?"

"When thirty-year-old men date twentyish-year-old women, that's when."

"Wow, does that bother you?"

"I just worry it bothers you."

"Well, you're wrong. I'm not really sure what my mom is going to say, but she'll get over it. She loves you."

Travis's phone beeped and he quickly got up to check it. I was getting used to the many phone calls, texts, and emails that interrupted us.

"Client?"

He stared at his phone and it took him a minute before he replied. "It's Missy."

I climbed to my feet to see what was distracting him. "Missy?"

"She's here. She wants to talk."

"Here, here?" I said, looking around.

"Yes, here. Outside. Why is she here?" He put down his phone and pulled open the curtains.

"Do you see her?"

"Yeah, I see her. I'm going to send her away," he said. "I'm so sorry about this."

"Do what you gotta do. I trust you."

"Thank you." He kissed my head and slipped his shoes on. "I can't believe she just showed up like this."

He opened the door, and I heard Missy yelling at him before he shut the door. Their voices were muffled. I couldn't make out anything they were saying. I sat on a chair and chewed my nails, peeking between the blinds.

Missy was beautiful with long brown hair and a big puffy pink jacket. She was crying.

My phone rang and I jumped. "Matt?"

"I'm sorry to bug you, sis. I know you're in Duluth, but Emily is in labor."

"You didn't bug me at all. I'm on my way."

"Thanks, Gabby."

The fear in his voice traveled through the line. "I'm going to be a dad."

"You're going to be a great dad. Is everything okay?"

"So far, so good. She's been asking for you."

"I'm on my way."

I hung up the phone and grabbed my jacket and purse. My suitcase could wait. I slipped on my shoes and jacket and met Travis on my way out.

"Where are you going? Are you mad?"

"No, no, Emily's in labor. I gotta go."

"She is? Can I drive you?"

"To Hibbing?"

"Yes."

"I need to take my car; I work tomorrow," I said, pushing past him.

His eyes were red and glossy, and he was obviously very shook up.

"I can meet you there."

I grasped his hand. "I can call you later. I really gotta go."

He nodded and followed me to my car. Missy's car was still in the driveway, and Travis ran over to her.

I began backing out, swearing at her to move until I saw her running toward me.

"Not now. I don't have time for this," I mumbled under my breath.

She knocked on my window, a sad smile spread across her face.

Travis called to her. "Missy, she needs to go. She's in a hurry. Let her go!"

She ignored him.

She extended her hand through my open window. "Hi, I'm Missy."

I was at a loss for words.

"You know, I'm not sure what's going on between you and Travis, but I really need to go. I'm in a rush."

"It will only take a minute. I just wanted to let you know this man is a lying, cheating bastard, and you have no idea what you're getting into."

I checked my rearview mirror and my side mirror, searching for a way to back around her car.

"I'm sorry. I really don't have time for this. You need to talk to Travis, not me. I really need to go."

"You don't understand--"

"No, you don't understand," I said through clenched teeth.

I put my car in reverse and drove right through his yard. I saw the bush and heard it beneath my car as I dragged it out of his yard. I did not have time to sit and chat with a jealous woman while my brother was having his first baby and I was more than an hour away. I shifted the car into drive, squealed my tires, and left the bush in the middle of the road.

Missy threw her hands up in the air. Travis just shook his head with a grin.

"I told you I was in a rush," I said beneath my breath. "You're lucky you weren't in my way."

As I made my way up the hill, I had to remind myself to slow down multiple times. Approaching Cotton, my phone rang. Travis. I was expecting his call. Had Missy left?

"Hey."

"Gabby, I'm so sorry about that. She just showed up and would not leave until she met you. I promise, I'm not like what she told you. She's mad because I kicked her out, and well, she thinks I cheated on her with you and you didn't know. I had no idea she--"

"I really don't care, Travis. It sounds like you need to tie up some loose ends anyway."

"I told her it was over. She knows we are done."

"Obviously she didn't get the hint. Listen, we can talk after Emily has her baby, okay?"

"Promise you won't let this scare you off?"

"What did she even say to you?"

"Well, you need to understand she is a compulsive liar."

"Travis."

"She said she is pregnant...with my child."

# COTTON CANDY ICE CREAM

"Hey, Mom." I wrapped my arms around her. "Did she have the baby yet? Did I miss it?"

Mom's eyes sparkled and she glowed. "She just delivered a beautiful baby girl; my first grandchild."

"Can I see her?"

"We need to wait a bit. They're making sure she's okay, and then Emily's going to nurse the baby."

"Okay, I guess I'm just going to have to wait my turn. That's what I get for being out of town."

"They said they'll come get us as soon as she's ready." She clasped her hands together. "Oh, Gabby, she's absolutely beautiful."

"Were you in there for the birth?"

"No, but I stood outside the curtain, and then they let me hold the baby before they took her measurements. They said she's a little jaundiced, so they wanted to put her under the bili lights for a bit. Lucky she decided to come back from Duluth early or she would have had the baby in Duluth and Matthew may not have made it in time."

It was a good thing I cut our day short to get back to Travis. Oh, Travis. The thought of being caught in the middle between whatever was going on with him and Missy had me sick at the thought. A woman making up being pregnant just to lure a man to date her is a scary type of woman.

I looked around. "Where is Matthew?"

"He's in a little bit of shock. He should be out soon. He'll be so glad you made it. Jill just left. She has a cold, so she didn't want to chance giving it to the baby."

"I bet it's killing her she can't hold the baby."

"You know it. So, what were you doing in Duluth? Were you there all weekend?"

"Hey there, Auntie."

I turned around to give Matthew a big hug, grateful he interrupted us just in time. "Congrats, Daddy."

He rubbed his eyes. "She so beautiful. Oh, Gabby, just wait until you see her. She looks just like her mom. How can I be so excited and yet so petrified at the same time?"

"Because you know one day she's going to be a teen."

"Isn't that the truth," Mom said, laughing.

She hugged Matt. "I'm so proud of you, son. You've overcome so much in your life and found a great woman." She looked at him with such pride in her expression it made my heart melt.

"Thanks, Mom."

"You've come so far, Matthew, so far."

"I have."

Matt never used to be so sentimental. Before Emily, he loved to go to parties and get drunk, and then at nineteen he became addicted to meth. We all knew he was partying too much, but his grades were good and no one suspected he was into meth. He even graduated from college, so we just backed off until he met Emily and soon checked himself into rehab.

Them meeting was quite a coincidence. Matt had to get his license renewed, and when he received it in the mail, Emily's picture was on the front with his information. He called the DMV, but they just told him to cut it up and they would send him a new one.

A week later he was on a low, desperate to buy more meth. He hated himself for what he was doing, but didn't know how to tell us. He ran to the gas station, and as he opened the door, he ran right into her. Her purse went flying, and she sprained her ankle and couldn't walk. Matt was her hero. As he sat in the waiting room staring at his license with her picture on it, he could not help but laugh at the coincidence of it all. Once she was discharged, he showed her the picture, and she couldn't believe it. He brought her home and sat there all day and all night talking to her, and he finally broke down and told her about his drug habit. She convinced him to get help and promised she'd wait for him to get out of rehab, and she was true to her word. If it wasn't for Emily, we would have lost my brother sooner or later. She was his angel and the reason we got him back.

He and Emily went to NA meetings together, and he took responsibility for his past. They were very big on going to church on Sunday mornings and when Emily was out of town, Matt would go to church by himself or ask Mom to come with. Now I wasn't so sure how he was doing or if Emily knew he was drinking too much lately when she was away.

A nurse broke into my reverie. "You can come in now."

We walked in behind Matt as he led the way to his wife and beautiful baby girl.

He placed the baby in my arms. "Gabby, would you like to hold your niece?"

Her little hand wrapped around my finger as I stared at her tiny face. Her eyes kept closing. She was swaddled in a blanket with pink and blue giraffes on it and a tiny pink hat. It made me think about my future, my children. Would it just be Melanie and Ben? Would I have more?

Emily's long blonde hair was snarled and her mascara was smudged under her eyes, but she was still glowing. She sat up in bed. "She's perfect, isn't she?"

"Absolutely perfect in every way."

I woke up early Monday morning to get ready for work and turned on my phone. I had three missed calls and two text messages from Travis because I spent all day Sunday at the hospital with Matt and Emily holding the baby and didn't want any distractions. I was not ready to talk to him yet or hear any of his messages.

Phillip was waiting outside the bathroom door. "So, how was your weekend?"

I secured the towel around my chest. "You can't even wait for me to get dressed, can you? You are up early."

"I'm sorry."

"Did you hear Emily and Matt had their baby?"

"No, I had no idea. What did they have?"

"A girl," I said. "I've got to get ready for work. How was the shelter this weekend?"

"Well, I met Melanie and Ben."

"And?"

"They are every bit as cute as you said, except Melanie isn't feeling very well."

"What's wrong with her?"

"She's complaining that her leg hurts. Not sure if she just wanted attention or if she is having growing pains. She was crying most of the day, so Denise had me take her to the emergency room last night."

"Oh no. What did they say?"

"They did some blood work and said they would call us with the results when they came in and said if it gets worse to bring her back. Are you still considering fostering?"

"I'm not really sure. I have a lot to think about. We have a lot to think about."

"Yes, we do."

"Not tonight. Jill is having a dinner tonight since Irene arrived a little early and they couldn't last night. Can you come?"

"I'll be there. I have to pay some bills, but I shouldn't be too late."

"Okay, how's everything with you and Lucy?"

"How is everything with you and Travis?"

"Point taken," I said, shutting my bedroom door.

I arrived a half-hour early for work, eager to check on Melanie, but at seven-thirty in the morning, she probably wasn't awake.

I knocked on the door. Denise answered it.

"You still here?"

"No, I came in at four in the morning after receiving a phone call that our midnight employee was sick."

"Sucks to be you," I said. "How's Melanie?"

"She's eating breakfast already. She's like a whole new person. She's happy and says her leg doesn't hurt anymore. Even the color is back in her face."

I pushed my way past her. "That's great."

Melanie was sitting at the table eating Cheerios and humming to herself.

"Good morning, Melanie."

She turned around, and a smile spread across her face. She jumped up and wrapped her body around my leg. "Gabby, you're back!"

I grabbed my leg to help lift the extra weight and began walking around with her holding on tight and giggling. After a few steps, I was sore and pulled her off.

I picked her up. "You must be feeling better, huh?"

"I'm all better. The doctor cured me. I'm Doc McStuffins today. Can I look in your ears?"

"How about you eat your breakfast first, little lady? Then I'll definitely take a trip to the doctor."

"Yay!"

She sat down and scarfed her cereal as fast as she could.

"Slow down, Melanie, slow down."

Her lower lip stuck out. "Sorry, I forgot."

She finished breakfast, and Denise got her dressed while I finished up some paperwork. We played Doc McStuffins for a good hour. According to Melanie, I broke everything in my body, but luckily the Doc was in the house to fix it. She even said I had a temperature of one million, to which I replied, "And I'm still alive."

She was in good spirits as the morning progressed. Just as we were setting up to play Barbies, the phone rang.

Denise hurried into the office to answer it. A few minutes later she asked for me to follow her back into the office.

"Is everything okay?" I said. "You look a little pale."

"Sit down." She stared out the glass at Ben and Melanie. "That was the doctor."

I stopped breathing and stared at her mouth. "Is everything okay? Please tell me everything is okay."

"The doctor said the results of her blood test were abnormal. He said we need to bring her in for more testing today."

"What does that mean exactly?"

"I don't know, but she needs to go there now."

"But she's fine today," I said. "She's fine, just look at her."

"I'm sorry, Gabby. Would you mind taking her? I'm not sure how long it's going to take. I'm exhausted. I'll call social services so they know what's going on."

I took a deep breath. "I can take her."

"You sure?"

"Without a doubt."

"I'm pretty sure social services will put a rush on fostering her, if you are still considering it."

"I'm not sure. I still need to talk with Phillip more about it, but with or without him I'm probably still doing this. Poor thing. No little kid likes going to the doctor. Is it serious?"

"I'm not sure, but the doctor seemed to think so."

"What does he think it is? It was just a sore leg, right?"

"That's all I heard from Phillip, but the doctor must have some worries or they wouldn't make us bring her back."

"Okay, well let me know what you hear. Am I just supposed to bring her in right now?"

"Yeah."

After a full day of tests, Melanie finally hit her breaking point.

I hugged her. "Just a little while longer, sweetie."

"You keep saying that. I wanna go. I wanna go now. I want my mommy."

I hugged her. "It's going to be okay. I'm here for you, honey."

We finally wrapped up the next test, and the doctor asked us to wait in the waiting room. Luckily Doc McStuffins was on.

I texted Denise to give her an update, and she told me that everything went well with social services. All I needed to do was sign the paperwork once Phillip and I decided if we were going to be her foster parents and then they could move forward with getting me licensed. It was all happening so fast.

Melanie pointed at the cartoon character. "Look, Gabby, it's me. Doesn't she look just like me?"

I smiled, admiring that she didn't see a difference between herself and the African-American cartoon. She was so innocent and sweet. She saw the world differently and it was a breath of fresh air. "You definitely do."

"Melanie," a nurse said.

We jumped to our feet. "Melanie, you can wait right here. The doctor wants to talk to your mom real quick."

She giggled. "My mom."

"I'm not actually her mom," I whispered to the nurse.

The nurse frowned. "Is there any way you can get ahold of her parents?"

"They are kind of unreachable. I don't really think that's possible. She is in the custody of the state right now. Both parents are incarcerated."

"How about a close family member?"

I shook my head. "Not that I know of. I'm from the shelter and am possibly going to be her foster mom."

"Okay, wait here. The doctor will be right over to talk to you. I'll take some stickers and hang out with Melanie until you're done, if that's okay with you. I'm just going to touch base with social services to make sure the doctor can talk to you before I go see Melanie."

I nodded. The waiting area was empty. I glanced at my watch. It was after five and the clinic closed at five. I bit my nails, then stopped when the doctor walked toward me a few minutes later.

"Hi Gabby. I have been trying to get ahold of Melanie's social worker and I finally reached someone from their office. They told me you are in the process of becoming her caregiver and I can speak to you about what's going on."

"Yes, she's in my care. I work at the shelter."

"Well, we've determined the reason for the pains Melanie is experiencing in her leg."

"She's fine today."

"I know it seems that way, but the pains will come back."

"What do you mean?"

"Melanie may have leukemia."

I took a step back and covered my face with my hands and rubbed them hard, like I was trying to wake up from a dream. I gasped for air.

"B-but she's only five years old. What do you mean, may have leukemia? Wh-what do we do from here?"

"I recommend taking her to a children's hospital where she can get a second opinion from a doctor who specializes in this."

I could not believe what I was hearing. I cleared my dry throat and whispered, "Is there a chance she doesn't have it?"

"It's highly unlikely that I'm wrong, but they will do more testing at the children's hospital that will give you more answers."

"Will she have to undergo like chemotherapy or radiation?"

"Most likely, but you will have to talk to them. I talked to her social worker, who is contacting Melanie's parents to let them know what is going on. She said she will get ahold of you as soon as she can."

The tears rolled down my cheeks and my chest heaved. It felt like a punch in the gut when he said the word cancer. I was so glad Melanie wasn't here to see me like this. It wasn't fair she didn't have her mom and dad to be here with her through this. I thought of my mom and I couldn't imagine not having her around if something like this would have happened to me. My heart broke at the thought.

"Do you have any questions?"

"I have a million. I just can't think of them at the moment."

"You'll know more once you go to a doctor that specializes in childhood leukemia. Here is a list of a few places I recommend in The

Cities. She needs someone by her side as she goes through this. I'm not sure what your roll is here, but it is going to be an emotional roller coaster."

He shook my hand. "Good luck. Remember, if you need anything, give me a call."

He looked over at Melanie and pursed his lips together as he opened the door to the waiting room for me.

I crouched down beside Melanie. "How about some ice cream?"

Melanie's eyes lit up. "Cotton candy ice cream is my favorite. Can we get some please, please?"

I blinked away the tears and smiled as she put her little hand in mine. "Cotton candy ice cream it is."

"Thanks, Mommy. You're the best."

# HELLO, PRINCESS

I tried to sneak past Mom, but she could see I was upset and followed me into the living room where Uncle Mike and Phillip were watching television.

She pointed to Jill's bedroom. "Gabby, come here for a second. I want to talk to you about something."

"Okay?"

There was no getting away with keeping this from her. My mom had these instincts that were beyond normal, and growing up it was horrible. When I was younger, I thought she had magic powers because she could always tell when something was wrong or bothering me, and then the interrogation would begin. Of course, it was loving, but she always saw right through my poker face.

"Is everything okay? You look down."

"No, I'm not down, Mom. I just have a lot on my mind. I'm thinking about being a foster parent for two kids from the shelter, and Phillip is going to do it with me and..." I stopped talking and looked down, realizing I was fidgeting and looked back up to stare her in the eyes. "I've been meaning to talk to you about something else, too. I'm seeing someone."

She smiled. "I know. What's he like?"

"You knew? Why didn't you say anything?"

"I knew you'd tell me when you were ready," she said, holding my hands.

"I'm seeing Travis."

"Travis who?" she asked, scrunching up her eyebrows.

"Olivia and Casey's son."

"Oh, Travis," she said in a high-pitched voice. "I would have never guessed. Is he good to you? You know I've always liked Travis."

"Yes, Ma, he's pretty good to me. We just started seeing each other not too long ago."

She leaned forward. "And why are you hesitant?"

"I don't know. I guess he wants me to move in with him already and it makes me nervous."

"Is it his age that bothers you?"

"No."

"It doesn't bother you who his parents are, does it?"

"Maybe a little bit."

"Don't let our past get in the way of your happiness. It has nothing to do with him. His parents really aren't that bad." She smiled at me. "When people are mean, maybe gossip too much or start trouble, they are usually the ones who have unhappy home lives. Gabby, those are the ones we need to help the most."

"I knew you were going to say that."

"It's true." She scooted closer to me on the bed and nudged me gently. "I know it was hard growing up without your father. And I know you blame Olivia and Casey for what they did, but you need to start trusting again. What happened to him isn't their fault."

"I guess."

"You are very devoted to your job and you love those kids from the shelter, but you need to start thinking about yourself, too. It's time you let yourself fall for a guy, and Travis is definitely a great one."

"It isn't easy. I even told him I wasn't looking for anything serious."

"And he is still fighting for you? Do you know how many girls would kill for a man like that?" Mom got up, grabbed her purse off the floor, and began sorting through it until she pulled something out.

"What is it?"

She handed me a picture of her and my dad when they were young in athletic gear and tenner shoes standing in front of a school. The trees were full of pink, green, and orange leaves, the sky bright blue. I smiled.

"This is your dad and me at Bemidji State. I always had the biggest crush on him in high school, but I never thought I was good enough. He was a senior and I was a freshmen. I know you, and I'm sure it bothers you that Travis has a lot of money, and it can be scary. I felt that way about your dad."

"Did Dad have money?"

She took the picture away and studied it closer, her eyes filling up with tears. She wiped them away and smiled. "He didn't have money, but you know I didn't have the best childhood. My dad was a drunk and my mom ran away in the middle of the night for a better life for Jill and me. I had trust issues, and it wasn't easy to date your dad. I felt like he was so much better than me, and how could a man like this love little old me. I thought eventually he'd see right through me and stop loving me."

"How did you get past that?" I said, putting my arm around her and resting my head on her shoulder. I heard her say bits and pieces about growing up, but this was the first time she really opened up to me about her past and my father. I felt closer to her than I ever had before.

"I let myself fall. Your dad had his faults just like I did, and he wasn't near perfect. I began to love myself, and I loved him. Every time I run, I think about this day running with him at Bemidji State. We talked for hours. And he loved me for who I was. Our marriage wasn't perfect, but it was no fault of Olivia's. In the end, we only grew stronger together."

"That is so sweet, Mom. I miss him so much."

Mom lifted my chin. "I do, too, honey, but it is important that you also understand that he would want you to be happy. Stop running from your fears and start embracing them. Your dad died saving my life."

"There is nothing he wouldn't have done for you."

"Exactly. He had a heart of gold, but I would have done the same for him. Stop living your life for what you think would make your dad happy and start living it for you. Embrace the past, but also continue building happiness into your future by letting yourself fall in love."

She reached over to hug me and there was no stopping the tears that followed. "I want you to have this picture, to remind yourself that happiness is a choice only you can make."

"Are you sure? This picture means so much to you."

"I want you to have it."

"Thank you. I love you, Mom."

"I love you, too. You got this. Listen to your heart. And remember, if it's meant to be, it'll be."

"There is one more thing."

"What?" she asked with a concerned expression on her face.

"The little girl has cancer."

I waited until dinner to share my news about Melanie's diagnosis to the rest of the family. There wasn't a dry eye in the room, and everyone was very supportive.

Jill looked over to Phillip. "Are you sure you're both ready for this?"

"We haven't decided yet," he said.

"I guess we wanted to talk to all of you about this before we make our final decision. It's really hard to say no at this point," I said.

"I can't imagine that poor little girl being diagnosed with cancer and not having anyone to help her," Mom said.

"I know, but it will also be a lot to bring her to her appointments and watch her go through all that pain. It's a big commitment for both of you," Jill said.

I looked at Phillip and he shot me back a comforting smile.

"How does Lucy feel about this, Phillip?" Jill asked.

"Lucy isn't exactly in agreeance with all of this, but I told her this needs to be my decision."

"And?" Mom said.

"And it is my decision and Gabby's, of course."

Lucy was not understanding or approving at all of the relationship Phillip and I shared, and she threw it in my face whenever she could. We all knew their rocky relationship wouldn't last long, or hoped it wouldn't.

"Well, you know we are here for you whether you decide to foster them or not. We are family and this is what we do," Mom said.

I took off my shoes and sat on the couch at home next to Phillip, emotionally drained from my day. Emily and Matt were still in the hospital with their baby, and I was bummed they couldn't be there as we shared the news with our family.

"I think that went over well with my family. What do you think?" I asked.

"You know you are my best friend, right?"

I scrunched up my eyebrows and gave him my full attention. "Yeah."

"I would love to be a part of helping you with the kids, but I just don't think I want to sign up to be their foster parents. I'm just not ready, you know."

"What are you saying, Phillip? You've changed your mind?" I could feel my heart beating fast in my chest as I stared at him, trying to understand why he would do this to them.

"I didn't really change my mind. I just don't think I can sign the papers."

"Melanie has cancer, Phillip. How can you not want to help?"

He put his hand on mine, but I pulled away. "I want to help, and I'm here for you and for them. I just don't think I can make that commitment right now."

I stood up abruptly. "It's Lucy, isn't it? I can't hide it anymore. She's controlling and evil and if you let a girl like that come in the way of helping two little kids with no parents who have had the worst life imaginable, you aren't the person I thought you were."

"It's not Lucy. I don't care what Lucy says. I just think this isn't something we should sign on to do together. We aren't a couple, Gabby."

"You are a coward," I said, unable to hide my emotions. A part of me wanted to hit him right in the face, but I controlled myself.

"I want to help you raise them, but I just can't sign the papers. Can you please understand that? I will do whatever it takes to be there for them and help you, but I just can't be their father."

I was inches from his face. "No one is asking you to be their father. I don't want you to sign if you don't want to sign, but I'm doing this with or without you." I turned away and headed toward the kitchen.

Phillip grabbed my arm and turned me around. "I want to be the uncle."

"What?"

"I want to be the uncle-like figure in their life. I'm not running away. Don't run away from me."

"What if Melanie dies? I need you, Phillip," I cried out in frustration.

"She's not going to die, and I will be right by your side no matter what happens. Can you understand where I'm coming from?"

I covered my eyes with my hands. I didn't want to see him, didn't want to talk to him. How could he back out like this? What was wrong with him? I felt like I didn't know him at all.

"Look at me, Gabby."

I did as he said.

"You are stronger than you think you are. I'll be right by your side."

"You promise? I can't do this alone, Phillip. I'm scared. What if I'm a bad mom?"

"I promise you are going to be a great foster mom. Look who raised you."

"I'm mad at you."

"I'll even help you paint the bedrooms upstairs."

I laughed through my tears; he wiped them away.

"I do think Melanie should get the bigger room though. Girls need a large closet for all their clothes."

"I think that is a great idea."

"You really promise you will help?"

"How long have you known me? I promise."

"I'm going to hold you to that."

He smiled. "Now go get some sleep."

I nodded, and without another word I made my way up the stairs, glancing at the first empty bedroom on the left. I turned on the light and stared at the twin bed and smiled. I can do this. I can do this.

For the next week, Phillip and I spent every free minute shopping and getting the rooms ready for the kids while we waited to hear about when we could bring Melanie to the hospital or when they could come home with us. Phillip was in charge of buying everything for Ben, and I was in charge of Melanie's room. We worked together while blaring our favorite Bob Dylan songs. Bob Dylan was from Minnesota and raised right here in Hibbing. Phillip and I were proud of that and constantly listened to his music when we were on a mission to get stuff done around the house.

I woke up at five in the morning and began painting again. Phillip joined me as we painted until just before the sun went down. We stood in Melanie's room with paint splattered all over our clothes and ate pizza and drank Merlot in celebration. I stared at our finished work, imagining what it would be like when they were finally sleeping in their rooms. No longer would they have to worry about being hit, and hopefully Melanie's diagnosis was wrong.

⟂

"Are you getting nervous?"

"I don't know, Mom. I know it's going to be tough getting to know them, then having to let them go eventually, but I just can't imagine Melanie going through this alone."

"I understand that you feel responsible, dear, but you can't feel like you have to do this."

"I don't. I want to."

"Okay, well you know I support you no matter what. How are those bedrooms coming along?"

"They are looking nice. Me and Phillip went and got wooden letters to go on their walls. Phillip has been adding to Ben's room and it looks great. You have to come see it."

"I'll come see it as soon as they are settled. How long did they say it was going to take?"

"With everything going on with Melanie, it could be any day. I'm really not too sure how long we have to wait for Ben. Sounds like I'm going to have to bring her to the hospital to see an oncologist. She doesn't even know what's going on yet."

Mom let out a sigh. "Those poor kids. At least they have a chance now that they have you."

❧

"Gabby, I wanted to let you know that the kid's maternal grandma contacted me. She's talking about custody, so just be aware. Most likely it won't come to anything, but I wanted to give you a heads-up," Renee, our social worker, said.

"Oh, no, so I might not get them anymore?"

"You are definitely getting them, but I'm just not sure how long. Nothing is for sure. I'll let you know if it turns into anything, but our number one priority is to keep kids with their families, as you know."

"Thank you for letting me know. I just want what's best for them. How long before I can take her to the children's hospital?"

"I'm putting an emergency order on this whole thing, and you should be able to take her tomorrow. She needs the treatment now. Every day we wait is another day lost. We need to know how far her cancer has progressed."

"I'm just so scared for her."

"I understand that. It's not going to be easy."

"Poor little Melanie. She doesn't even know what is coming," I said.

"I know. It's going to be a long road for all of you."

"She's just been through so much. What about Ben?"

"You guys will be able to get Ben at the same time."

"Oh, that's wonderful."

"They are both lucky to have you and Phillip be there for them through all of this."

"There is something I need to tell you about Phillip."

She stared at me, her smile so warm, I didn't want to tell her.

"He doesn't want to be their foster parent but wants to help me with them."

"And how are you feeling?"

"A little nervous, but I want to do this. I want to help them."

"That is not a factor of you not getting the kids. It is great that he wants to help, but you don't need him to sign anything to be able to foster them."

"Oh, good."

"If there is anything you need or any questions, please give me a call. Good luck, Gabby. I'll be in touch."

"Well, somehow Renee pulled it off and we can pick up Melanie today and head to the Cities to meet with Melanie's oncologist."

"And how is Phillip doing with all of this?" Mom said.

"He's doing okay. He feels horrible about not signing the paperwork, but he'll be picking up Ben today while I bring Melanie to the hospital."

"How about their parents? Do they know Melanie is sick and they are being transferred into foster care?"

"Renee said they know. I really don't know much about them. All I know is that they are both stuck in prison for quite a while. I guess their maternal grandmother wants to be a part of the children's lives. Makes me nervous, you know."

"Hopefully she's good to them and doesn't do any drugs. Just remember, their grandma could come take them at any time."

"I know. I'm just so glad I can be there for them."

"In case I haven't told you, I'm so proud of you, Gabby. I've never had grandchildren before, and now I will have three. I can't wait to spoil them."

I laughed. "Thanks, Mom."

Travis called me six times, and I finally had a chance to answer.

"Hey, sorry about that. I've been quite busy."

I switched his call to the speaker system in my car so I could talk hands-free.

"Are you mad at me? Mad about what Missy said? I know she's lying. I just know it. I'm making her go to the doctor with me. We haven't slept together in months, I promise. If she really is pregnant, I'm taking a DNA test."

"I can't imagine what you're going through right now, but I've had a lot going on. I'm not avoiding you, I promise."

"What's going on? Is everything okay? Is it Emily? Please tell me the baby is okay."

"No, no, the baby is fine. Remember how I told you about that little boy and girl from the shelter and how I had considered fostering them?"

"Yeah."

"Well, Melanie was having some pains, so they brought her in to the doctor, and they had some tests done and we found out she has cancer. I decided to foster them, and I am going to bring her to the Cities to see an oncologist. Help her through this difficult time."

"Are you serious? That's horrible. Wait, so you are taking them in?"

I paused. "Yes, for now anyway."

He groaned and I could tell he was not happy.

"Why didn't you call me?"

How could he be so selfish? "I was a little busy. I'm sorry."

"I'm not mad for what you did, Gabby. I'm mad that I wasn't a part of your plan. I'm sad you didn't tell me. I bet you told Phillip."

"Phillip is my best friend, and he is going to help me with them. If this is going to work with us, you need to understand he is no threat to you. He's like one of my girlfriends. I'm not upset with you for Missy dropping by, and I totally trust that you don't think she's pregnant with your child. Travis, you need to trust me."

"You're right. I'm sorry, but I feel like a distance is between us, and I don't like it. I...I miss you."

"I know. I promise I'll let you know when I find anything else out. This is something I have to do. I hope you can understand that."

"Yeah."

"What's going on with your house in The Cities?"

"I'm on my way there now, but I'm still living out of both houses at the moment. I decided not to sell my house in Duluth, for now anyway. I can come back if you need me to."

"No, that's fine. Actually, I am heading to Minneapolis to take Melanie to the children's hospital. Maybe you can come tomorrow, after she is a little more comfortable. I'd really love for you to meet her, if you want to."

"I'd love that."

"Listen, I gotta go. I'll call you later, okay?"

"Okay. Drive safe."

I knocked on Melanie's door to find her waking up from a short nap. I smiled. "Hello, princess."

She was wearing a beautiful red dress with white polka dots and her navy blue tights.

She jumped into my arms. "Mommy!"

She was calling everyone who worked at the shelter Mommy.

I hugged her close and then pulled my head away so I could look right into her eyes. "How would you feel about going on a road trip with me?"

She jumped up and down and screamed. "Yay! Where we goin'? The movies, sledding, please tell me we are goin' to Dave's Pizza."

I kneeled down next to her, took her hands in mine. "We're going for a long drive to a place with a lot of nice people who are going to take care of you and make sure you are healthy. We can call it an adventure, okay?"

"Is Ben coming?"

"Not today. It's just me and you, if that's all right?"

"Okay."

She skipped into the living room to tell her brother.

Ben was watching <u>Pokemon</u> and wasn't paying attention as she gave him a hug and told him she was going on an adventure.

Phillip came out of the kitchen, and we all went into Melanie's room together.

"How would you like to come home with us?" Phillip said to Ben. "Like for the day?"

"No, like for a while. Come stay at our house?"

Ben sat there, staring at his foot while he played with his shoe, taking it on and off. He looked up, his big blue eyes glossy and broken. "No. You are trying to take us away from our parents."

"Ben, Gabby and I will never try to take the place of your mom or dad. We want you to stay with us for a while instead of staying at the shelter. Until your parents can come back."

"You aren't trying to take us away?" Ben said, looking at us from the corner of his eye as if debating whether or not he could trust what we were saying.

"No, I promise," I said. "I'm taking Melanie to Minneapolis to see a doctor for the pain she is having in her leg, and Phillip was hoping to take you to see your new room and maybe you guys will come down and see us if we have to be there for more than a day."

He put his shoe back on and stood up. "I guess I'll go, but only because I want to leave this stupid place. And you best not be lying to me or I'll be so mad."

"Cross my heart," I said as Phillip and I exchanged glances and followed Ben out the door.

"You better have toys."

Phillip followed Ben into his bedroom, and I watched Phillip pick up the small bag and ask Ben where the rest of his stuff was. I stopped to watch as Ben grabbed a pair of pajamas out of the drawer and then said, "This is all I have."

I signed some paperwork in the office, and Gloria and Denise gave me a hug and wished us well. I gave Phillip a stiff wave goodbye. His eyes looked so sad as he put the only thing Ben owned in his bag and got up to go. Melanie didn't have much more in her bag either.

Melanie insisted we stop at McDonald's on the way, but I was hoping for a sit-down restaurant so I could talk to her a little more about the hospital we were going to. Then again, why get her upset before we even get there? The light snow came down on the car as we left the drive-through with a happy meal for her and a coffee for me.

"I love snow. I told Ben snow is Santa's frozen tears, but he doesn't believe me. Do you believe in Santa Clause?"

"Of course I believe in Santa Clause," I said. "Who doesn't?"

"Ben. Santa Clause doesn't come to our house, and Ben says all the other kids at school get presents from Santa. Do you think we're on his naughty list?"

I held my breath. I needed some practice with this parenting thing. "Oh, Melanie, sometimes Santa gets a little lost when he's flying all over the world. I'm sure he would never do it on purpose. Have you tried writing him a letter?"

"I don't know how to write yet, but I can write my name." She puffed out her chest and lifted her chin.

"That's very impressive. Maybe we can write a letter together."

"But isn't Christmas a long ways away?"

"Yeah, but it's never too early to write to Santa. Now tell me all about kindergarten."

"Well, I'm in Mrs. Meghan's class. She's really pretty," she said.

"She is, huh?"

"Yes, and really, really, really nice. Sean isn't very nice. Sometimes he yells at Mrs. Meghan and tells her he hates her. Sometimes he even throws stuff, and one time he hit me right above the eye with a pencil and even punched Johnny in the nose. Sometimes I get really scared," she said, biting her nails.

I laughed and then caught myself. "That doesn't sound very nice, does it?"

She stared out the window. "No, but I think he's just really sad."

"Why do you think he's sad?"

"Because Ben does that sometimes when he's real mad, and so does Uncle Frank, and Mom and Dad, too."

"They do? Have you ever been hit with anything before?"

"Are you kidding? All the time. I know it's not on purpose. Sometimes people just get mad and hurt you."

"You know it's never okay to hurt anyone, right?"

She nodded and looked away.

"If someone hurts you, you tell an adult you can trust, okay?"

"Mmm hmm."

# KNOCK, KNOCK

We walked across the walkway high up above the road. Melanie pointed at the buildings while I stared at the one-foot glass squares we were walking across, silently appreciating that I couldn't see through them due to my extreme fear of heights. It was hard for me to take in the beautiful view when all I could think about where these squares falling and taking Melanie and me with them.

We entered the long narrow hospital hallway and reception desk where I had to show my ID and they had to make sure Melanie was a patient there. The lady then gave us directions to where we were supposed to be going. We had no problem making it to the oncology wing with all the signs along the way. We stopped and rested our hands on a railing as we looked at the five-story-high ceiling with huge glass windows covering one whole wall.

I glanced up at the ceiling and pointed out the huge skylight above our heads to Melanie.

Her jaw hung open and she let out a joyous squeal of excitement at the open view below.

"Look down there. Look down there." She pointed at the kids after only a short glance at the skylight.

Red, black, and green chairs and white tables were spread around the floor. Big teddy bears were painted on the floor and a snail slide and snake climbing wall for young kids sat right in the middle of the floor. Kids were hopping in and pushing a small play fire truck with their feet, while others played in the miniature kitchen. Tired mothers and fathers were relaxing on big couches while their kids played. A huge television hung on the wall in front of the couches, and a gigantic dance pad lay open on the floor. Children in wheelchairs wheeled themselves around a maze. Their cheers of excitement had Melanie's attention.

How did these kids have enough energy to play?

Melanie jumped up and down and nearly fell into the railing. "Can I please play down there? Pretty please?"

I looked at my watch. "Okay, but just for ten minutes. We don't want to be late to see the doctor, okay?"

"Okay. I promise."

She made her way down two flights of stairs to the play area.

I tried to stay right behind her. "Careful," I yelled out to her when she almost missed a stair.

She played with a little girl her age with a bandana around her bald head. She seemed a little tired, but kept up with Melanie.

I called Melanie, and she pouted a little bit, but quickly said goodbye to her new friend and ran over to me.

"Why was she wearing a bandana?" she asked, pointing to her own head.

"I'm really not sure. We will have to ask her the next time we see her, okay?"

No way was I going to scare her before we even saw the doctor, and I wasn't lying because I did not know for sure what the little girl was diagnosed with.

The waiting room had the same couches and chairs as the play area, and all the walls were white with bright-colored paintings. We were taken into an exam room to wait for Melanie's doctor. The room was full of tiny handprints with names on them.

Melanie fingered them one at a time. "Do you think I'll be able to write my name on the wall with my handprint?"

I did not answer her, but she didn't seem to notice.

"What does this say?"

"Tiffany," I said.

"And this name?"

"Sandy."

"And this name?"

"Zeke."

"Do you think my friend has her name on the wall in here?"

"I don't know."

The door opened.

I was relieved to have a little break from the questions I wasn't sure how to answer.

The doctor strolled in. He had a foam red nose on his face and glasses with Slinkies drooping down, reminding me of Patch Adams.

We laughed and he turned around looking for what we were laughing at. He shook my hand. "You must be Melanie," he said, looking at me.

Melanie giggled. "No, silly, I'm Melanie."

"Oh, I'm sorry. I thought you were the parent and she was the kid."

"No, silly, I'm a kid."

She jumped up to shake his hand, obviously feeling very comfortable with him. It helped me relax a little bit more.

He looked surprised as his hand met hers. "It is great to meet you, Melanie. My name is Doctor Bruce. Sorry, I'm so embarrassed. That has never happened to me before."

She gave him a two-eyed wink. "It's our little secret."

"I heard your leg has been bugging you. Does it hurt right now?" he said.

"No, but it hurt yesterday."

"So it doesn't hurt now?"

"No."

"Well, I was wondering if you could help my friend Angela out. She's trying to learn how to become a nurse, and I was hoping you might want to be her patient. What do you think about that?"

"Really? What do I have to do?"

"Well, I've been looking for a friendly little girl to show her how to give tests, and you look perfect for the job. What do you think?"

She stood up and chewed on her blond hair. "What kind of tests?"

"Yucka, you don't want to chew on your hair. Here, chew on this." He pulled a sucker out of his pocket.

Her eyes lit up. She looked at me, and I nodded in approval. She opened it up and gave him her full attention. He was good.

"Well, you would need to wear my glasses."

He took off his glasses and put them on her. "Oh, and this nose, of course."

She relaxed and sat down again. "Why?"

He shot me a questioning look. "Because she's nervous, and you need to cheer her up. Do you think you're the girl for the job?"

She squealed and clapped her hands. "Uh huh."

"Are you sure? I'm not sure. You look very funny. Um, do you know any good jokes?"

"Knock knock."

"Who's there?"

"Duane."

"Duane who?" he asked, as if he had never heard the over-told joke in his life.

"Duane the tub, I'm dwowning." She laughed, slapping her knee.

The doctor was laughing harder than she was.

"Here's another one, just in case she doesn't laugh for some reason. Why was six afraid of seven?"

She seemed to really think about this one. "I dunno, why?"

"Because seven, eight, nine," he said.

His belly laugh grew louder, even though we weren't laughing with him.

I whispered in her ear, "Did you get that one?"

"Not really."

"Yeah, stick with your first joke," he said. "There is a machine my friend Angela will be asking you to get into. It's a really cool tunnel, and there's a really cool picture you get to look at when you lay on the bed. But you have to stay really, really still. It's a great way to practice your skills for hide-and-seek. Do you think you can do that?"

She stuck up both thumbs and he did the same.

"Now, there is a secret picture on the ceiling, and I need you to tell me what it is when you get back into my office, because I forgot. Okay?

And you have to be really still."

"Okay."

"Melanie, have you ever had blood work done?"

She looked up at me with a confused look on her face. I put my face close to her.

"Remember how you went to the doctor and they had to test your blood to help with the pain in your leg?"

"Yeah."

"That's what he's talking about."

She nodded her head.

"Do you mind if we test you again?" he asked, shining a laser pointer on her hand.

"It depends. You got another sucker?"

We all started laughing, but Melanie's face didn't show any excitement.

"Sounds fair. Blue okay?"

She tapped her chin, deep in thought. "How about red."

"Red it is. So you don't mind helping my friend first then?"

She nodded at him in fast motions.

He headed for the door with the clipboard in his hand. "All right, if you can make Angela laugh, I'll juggle for you after the tests, okay?"

"Really? Promise?"

Melanie turned around to look at me with excitement in her big blue eyes that I could see clearly through the spaces in the glasses.

He tapped her on the shoulder. "I promise."

The day dragged on with all the testing, but Melanie didn't seem too bothered by all of it. She had Angela laughing hysterically. Angela had on Minnie Mouse ears and Minnie Mouse scrubs and even mimicked the way Minnie talked. Even with all the needle poking, Melanie was still in the best of spirits.

Dr. Bruce came into the exam room while Nurse Angela checked her blood pressure and heart rate. Dr. Bruce instructed her to lay on her side while he numbed the area on her lower leg where he would be inserting a needle to first conduct a bone marrow aspiration to collect fluid and then a bone marrow biopsy to collect a sample of solid bone marrow tissue. He said it would take about a half an hour and she may feel a brief sharp pain or stinging. He asked her if she was nervous and said he could sedate her if needed, but we declined because we agreed she didn't need it.

I watched him pull out the big needle and I sqeezed my eyes shut. Melanie cried out in pain, and I held her tight from behind.

"It's almost over," I reassured her.

"I need to be strong, right Dr. Bruce?" she asked him after she wiped her tears.

"You are doing a great job, and your mom's right, I'm almost done."

The nurse gave us the go ahead to play in the play area until the doctor had the results. She said to be careful, her chest will be sore for a while. She gave her a children's Tylenol and told her to take it easy. We ate lunch in the cartoon-themed cafeteria, then we played in the kid's area for an hour or so before Melanie fell asleep on the couch.

Around six, the doctor motioned for me to meet him over by the far wall. Melanie's head was resting on my lap, so I picked it up gently and placed it on the couch before walking over to him.

"The tests came back. She has acute lymphoblastic leukemia, which is also known as ALL, much easier to remember. It is the most common form of cancer in children."

I closed my eyes. This was so bad. I felt my chest collapse.

"She's going to need surgery immediately to have a port placed under her skin. It's the least painful way for us to give her chemotherapy because we can just inject it into the port and avoid poking her all the time. She will probably be in the hospital for a couple days, if not more."

I cleared my throat and wiped away tears. "Is this really serious? I'm not even sure what questions to ask right now. I'm only her foster parent, and this is just so much." If only Philip was here with me right now.

"Well, she will be receiving six to twelve months of chemo, depending upon how well her body reacts to the treatments. The side effects can include anemia, bruising and bleeding, diarrhea or constipation, high fevers, mouth and throat sores, nausea and vomiting, organ damage, hair loss, and others. These are the most common."

I shook my head and covered my mouth, letting out a loud exhale as my heart dropped in my chest.

"Don't let all of this scare you. It's better than the alternative, but she will need you during all of this."

"Organ damage?"

"Yes, chemotherapy is very toxic. It can affect the heart, lungs, kidneys, liver, and brain, and can cause temporary or permanent damage. It can also affect her hearing."

I exhaled and rubbed my face with my hands again. "Do we have to do chemo? Are there any other options?"

"Gabby, the chemotherapy will control the cancer and enhance Melanie's quality of life. It interferes with the ability of cancer cells to divide and duplicate themselves. It is given through the bloodstream, so it can reach cancer cells all over the body. It stops the cancer cells from dividing by eliminating and replacing essential enzymes the cancer cells need to survive. It's the only option. I'm sorry. She will need to come back tomorrow to have a port put in her chest. We will need to put her under for that. No food or drink after midnight. We will also do a spinal tap while she is under to check to see if the cancer spread to her spinal fluid."

"That sounds painful. It all just sounds so horrible. She's only five."

"She will be asleep and won't feel a thing. She may be a little sore when she wakes up. Anesthesia takes a lot out of children her age. Plan on keeping her down most of the day. ALL is cancer of the blood, which in turn affects her entire body. Gabby, this is going to be very hard and exhausting for both of you. You really need to just make sure you are able to do this for her. No one would look down on you if you decided to walk away."

"No way. I'm in this for the long haul. She needs me."

He nodded his head and put his hand on my shoulder. "If you need anything, you just let me know." He handed me his card. "I'll see you early in the morning. I need her back here by eight o'clock. I'll talk to her more about it tomorrow. Would you like me to talk to her today?"

"No, don't wake her."

"Okay," he said, patting my back. "Would you like me to come back when she wakes up and explain it to her?"

"Don't you think I should be the one to tell her?"

"It's up to you, but sometimes it is easier coming from the doctor."

"Okay, you don't mind?"

"Not one bit. I'll be back in a little bit. I just need to get something."

I stared at the card he gave me as he walked away. Once he was out of sight, my emotions brought me to my knees and I cried as quietly as I could while keeping an eye on Melanie sleeping so soundly. She mustn't see me break down.

Grabbing my phone to call Phillip, I noticed the missed call from Travis and swiped it to call him back.

"Is everything okay? How did it go at the hospital?"

I explained what the doctor had told me, and he was silent for a moment.

"Are you sure you want to do this?"

"Yes, Travis, I'm sure."

"Dumb question. What do you need from me?"

That was the best thing he could have said.

"I'm not sure. As soon as she wakes up we're heading to the Ronald McDonald House to stay for the night, then back to the hospital for more tests in the morning."

He asked me if I wanted him to come down, and I told him he didn't have to, but he was pretty insistent. I hurt his feelings, but I had too much to worry about and did not have time to worry about anything but Melanie right now. I told him I would call him in the morning and quickly hung up to update Phillip.

"How'd it go?" Phillip said.

I explained her diagnosis. He sighed.

"That's horrible."

"Well, the hospital set us up to stay at the Ronald McDonald House."

"Okay, we'll be there in about an hour. We're just getting into The Cities."

"I'm so worried about her. How's everything with Ben?"

"He's doing great, actually," he said. "I told him I'd take him to the Mall of America tomorrow, if that's okay."

"Sounds perfect. I'd hate for him to have to sit here all day in the hospital waiting for Melanie."

"Are you sure you don't need me?"

"I definitely need you. I need you to take care of Ben. I think Travis will be here tomorrow anyway."

My mom and Jill were walking down the steps with daisies and a present in hand. "Gotta go. My mom just showed up."

Looking up to greet them, I saw Melanie sitting up and rubbing her eyes.

"Melanie, we have visitors," I said, helping her to her feet.

She rubbed her eyes and smiled. "Doctor!"

Behind me, the doctor was juggling bean bags, at least six. We stood there watching until he stopped, catching them in his hands as they came down and then he did a bow. Everyone was circled around him clapping, including my mom and Jill.

"Angela told me you made her laugh more than anyone ever has, so I had to keep my promise."

"That was awesome," Melanie said, running up to hug him.

"I don't break my promises. Let's go for a little walk. Gabby, did you want to come with?"

"I'll be right here. You two go ahead. Unless you want me to come with."

"I think we're okay. What do you think, Melanie?"

She grabbed his hand and they walked together toward the slide. Her smile said it all.

"Now tell me what you saw on the ceiling..."

Mom came up behind me. "Where are they going?"

"There is some bad news. He's going to talk to Melanie. Maybe I should have went with them."

"Do you want to go?" Mom said.

"He's really good with her. It gives me a chance to tell you what's going on."

"What's going on?" Jill said, her voice pitchy.

"It's official. Melanie has cancer."

# CANCER SCHMANCER

Melanie didn't look too worried after she got done talking to the doctor. I wondered what he told her when she skipped over to us.

She won Mom's and Jill's hearts as they watched her open up their gift.

"A Belle doll!"

She hugged the doll, a huge grin spread across her face.

She gave them both a hug. "I love it!"

They followed us to the Ronald McDonald House.

"How did your talk go with the doctor?" I asked Melanie.

She patted my arm gently, catching me off guard.

"I'm not scared, Mom. I know you will be right beside me. Cancer shmancer," she said, shrugging her shoulders.

I shook my head as we pulled into the Ronald McDonald House. The sign and giant house made me feel a little better.

Melanie looked out the car's front window. "Is that where we're staying?"

"That's the place."

"It's huge!"

I wasn't really sure what to expect as we entered the gigantic house. The walls were lime green and a set of double doors led to a giant living room with a huge brick fireplace. The brown leather couches and dark wooden table were empty, and a woman greeted us when we entered.

Mom stared at the high ceilings and wooden tongue and groove floors in disbelief. "How much does it cost to stay here?"

"Nothing, Mom," I said quietly so Melanie wouldn't hear me. "They get donations for circumstances like ours."

"Well, this is definitely a great place to stay. Is this just for one night?"

Melanie found the playroom and began looking through the bin of dolls.

"I'm not really sure. I'm taking it one day at a time."

"Wow, I don't think I'll be skipping the donation box at McDonald's anymore. This place is exquisite."

Jill nodded and made her way over to Melanie to look through the dolls with her.

The woman who had greeted us smiled. "Right this way. I'll show you to your room."

Jill told us to go ahead while she stayed to play with Melanie.

When we came back, I heard Melanie jumping with joy. "I love it. Thank you so much."

I turned the corner to find Matt, Emily, and little baby Irene by Melanie's side as she held her new white teddy bear.

She came running up to me. "Look what they brought me, Mommy! Is this what it's like when Santa Clause comes?"

Smiling back, the thought of how supportive my family was warmed my heart. "It's even better when Santa comes. I see you met Irene."

A grin spread across her face as she got down on her hands and knees to get closer to her. "Hew-ow, I-wene," she said in a high voice, touching her toes.

Irene stared back at her from her carrier.

Melanie tugged on my shirt. "I think she likes me."

I laughed. "I think you're right."

She giggled and returned to digging in the toy bin.

I turned to hug my brother and his wife. "I'm so glad you came. Can you hang out for a while? We were just going to show Melanie the room she will be staying in."

"Of course. There is nowhere else we'd rather be," Emily said.

By eight o'clock, Melanie was fast asleep in her bed. The rest of us were in the next room discussing the day, Irene asleep in the carrier at Emily's feet.

Phillip and Ben arrived a little after eight. I started a bath for him right away. Mom and Jill announced they were tired and needed to go find their hotel.

Emily picked up the carrier.

"I think all this excitement is really getting to her," I said.

"She's adorable," Emily said, gazing at sleeping Melanie.

"I can understand why you fell in love with her so quickly."

"Can you imagine fighting for your life at just five years old?"

"No, I can't. It doesn't seem fair at all. I look at Irene and I can't imagine what you are going through."

I shook my head and tried to hold in the tears, but they overflowed my eyes. I sat down on the floor. Emily sat down beside me and wrapped her arm around my shoulder.

Matt peeked into the bedroom. "Travis is here."

I pulled myself together and stood up. "Do I have any mascara running?"

"No, you look beautiful. Remember, these tears aren't a sign of weakness; they are a sign of love."

I thanked her and hugged both Emily and Matt before they left.

Travis stood in the doorway and watched them pass by, saying hello. "Are you okay?"

I headed for my bedroom. "It's been a long day."

He pulled me in close and kissed the top of my head. "I bet. What can I do?"

"Stay for a while?"

"That I can do."

Ben got out of the bath, following Phillip to the third bedroom. Phillip decided to sleep on the floor so Ben could have the bed to himself.

"You're going to have a great time at the Mall of America with Phillip tomorrow," I said once Ben was dressed.

"I've never been there before. I want to ride all the roller coasters and eat pizza."

Phillip laughed. "Funny, that's exactly what I want to do."

I kissed the top of Ben's head as he got ready to get into bed.

He pulled away and folded his arms.

"I'm sorry. I hope I didn't make you feel uncomfortable."

He turned his head to glare at me.

"If you don't want me to kiss your head, I understand. I don't want you to feel uncomfortable."

"I don't like it."

"Thank you for telling me. Would you like to talk about it?"

"No," he shouted. "Leave me alone. I want my dad."

He jumped on the bed and turned his body away from me. I watched his shoulders rise and fall with each tear. I sat down on the bed, careful not to touch him.

"I'm sorry your dad can't be here, Ben. I want you to feel safe when you are with Phillip and me."

"She means well, promise," Phillip called out from behind me.

"I wanna go to bed. I'm not Melanie. You can't 'nipulate me like you can her."

I stood back up. "I'm sorry you feel that way, buddy. I really want to get to know you better, and I want you to know I am always here when you are ready to talk to me."

"I don't ever wanna talk to you!" he yelled, kicking his feet and pounding his fists into the pillow.

"But--"

"Get out, get out. I only want Phillip."

"Okay, buddy, I'm going." It hurt my heart, but I knew this little boy was going through a lot and he would come around when he was ready.

I closed the door and listened for a moment as he opened right up to Phillip.

"Is Melanie going to be okay?"

"Yeah, the doctors will take great care of her."

"Do you think she's going to die?"

"We are doing everything we can to keep her healthy."

"I hate God. I hate Gabby, and I hate this stupid place."

I hung my head and walked away.

⁐

Travis and I went to the fireplace downstairs, and I made us both a cup of tea.

"How are you holding up?"

"I'm doing fine. It's Melanie and Ben I'm worried about. Let's talk about something else. How's your new house?"

"Well, I'm not really working in Minneapolis yet. I'm working with some clients and referrals, but I'm still mainly out of Duluth. I'm thinking about just traveling back and forth for now."

"That'll keep you busy. And Missy?"

"She said the doctor insisted we wait until the baby is born to take the paternity test. He said it can put her into labor too soon or cause other problems."

"So, she's definitely pregnant then?"

"That's what she said, but I haven't seen her since the day you were at my house in Duluth. I don't know if she's even showing yet."

"What would you do if it was your baby?"

He stood up, shooting me an angry expression. "You don't believe me, do you?"

"I believe you don't think it's yours, but what if it is? I'm just asking. If it is your baby, what would you do?"

"It's not my baby. I don't know how many times I can tell you that."

I stood up and put my hand on his shoulder. "I'm sorry if it came off that I didn't believe you. What I mean is even if it is a very small possibility, what would you do if it was your baby?"

"You aren't getting it, Gabby. It's more likely she's lying about the whole thing to trap me. It's not my baby."

I shook my head and stepped away. "You know what, forget I even asked. That isn't what I'm saying at all."

I went to pull my hand away and he put his on top of mine. "I'm sorry. I'm just scared, that's all. I'm sorry I'm being such a jerk."

"It's been a long day for the both of us. Let's talk about this tomorrow, okay? Thank you for coming tonight."

He stepped closer to me, his eyes looking deep into mine. "What can I do to help you?"

"I don't know."

We stood there staring at each other, his hand brushing against my cheek. I closed my eyes and relaxed as his touch gave me goosebumps.

I heard Melanie's voice from down the hall. "Mom, Mom."

"I'll come back in the morning. I think your little girl needs you."

"Thanks, Travis."

I woke the kids at seven-thirty.

I watched Melanie's foot come out from under the blanket. A huge bruise had formed around her ankle.

"What happened?"

Melanie panicked and looked everywhere but at her leg. "What?"

I ran over to her side and pulled out her foot.

She shrugged it off. "I don't know."

"Did you bump it? Do you remember hurting it somehow?" I asked.

The room was quiet until Ben and Phillip came running in.

"What's wrong? What's wrong?" Phillip and Ben said in unison.

I pointed at the bruise. "Look at her leg!"

Phillip went to the door. "Hey, Gabby, can you come help me with something?"

"No, this isn't a good time. Look at Melanie's leg."

He waved me to the door. "Real quick."

I followed him, but I wasn't happy about it. I wanted to be with Melanie, not to leave her when her leg looked that way. I was about to open up my mouth and yell at him for wanting to leave the kids alone when he turned around and stared at me. He took my hand, but I pulled it away and shot him a death glare.

"I know you love Melanie, and you're nervous about today, but Gabby you are scaring her."

I clenched my teeth. "What do you know, anyway? You just walk in here and act like you know what's going on, but you aren't helping."

"You're right, I have no idea what's going on, but I can tell you that little girl is scared to death. She is getting ready to go to the hospital and have a dangerous procedure, and the only person that has ever seemed to care about her is freaking her out."

He gently put his hand on both my triceps. "Gabby, it's okay to be upset and even scared. You can take it out on me, but don't let her see the fear in your eyes. You are what's keeping her sane right now. You."

"And you are making Ben promises you can't keep."

"What?"

"You told him we won't let anything happen to her. Don't you see that you are the only person he trusts right now and if something happens to her..."

"Nothing is going to happen to her, you hear me."

I dropped my arms out of his grip. "You don't know that."

"You have to believe."

Fire burned in my chest as I began to hit him in the arm, not physically trying to hurt him, but letting out the anger and frustration in my life. Why Melanie?

I cried into his chest. "It's not fair. It's not fair. She doesn't deserve this. What if she...I mean, what would I tell Ben? She has no one, no one."

He pulled me in tighter, shushing me while rubbing my head, and then his body stiffened and he stepped away.

I turned around. There stood Travis with pink roses and a big brown teddy bear sticking out of a gift bag. "Get well soon" balloons soared above his head.

I stood there, frozen.

He handed me the gift bag dangling from his arm. "This is my gift for Melanie."

I thanked him and walked into her room, leaving him in the hallway with Phillip.

When Phillip finally entered the room, he handed me the gift bag and balloons Travis had been holding earlier.

"I need to talk to Travis. Did he leave? I'll be right back. Will you get jackets on the kids?"

His gentle demeanor turned sad. "He went down the hall to get coffee."

"I'll be right back."

He nodded.

I smiled gently and picked up my pace to catch him. "Travis, Travis wait."

He turned around and looked at me. "I didn't mean to show up without calling."

"No, it's fine."

"I guess I'm just selfish because I feel like you and Phillip have this family now, and I'm out of the picture."

We watched as a kid in a wheelchair waited to get into the elevator at the bottom of the stairs with what looked to be his father pushing him. We both watched him in awe. Neither one of them had any hair, and the boy was quite pale, but the smile on his sweet face warmed my heart. Was this going to happen to Melanie? It was a question I kept asking myself.

Travis and I exchanged glances and I knew we were both thinking the same thing.

"Do you want me here, then?"

He made his triceps bulge beneath his shirt, and as the muscles in his jaw tensed, I studied his strong body.

He caught me staring and quickly made his pecs dance by flexing them one at a time, back and forth.

I shook my head and began to laugh under my breath. "Stop doing that. I really have to get to Melanie's appointment. Come by later if you want."

He smiled at me, putting his hand behind my neck and pulled me into a warm kiss. "You know I will."

# THE HOUSE

Phillip and Ben took off to go to breakfast and then to the Mall of America. My mom, Jill, Emily, and Irene came to the hospital for support while Melanie had her procedure done. Phillip asked me over and over again if I was sure he should take Ben to the mall instead of being there for Melanie, but we both knew this was in the best interest of Ben. He should not sit in the hospital all day, worrying about his sister.

The doctor said the bruising was an effect of the cancer, and I should expect to see more as the days progressed. He told me I should let him know when I found new bruising or saw any other side effects.

The nurse wore bright yellow minion scrubs and big minion goggles on her head. She was telling Melanie a story about how she woke up this morning and her three-year-old daughter was jumping on a banana and it smeared all over the carpet.

"When I asked her why she did it, do you know what she told me? She thought if she jumped on one end she could catch it when it came out the other. Can you believe that?"

Melanie laughed and didn't notice the nurse putting an IV in her hand.

"Too many cartoons."

The nurse taped it up and said, "All done."

"It's over?" Melanie asked, surprised.

"I told you it wouldn't hurt."

After making sure Melanie hadn't had anything to eat since midnight last night, they took her into surgery to place the port in her chest and do the spinal tap. I paced around the waiting room for an hour-and-a-half until the nurse told me Melanie was awake. The nurse pulled down her gown a little bit to show me what Melanie's port looked like. It was about the size of a small coin with a silicone center. She explained Melanie could be pricked with a special needle many times without poking her with needles in her little arms and legs. The doctor told us it has a thin flexible silicone tube attached and that the port and the line is completely implanted under the skin.

When the drugs wore off, it was painful, and it took everything I had not to cry with her. I hated every minute of it. I just wanted to take away her pain.

"Ben is going to think this is so cool," Melanie said once it was all over.

"It does look pretty cool," the nurse said.

We went home for two weeks to wait until the area around the port healed enough so she could go back for chemo. Travis took some time off to help around the house, and I did my best to help Melanie keep the area clean. Travis and Phillip both helped to take care of Melanie, and Ben kept his distance. He loved his new room, but didn't want to leave it unless it was time to eat.

I drove Melanie back to the hospital, her teddy bear in her arms as we met with the nurse.

The nurse showed Melanie a tube of cream. "Now, this cream is called anesthetic cream, and we will put it on your skin to numb the area before we begin treatment, okay?"

Melanie closed her eyes, but not before I saw her worried look. She squeezed my hand. "Is it going to hurt?"

"It does sting a little bit. Would you like it if Gabby sits behind you and you can squeeze her hand?"

Melanie looked into my eyes and nodded. She looked so scared.

The nurse put the cream on the circular port, which was about an inch below the center of her right collarbone. Her skin was raised about a half inch, and I was glad it wasn't too big. They assured us it would only leave a small scar. The nurse told Melanie not to touch it or it could get infected.

The doctor came in and filled Melanie's pockets with suckers. "How are you feeling, Melanie?"

She smiled at him. "Good."

"We have to wait about a half an hour or so before it's numb, okay?"

She nodded.

I sat behind her as they washed their hands, placed gloves on, and talked to her about her favorite color and her favorite food. They talked us through the procedure. The nurse opened up a small white package and told us they were accessing the port. They all put masks on and had me put a mask on while they pulled out a needle and connected small parts before bringing it toward her. I closed my eyes and felt her hands squeezing mine. I opened my eyes to see them cleaning her skin with a big Q-tip and telling her this was to make sure she didn't get an infection. They rubbed it all over her chest and waited for it to dry. They used their hands to spread her skin and brace the port. I then saw the needle come closer. Melanie turned her head and cried out in pain.

"It's all over, Melanie," the doctor said. "Stay still for one more second, okay?"

They turned the tube and then put some gauze under the tube and then put the dressing over it. They then put a window-like bandage over the top so we could still see where the needle was placed. Carefully, they worked their gloved fingers around the edges, pressing it down. I noticed I wasn't breathing.

"Almost done, Melanie. How are you doing, sweetheart?"

She cried harder. "That hurt." After the sealing was done, the doctor told her what a good girl she was and how proud of her he was. She looked down to try to see it. "How long do I have to have this needle in me?"

"Just until the end of the day, and then Gabby can take you to play downstairs if you are feeling up to it, okay?"

Melanie slept most of the day as I sat there staring at her, replaying the needle in my head. It seemed so big and the way she cried just ate at me. I didn't want her to have to go through this again. At the end of the day, the doctor came into the room to remove the needle. Melanie was scared and held my hand, even though the doctor said this wouldn't be as painful.

They put fluid into the needle through a syringe. They flushed the port after with medicine they called Heparin. They said it helps to prevent the port from becoming blocked so that it will work well every time we come to the hospital.

I kissed the top of her head. "You were so brave."

After it was done and they removed the needle, they checked the port for redness and said it looked really good.

The doctor smiled at Melanie. "Well, maybe you can get Gabby to take you down to the play area now."

Her face broke into a big grin. "Yeah! Can we, Gabby? Can we, please?"

I winked at her. "As long as it's okay with the doctor."

The doctor pointed to the incision and port area. "You just need to be careful not to bump this area, okay?"

"I promise."

"Now, I'm going to talk to Gabby for a minute, if that's okay with you."

"Okay."

We stepped outside the door. "As you know, we've begun the chemotherapy. We're doing lower doses of chemo over a longer period of time. In four days you will need to come back for a follow-up checkup."

"Why does she need to do this?" I said.

"She needs this done so we can determine the stage or progression of her leukemia, check her iron levels, and monitor how well the treatment is working."

"Why does she have so much energy after her chemo? What should I expect from it?"

"Well, the chemo attacks cells that are dividing quickly, which is why they work against cancer cells. The side effects come from other cells in the body, like the lining of the mouth and intestines. Hair follicles divide quickly and can be affected by chemo, which can lead to hair loss, mouth sores, loss of appetite, diarrhea, nausea and vomiting, increased risk of infections, and more bruising and bleeding, and also fatigue. It varies from patient to patient."

I nodded again and chewed on my thumbnail.

"Gabby, you need to stay strong for Melanie, okay? You can't do this on your own, so don't expect to. Ask for help. You have a lot of family support. She is going to be in a tremendous amount of pain."

"Okay."

I followed him back into the room, where Melanie was once again giggling and chattering like it was just another day.

"Are you ready yet, Mom? I wanna play."

If she only knew how the way she sometimes called me Mom made it hard to ever be able to say no to her.

I held Irene tightly in my arms while Emily and I watched Melanie play. I thought back to the children I'd seen since I'd been here that didn't have any hair, and I wondered how long it would take for Melanie's hair to fall out. The doctor was great at explaining to her what he was doing so she could understand what might happen. She was scared and cried, but he assured her she was going to be okay.

After she was done playing, we all went back to the Ronald McDonald House that we started calling The House.

Melanie and I snuggled in the bed and watched <u>Frozen</u>. I texted Phillip to let him know the procedure was over and then I texted Travis.

Travis wanted to come to The House and meet with us, but I told him she was pretty exhausted and that he should come by tomorrow instead.

After Melanie fell asleep, I shut her door and joined Emily at the table.

"How is she?"

I rubbed my eyes. "Sleeping."

"And how are you doing?"

"I'm emotionally drained. I'm so worried about her. Where are Mom and Jill?"

"They went back to their hotel. This place is amazing, and there is so much food. Would you like me to get you something to eat?"

"No, I'm not that hungry. Where's Irene?"

"Matt took her to meet up with Phillip and Ben at the mall."

"I'm so glad you stayed with me. How is the fundraiser planning going?"

"I think we're pretty much set. Everything is booked and ready to go. Don't you worry about a thing. Tickets and invites are out, and we've gotten a lot of community support."

"I'm so glad to hear that. I never doubted you. I'm thinking about telling Melanie's story in my speech."

Emily smiled. "I think that's a great idea."

I heard my phone and pulled it out to see Renee's name.

"It's my social worker. Hang on."

Renee told me Melanie and Ben's grandma would be stopping by tomorrow to see the kids. She was glad to hear Melanie was doing well, considering the whole situation. As I hung up the phone, I wished I could take her cancer away. How much was too much for this poor little girl to take?

⌘

"Can I go to the playroom?" Melanie asked when she woke up.

I couldn't believe the energy she had after beginning chemo. "As long as you promise to be careful."

Emily and I followed her to the playroom.

"Gabby!"

Ben came running down the hall and caught up to Melanie.

"The Mall of America was so awesome, Mel. I rode roller coasters and ate pizza and, oh, I wish you coulda been there! You would just love it. I even saw Dora and Boots."

Melanie pointed to the circle beneath her collarbone. "Oh Ben, you have to see my cool scar. Look, look."

Ben got closer and covered his mouth with his hand. "You finally got all the bandages taken off? Wow, that's cool. Does it still hurt?"

"A little bit when they stuck the needle in."

"A needle?"

"Yep, it all goes right into my port. I'm on chemo and I might lose my hair and get to wear cool scarves."

"Are you scared?"

"Nah, it's just hair. Wanna play Chutes and Ladders with me?"

"Yeah."

They ran off to set it up at the kitchen table.

Phillip came up and hugged me. "How are you holding up?"

"It's been a long day."

"Why don't the two of you get a bite to eat at that pizza place down the street," Emily said. "I can keep an eye on the kids. It'll be fun."

"I can't do that. I can't leave them. Ben isn't exactly--" I tried to find the right words. "He doesn't like to be without Phillip."

"It'll be good for the both of you," she said, cutting me off. "Plus, you have some catching up to do that I don't think you want the kids to overhear."

I looked at Phillip for approval. He nodded in agreement. "I think it's a great idea, don't you?"

"As long as the kids are okay with it. And only for a little bit."

"How did everything go today?" Phillip asked.

"Well, we started the chemo today, as you know. It will be given to her in cycles with each period of treatment followed by a rest period to give her body time to recover."

"I'm just glad she's getting lower doses of chemo, even if it is over a long period of time. I can't believe she has that much energy after her first day on chemo."

"Me neither. The doctor said it may take a few days for the effects to kick in. I just hate that they are pretty much putting poison into her body to kill not only the bad cancer cells, but her good cells, too," I said.

The waitress took our order of pizza and martinis.

"It doesn't seem right, does it? I wish there was a better way, but I guess we need to trust the professionals. I can't help but wonder what consequences it will have on her health when she gets older."

I nodded.

An older woman with a cane walked by our table and picked up something off the floor behind me. She held it in front of me. "Excuse me, ma'am, is this your phone?"

"Yes, I must have dropped it. Thank you." I took my phone and shoved it in my purse, making sure the ringer was on.

She stopped and stared at us for a moment with a big grin on her face. "I must say, you two make a really cute couple. You look so happy."

"We aren't--"

"I'm sorry to bother you, but this is the anniversary of the day my husband passed away. We were together fifty years."

"I'm so sorry to hear that. How many years has it been since he passed?" I asked.

"This is the first anniversary. I made it a whole year without him, but I'm not sure how."

Her silver hair perfectly wrapped around her head and stopped at her shoulders. When she smiled, she smiled with her whole face, which made me forget for just a couple seconds what was going on in my life.

"I came here to think about him, and I prayed he'd give me a sign he was here with me. I look at the two of you together and I realize that you are my sign. The chemistry you share is just like me and my Frank." She put her hand on my shoulder. "Don't take each other for granted. Give yourselves to each other each and every day. For tomorrow, it may be gone."

She walked away, and Phillip and I stared in silence until he started laughing. I tried so hard not to laugh, but our laughter became hysterical.

"Why do we seem to give everyone that reaction?" I said.

I took the martini from the waitress as she came back to our table.

"Is there anything else I can get you?"

Phillip and I tried to keep ourselves from continuing to laugh. "No, I think we're good, thanks," I said.

He held his glass up in the air. "To Melanie and Ben."

"To Melanie and Ben, and to us," I said.

"To us."

# WHY ME?

It felt good to clear my mind and not think about the procedures for a little while. Phillip had me in tears laughing about Lucy walking into our glass door.

I laughed. "No way. She thought the door was open? It's March."

"She went to bring our mail in, forgot the door was shut, and bam, broken nose."

"That is unbelievable. Is she okay?"

"I don't really know. She called me to yell at me after it happened."

We made our way back to The House. "It's horrible that we're laughing, but it just makes no sense. How are the two of you doing anyway?"

"How are you and Travis doing?"

"Good point," I said. "It's all a mystery, I guess."

"Yeah. Who knew two sweet kids would make our significant others so insecure?"

"Well, there seems to be something about our friendship that makes everyone think we are in love. You are like my brother. I just don't understand."

He opened the door for me. "That's the point. No one understands that a man and a woman can be best friends without screwing. It's their problem, not ours."

I heard Melanie's screams echoing down the hallway, and I raced to her room.

She was throwing up in a bucket on her lap. Emily was holding her hair back and helping her hold the bucket in place.

"Are you okay, Melanie? I'm so sorry. I shouldn't have left."

"She's fine. She's just a little nauseous, right honey?"

Melanie nodded her head, her face looking a little green. "I don't feel good."

Her eyes filled up with tears and she moaned again.

I ran into the bathroom for a wet washcloth and held it on her forehead. She opened her eyes and forced a smile as she looked into my eyes, then she closed them again.

"Mommy, will you lay with me?"

"I'm right here, sweetie," I whispered.

I crawled into bed with her and snuggled her from behind as she moved onto her side. I began running my fingers through her hair.

Phillip squeezed her hand and then left the room with Ben.

I heard Ben from the hallway. "Why's she so sick? What happened?"

"Her body is fighting the infection and sometimes it's going to make her sick. She's going to be all right, bud."

Emily closed our door. "Who's up for a game of checkers?"

"Why did this have to happen to me? What did I do wrong?" Melanie whispered.

"Oh, honey, you did nothing wrong. Absolutely nothing."

"Then why is no one else sick? Why doesn't anyone else have to get shots and a thing in their chest?"

She rolled over and looked at me. She needed an explanation. An explanation I did not have.

"You didn't do anything, but sometimes our bodies get infections we have to fight off. Luckily you are such a strong little girl. We will get through this together. Why don't you close your eyes and get some sleep."

"Promise you won't leave?"

"I promise."

I laid in bed thinking about my father, who was shot and killed by my grandfather when I was her age. I remember my mom coming home from the hospital. I was there with Aunt Jill when she arrived. Her eyes were dark and swollen, no smile spread across her face when she saw me. She slept for almost a week when she got home from the hospital. Jill tried and tried to make her eat, but she was just so sad. I crawled in bed with my mom, rubbing her back and gave her lots of hugs and kisses. She never pushed me away; she just pulled me in closer. I'd tell her knock-knock jokes and draw her lots of colorful pictures. I even sang to her to try to get her to be happy again.

For a while, I thought it was me making my mom unhappy. One day she got out of bed and I began singing, "The Sun Will Come Out Tomorrow," and she sang with me. The next day she took me out for ice cream. She started putting on makeup again, and dressing up in nice clothes. She told me that I was the reason she was happy again. She always said I saved her life. Matt, too. She was pregnant with him at this time.

I often try to remember Dad's funeral, but I have no recollection of it at all. I wonder if there even was a funeral, but I was scared to bring it up to Mom. I worried she didn't have one for him, and she'd just get depressed about it. Even worse, I wonder if I blocked it out, that if I remembered it, I'd remember how horrific it was.

My favorite memory was watching my mother's belly expand and the day my brother was born. Mom let me hold him in the rocking chair as we sang "Tomorrow." I even played the lead role in Annie in high school. To this day, when I'm feeling sad, my mom will come over and sing that song as loud and off key as she can until I crack a smile. It works for the both of us.

Phillip thought it was the best thing ever. One time he even videotaped her on his phone. He said he was going to put it on social media, but he knew my mom would kill him, and she is not the kind of person you want to piss off.

Melanie moaned and held her stomach, bringing me back to reality. "My tummy hurts."

She began throwing up again, the sour smell making my stomach turn. I held the blue bucket in front of her and held her hair back.

Her eyes filled with tears when it turned to dry heaving. She laid back down, tucking her face beneath my chin.

I held her in my arms, and rubbed her back as I forced myself not to cry.

"It's going to be okay, Melanie," I whispered, but wondered if I was wrong.

She finally fell asleep. I got up to check on Ben and Phillip. They were in the other room playing the Wii.

I gave Ben's shoulder a squeeze and sat down beside him on the couch. "Who's winning?"

When he didn't answer me, Phillip chimed in.

"Ben is. Although he stacked his team with all the best players while I was in the bathroom."

Ben focused as Bowser batted the ball, screaming out with joy when he got a home run. Swinging his remote back and forth, Ben danced in front of us.

He pointed at Phillip and laughed. "Oh yeah, that's right, in your face." Phillip and I exchanged glances, and before I could begin lecturing Ben on sportsmanship, a tap on my shoulder left me jumping in the air.

I turned around. "Travis, you scared the crap out of me."

He leaned over the back of the couch and watched the game. "Who is Luigi?"

"I am," Ben said.

"Wow, kid, you're pretty good. I may have to challenge you sometime."

"Just don't leave him alone and go to the bathroom," Phillip said.

"Note taken."

Travis kissed my check. "Do you want to go for a little walk with me?"

"I don't know. Melanie has been a little sick tonight and I..."

"I got it," Phillip said. "Go for a walk. If she wakes up, I'll text you."

"Are you sure? I'm just worried she'll be upset if she wakes up and I'm not here. I promised her I'd sleep with her tonight."

"She'll be fine. Crawl back in with her when you get back. She'll understand."

Phillip groaned when his team struck out. "Ben, you're killin' me."

"We got this," Ben said, swatting at the air. "It's not like you're our mom or anything."

My throat tightened and my mouth opened, but no words came out.

Phillip paused the game and took my hand as he led me to Travis. I saw his forced smile as he patted my back as if to say Ben did not mean what he said.

I couldn't breathe until I got into the hallway. His words stung right to my soul. Why did he hate me so much?

Travis held up my jacket. "Where do you want to go?"

He didn't notice how much Ben's words hurt me. Phillip always knew what I was feeling by just looking at me.

"Let's just walk."

We found a park close by, and I sat down on one of the swings.

"Gabriella, you are so beautiful, you know that?"

I felt my heart beating in my stomach. I pushed off with the swing. "You are too kind." He got down on his knees in the pebbles so he was as close as a whisper. "You know Ben didn't mean what he said."

"What?" Did he just say what I thought he just said?

"He's scared. He doesn't understand why his parents aren't here. If he's bonding with Phillip, he will bond with you."

"I didn't think you heard him."

"I heard him. Open up to me. I'm here to listen."

"I'm sorry I underestimated you."

"I have never felt about anyone in all my life the way I feel about you. I worry I'm going to lose you."

"Lose me?"

"Yes, I love you so much, and I want everything to work out with us."

He pulled a box out of his back pocket.

My stomach flipped in my chest until I realized it was too big to be a ring.

"Travis, you shouldn't have."

"You may not feel the same way when you open it. It's just a very old bronze key."

"What's this for?" I said, holding it in the palm of my hand. It looked antique, important.

"I can't tell you just yet. I know you have a lot going on, and I wanted to do something special for you, to help with the hard days."

I pushed off the ground just a little bit so I could grab the neck of his jacket and pull myself into him. My lips curled around his and they locked together. I pulled away, leaving him breathless, needy.

"Wow, you really like gifts, don't you."

I shook my head and let out a groan.

"It was just a joke."

I smiled. "I know. So was that."

He shook his head. "You are trouble, you know that?"

I reached into my pocket and pulled out my phone to make sure it was on in case Phillip tried calling. "I love surprises, but this one really has me wondering. That was really sweet of you, you know that?"

"I have to fly to New York for a couple of days to speak with some potential clients. I feel awful leaving at a time like this. You say the word and I'll stay."

I grasped his hand and pulled him into me so I could rest my hands behind his head. I licked the tip of his slightly prominent nose, leaving him taken aback with the shock of what I did.

"If you don't stop doing that, I'm not going to be able to bring you home tonight," he said. "I will send you a couple gifts while I'm gone."

"I'm sorry. You are just too cute. Go to New York. You need to go. Can I open the gifts in front of Melanie?"

"Yes, unless it has two hearts in the corner, then that means it's for your eyes only."

"Wait, how many gifts are there?"

"A package almost every day I'm gone."

I raised my eyebrows. "How many days will you be gone?"

"Seven."

"Seven, huh? Are you trying to buy my love?"

"No. Why, is it working?"

I shook my head.

"Because I love you, Gabriella."

I felt the blood drain from my face. I stood there for a moment, then I opened my mouth to talk, but nothing came out.

He placed his finger over my lips to stop them from parting. "It's okay. Don't say the words until you mean them."

He pulled his hands away and kissed me again.

# FOURTEENTH FLOOR

The child life specialists came to play with Melanie at the hospital. I did not want to go very far, but I had to leave the room so they could have some time with her. I constantly had a list of questions for the doctors when they came in, and they never seemed sick of me asking, or made me feel as though they were dumb questions.

I couldn't stop thinking about Melanie's grandmother coming to visit today. Phillip promised he'd make it back by nine with Ben. Although they were just playing in the play area, I felt a bit nervous their grandmother would come and be angry that Ben wasn't there. Was she as bad as their uncle? Would she hurt them? Maybe she hurt them in the past. How could I protect them if she decided to take them? Did she know about the uncle and if he would be around them? All these thoughts increased my anxiety.

I walked into the hospital room and found a lady dressed in a black dress, wearing too much perfume and another lady with a badge around her neck, I suspected must be the social worker.

I forced a smile and extended my hand. "Hello, I'm Gabby. You must be Melanie's grandma," I said.

Melanie was sitting up in bed and she had some color in her face. The nurse was taking her vitals.

Her grandma's eyes were cold when she shook my hand. "I'm Sheri."

"And I'm Tina, the social worker from the Minneapolis area," said the other lady, shaking my hand. "I'm working close with Renee on this case. I will be a part of this journey while Melanie is in and out of the hospital."

We made small talk before Ben and Phillip entered the room. Ben jumped into her arms, and I couldn't help but feel a little jealous, but glad they seemed to like her. She couldn't be that bad. Maybe she's just a little bit overprotective.

"We will give you guys some time alone," I said.

Tina nodded. "I would like to talk to you when you come back. How does noon sound?"

"That sounds just fine."

Ben wouldn't even look at me, but Melanie smiled at me as we left.

"Well, she doesn't seem so bad," Phillip said as we made our way down the shiny white hall.

I swallowed my tears. "Yeah, I can't help but feel like Ben hates me."

"He doesn't hate you. He's just scared. You know how much he's been through. Let's go get some coffee."

He led the way to the waiting room.

"What did the doctor say?"

It helped my nerves that he did not try to push me to talk about Sheri or Ben. We were both scared we were going to lose them if this grandmother decided to take them. Where was she when their mother died and the kids were being abused? Why did she wait until now to see them?

Phillip handed me a cup of coffee with two cubes of sugar and one teaspoon of cream, just the way I liked it. All I could picture was the way Melanie made me feel when she smiled at me, the way Ben warmed up to Phillip. I needed him to see that I just wanted to be a part of his life. Why did he hate me so much?

"The doctor said he wants to do the bone marrow aspiration and spinal tap tomorrow to check the progress of her treatment," I said.

"Already? Is he sure he wants to do that right now when she's so sick?"

"He's a doctor, Phillip. You don't think he'd make her do it if he didn't have to, do you?"

I felt horrible as the words came out, but there was no taking them back now. A fire was building in my lungs and burning my insides. I could not help the anger I felt, and he was in my line of fire.

"Hey, I'm on your side," he said.

"It's not like you care. You're running around with Ben having fun, taking him to the Mall of America and playing with him in that play place. He hates me. I don't get to spend any time with him at all. You aren't here watching Melanie get sick and not able to do a damn thing about it. You just don't get it."

"You asked me to keep him busy so he didn't have to watch his sister get sick. If you want to switch, I'd love to be there for Melanie. Ben is hurting, too. Whatever you need, you just have to ask. I don't know what you want from me. I'm doing everything I can."

"That's the thing, Phillip. You decided not sign the papers, and I just feel so alone. We were so stupid to think this could work when you won't take any responsibility for them."

The fire turned to tears and the burning in my body became numb. Phillip pulled me into his chest as I sobbed.

"It's going to be okay, Gabbs. It's going to be okay. You know I love those kids."

"It's not fair. I'm sorry I keep taking it out on you. What if something happens to them, Phillip? I know she's going to take them and there is nothing I can do about it. How can I protect them? How?"

He held my head in his hands and tipped my chin up to meet his gaze. "We don't know she's going to take them for sure. We need to pray and work together through this. I won't let anything happen to them. I won't. We have to trust that whatever is supposed to happen will happen. We have each other no matter what."

"I'm just so scared."

"Me, too."

"I worry she's going to get a lot worse. The constant throwing up-- can this really get worse for her? I hate seeing her like this."

"I know."

I pulled my phone out of my pocket. "Travis should be here soon."

"Here at the hospital?"

"I sent him a text asking him how close he was, and he just replied he was just pulling up at the hospital. He's coming to say goodbye before he takes off for New York for business."

"Travis?"

"Yeah, do you want to come downstairs with me?"

"No, go ahead. I'll be right here."

"Have you called Lucy at all?"

"No."

"You should. Call me if you hear anything. Thank you for letting me vent."

"That's what I'm here for."

Thinking about Phillip sitting in the waiting room for two hours before we could go in and see the kids gave me guilt twinges. If the roles were reversed and Lucy was here, he would never leave me to be with her. But Travis was exciting and calming, and I needed him to distract me from watching the clock.

As the elevator doors opened, the little girl who played with Melanie the day we got here in the play area was standing in the elevator. She had a big grin on her face as she held her dad's hand. She was no older than ten.

She shook my hand, and I smiled at her purple and gold Vikings bandana.

"You're Melanie's mom."

"Hello again," I said.

"Where is Melanie? Can she play?"

"She has some visitors right now, but maybe another day. Are you a Vikings fan?"

She adjusted her bandana. "Yes, I never miss a game. Does Melanie have cancer?"

Her father gasped. "Sandy. I'm so sorry. You'll have to excuse my nosey daughter; she seems to have lost her manners."

"I'm sorry, Dad," she said, putting her head down in shame of her behavior.

"No, it's fine. Yes, she has cancer."

Saying it aloud was not an easy task. I breathed in deeply and fought the tears. An image of her lying in bed so weak caught me off guard.

"If you don't mind me asking, what kind of cancer does she have?"

The elevator door opened on the first floor, giving me a chance to change the subject, but I knew not answering her question would be rude.

Sandy and her father followed behind me to the main entrance where Travis was waiting. "You don't have to answer that question," he said.

I turned around to face them. "She has leukemia."

"ALL?"

My heartbeat began to race as my mouth fell open. "You've heard of it?"

Sandy giggled and shook her head. "I had ALL. I mean, I'm in remission now, but I was diagnosed with it nine months ago."

I finally looked at her, really looked at her for the first time. She was thin and pale, her eyes sunken in, and black rings seemed permanently bruised around her eyes. I gasped aloud and then felt embarrassed for my reaction. "I'm so sorry. I guess I didn't realize how common it was."

"It's okay," her dad said. "It's been a rough battle, but we finally get to go home next week, and we're excited."

"I even get to start school next month. I'm so excited. Tell Melanie that she's going to be okay. She can beat this. Make sure to buy her a juicer. It helps with the side effects of the chemo."

She sounded so grown up as she rattled off a bunch of advice. "Don't go wig shopping until she's completely bald because it may not fit the same once she loses all her hair. And tell her to ask for ice gloves and socks so her nails don't go black and fall off. And get a lot of sleep and plenty of water so she doesn't get horrible headaches. And most importantly, get an ice cold cap so she doesn't lose her hair." She then pointed to her head and said, "Although it didn't work for me."

My heart ached for this young girl. Sandy talked as if she was in her thirties, like all of this chemo made her appreciate the importance of life. She knew way too much about cancer when she should be playing with dolls and watching cartoons.

"Most importantly, keep her positive, this process will make her a better person, although she will be very ill first," her dad said.

"Oh, and don't forget to pray," Sandy yelled out as she waved and headed in the other direction.

I found myself still waving in their direction, even though they were no longer looking at me. I turned around and walked toward Travis as soon as they were no longer in sight. He was staring at me with a confused look on his face and hadn't moved from across the room since I first spotted him.

"Who was that?"

"A little girl who has the same kind of leukemia as Melanie. Well, had the same kind of leukemia anyway."

He put his arm around me and we made our way toward the car. "Had?"

"Yeah, had. She's in remission."

"That's wonderful!"

"I can't get over how positive she was, Travis, and she was so frail and thin and weak. I can't help but worry that is going to be Melanie soon."

"It's not," he said.

"And how do you know that?"

"Because meeting that little girl was a sign."

"If only it was that easy," I said with a sigh.

"Let me take you for a quick drive," Travis said.

I didn't argue with him about leaving, because I needed to get away. We were silent the rest of the drive, almost like Travis knew I needed some time to think. We passed children walking along the streets with their moms, so healthy and happy. I couldn't help being angry with God. Why Melanie? She had been through so much in her short life. She deserves a break. What if her grandmother took her from us, and I wasn't there to hold her when she cried or help her deal with all the side effects? Don't cry, Gabriella, don't cry.

We neared the Minneapolis skyline, but I had no idea where we were going. All I could think about was Melanie getting sicker and me not being there to hold her and comfort her. I stared at the skyscrapers, one in particular, the one with a circular top. It reminded me of Melanie and how she was different than all the other girls her age.

"What are you thinking about?"

I blinked back tears. "The skyline."

He looked up, as if seeing it for the first time. "Minneapolis is beautiful, isn't it? Have you been to New York City? Now that's a skyline."

"I've always wanted to go, but no. I love the building with the circular top."

"That's Capella Tower. It used to be called the First Bank Place. It connects to the Minneapolis skyway system, which is the biggest skyway system in the world."

"Really? I didn't know that."

"The first skyway opened in nineteen sixty-two. It's close to eight miles of walkways, and when the US Bank Stadium is complete, it will extend another mile. They say the elevated passages signify escape from traffic noise, weather, of course, and stoplights."

"Aren't you just full of knowledge."

"My new office is in that building, and I read an article about it in the Star Tribune."

"I see."

He grinned and interlocked his fingers with mine. "I'm full of useless information."

I rubbed my fingers along his hand. His nails were cuticle-free, but his fingers were rough, as if he did a lot of hard labor.

"Are you judging my rough hands?"

"No, I was actually wondering why they were so rough. I didn't think you'd have much time to do carpentry."

He laughed. "I like to pour concrete sometimes. I have a buddy in Duluth who does a lot of masonry." He patted his flat stomach. "It keeps me in shape." We pulled up to a large brick building several stories high.

"What's this?"

"It's my new place."

"I thought you bought a house?"

"Well, I bought a home."

I was surprised he hadn't bought a mansion. Maybe he wasn't as showy as I thought. "Hmm, not what I expected."

He laughed as I followed him inside. A doorman opened the door for us and pushed fourteen on the elevator. The elevator was clean, but not too fancy. The doors opened up and Travis guided me to his door. He waved me in and I stepped into a simple, yet elegant apartment. Artwork covered his walls and reminded me of a gallery. Red, black, and white was the theme throughout.

I strolled into the kitchen and fat chef figurines greeted me. Even his clock had a fat chef on it.

The apartment was beautiful, but not fancy like his home in Duluth. It was still a little empty.

"I have something to show you."

He took my hand and guided me to the red curtains that hung on his ten-foot walls. "Ready?"

I nodded.

The light blinded me for a moment, so I squeezed my eyes shut. Then I opened them and gasped. The Minneapolis skyline was about a mile or two in front of me, but it looked so much closer. I felt like I could just reach out and grab it.

"Do you like the view?"

He slid open the sliding glass doors and led me out on the patio. I put my hands on the silver railing. I could see the tops of trees and the highway that led around the high buildings. It reminded me of a movie scene, not real life.

The clouds stood still as a chill ran down my spine and I searched for words. "It's beautiful," I said, still trying to take it all in.

"I decided not to buy the big house and settled for a great view. I took your advice and I'm keeping my home in Duluth after all."

"You're going to keep both?"

"Yes. I want to be close to you since you can't leave Hibbing for a while."

I turned back to the view. It was one of the most beautiful views I had ever seen, and I found it hard to look away. A vision of Melanie and

Ben sitting on the deck with us, sharing this moment together, made me smile. I imagined my arms around them as we gazed at the buildings illuminated in the dark.

"It's beautiful. Absolutely perfect."

He pulled me in and we stared at the city together, my head on his shoulder.

"She's going to be okay, Gabbs. They are going to be okay," he whispered.

I turned and faced him, then took his hands in mine. "Who knew we'd end up together? I mean, we hardly knew each other as kids, but we sure spent a lot of time together. And now, now we haven't even been together that long, and I feel this gravitation toward you, no matter how hard I fight it."

"Why do you want to fight it?"

He stared so deeply into my eyes, as though he saw into my soul.

"I'm just scared, I guess. You have so much, and I..."

"Don't even say it. It's money, possessions, nothing more than paper."

I shook my head and glanced at the view again. "I know."

"Then let me in."

Our soft kiss became harder and deeper. I longed for him. Finally, I let him in and dropped my shield. His hands began to explore my body and our kiss made the blood rush to my head. I didn't want to let go.

My phone rang and I fumbled to answer it, my hands shaky as I fought to slow my breathing.

"Hello?"

# PROGRESS

"Am I going to die?"

Melanie climbed into my lap with <u>Goodnight Moon</u> in her hand.

The social worker had to leave in a hurry but called me to let me know Sheri wanted my number so we could talk. I told her that was fine.

"What, honey? Why do you think that?"

"I'm so tired, and I just hurt all over."

"I'm so sorry." I stared into those beautiful blue eyes and anger washed over me. I couldn't take her pain away or even think of anything to say to make her feel better.

"Are you an angel?"

I raised my eyebrows, once again unsure of what to say. "An angel?"

"My mommy told me you were my angel."

"Honey, your mom doesn't know me."

"I see her sometimes."

"You do? Like while you're sleeping?" She was getting delusional. It worried me. I wondered if I should call the doctor. Something was making her see things. Was it the drugs, the cancer? She had to be dreaming of her mother.

"Yeah. Will you lay with me, Mommy? I'm so tired."

"I'd love to." I crawled into bed with her and tucked the blankets up to her chin.

"My mom said it's okay to call you Mom. She doesn't mind."

I wiped her tears with the back of my hand and kissed her forehead. "Oh, Melanie, everything is going to be okay."

"Will you sing to me?"

"What would you like me to sing?"

"Anything," she said, closing her eyes.

"I know just the song. It's a song me and my mom always sing to each other when we are scared or having a bad day."

"Really? You have bad days?"

"Oh, honey, we all have bad days. Have you ever heard of <u>Annie</u>?"

She shook her head, and as I began to sing, her smile appeared and she hummed to it. When I finished, she smiled at me and asked me to sing it again.

We woke up when the nurse came in to take her vitals. I stayed with Melanie, and each time she woke up she asked me to tickle her back. I did so without hesitation.

She jumped out of bed around eight in the morning and asked if she could play downstairs. "Please, Mommy, please will you let me? I feel so good today. I want to play."

"How about this. The doctor will be in to check on you soon, and you can ask him, okay?"

"Yay! Grandma is coming to visit me again soon. She said she is going to buy me a Made-to-Move Barbie, one that looks just like me. Isn't that great?"

"Really? That is so sweet of her. You really love her, don't you?"

"She never liked Uncle Ronnie. He married my Aunt Lizze."

"Is your Aunt Lizze your mom's sister?"

She nodded. "Uncle Ronnie is mean and scares me. Grandma said he's sick. Is that true? Is he sick like me?"

"No...he's not sick like you. His brain wasn't formed the same way yours is. No one should ever hurt you, ever."

"It's mainly my fault, I--"

"It's not your fault," I said, a little too loud, and she jumped at my words. "I'm sorry. I'm just really sad. I won't let anyone hurt you again, I promise. But Melanie, it's not your fault, okay?"

I had no control whether or not she got hurt again or even if her grandma took custody of her. I was only her foster parent, her temporary parent. I had no say in the matter.

"Are we going to live with Grandma?"

Her words felt like a knife in my gut. "Would you like to go live with your grandma?"

She sighed, and her little face puckered into a frown. "I don't know. I do, but I also want to live with you and Phillip. Ben wants to live with Grandma until Mom and Dad get better."

I tried not to let her words hurt me. "You're a very honest little girl, you know that? I love that about you."

"Hello?"

The doctor poked his head in after he knocked. "How are you doing, Melanie?"

"I wanna go play downstairs, and Mom said I can if you say it's okay."

His eyebrows raised. "Well, I'm glad you are feeling so well. Are you dizzy at all?"

"No."

"Have you eaten anything yet?"

Her bottom lip quivered. "No."

"Well then, why don't you eat this banana, and if it's okay with..." He pointed at me, unsure of what to call me.

Melanie giggled. "My mom."

"Right, your mom, then I don't see why not."

His smile was so heartwarming it calmed me down, especially since Melanie was feeling good today.

"While you're eating that banana, I have a new joke for you."

She took a bite and studied him.

"Why did the chicken cross the road?"

She grimaced. "To get to the other side."

"Nope, to get to the dummy's house."

Melanie and I both shook our heads. His jokes really needed some fine-tuning. He was a horrible joke teller, and I wondered if it was on purpose. I would never have known he was a doctor if I would have seen him on the street. His broad shoulders and strong jawline were quite sexy, and even his nerdy glasses were kind of cute. The amount of energy he had was inspiring, and a sense of positivity entered the room with him.

"Knock, knock," he said.

"Who's there?" Melanie said, looking bored.

"The chicken."

He stood there staring at her and suddenly she started laughing hard and couldn't stop. Her laughter turned into a cough, a deep cough that took at least ten seconds before it stopped.

"I don't get it. Why is that so funny?" I said.

I moved closer to Melanie as the coughing began again. What if she would start coughing up blood or something? Melanie finally stopped, but a huge smile still remained on her face.

"The chicken crossed the road to go to the dummy's house, and then he said knock knock and that he was the chicken. I'm the dummy, Mom, get it?"

I laughed, too, but I still didn't think it was as funny as she did. It was so great to see her smiling again.

The doctor pushed her in a wheelchair until we reached the play area.

"Take it easy, Melanie, okay?"

She was gone before he could say anything else.

He pointed to the bench, and we sat down next to each other.

"Is it a good thing Melanie has this much energy today after being so sick since we started the chemo?"

Doctors seemed to sugarcoat everything when Melanie was within ear shot, so when she was gone I was anxious to hear what was really going on.

"Yes, it's normal. She'll have her good and bad days, but she's still weak, so you have to keep a close eye on her in case she gets dizzy. Make sure she eats on these good days before she runs around. I'm sure I don't need to tell you that though. You are doing so well with her, and you've obviously done your research."

"Thank you. I'm new to this whole parenting thing. You are the one that is so great with her. I can't thank you enough."

"She's a sweet girl. I want to talk to you about the results of her bone marrow aspiration and spinal tap. It's good news."

"Good news? Is the cancer gone?"

"No, the cancer isn't gone, but the tests were better than I expected, so she is progressing. The treatment is working."

"Is that why she is doing better?" I held my breath.

"No, but it's a very good thing. Make sure she doesn't play too long and she gets plenty of rest. Make sure she eats and stays healthy. We will continue treatment, and you should be able to leave the hospital in a couple of days as long as she continues to eat, then you can head home and be with her until the next round in a week or so."

"Thank you so much. I can't wait to bring her home to her own bed in her own room."

"She has another eight months of chemo, but I know it can be expensive, so you can just drive back for the treatments."

I thought about Travis's place. Four bedrooms, close by for treatments, a magnificent view. I wasn't sure he was ready for us, and this would be a touchy subject with Phillip. But the thought of her out on the deck, staring at the beautiful Minneapolis skyline brought a smile to my face. I still had a few days before he came back from New York to think about it.

"Yeah, that sounds good."

"It will need to be a pretty sterile environment at home. You have to keep the germs to a minimum. Her immune system isn't very strong while she's receiving treatments."

"Okay."

"It's something to think about." He got up and headed for Melanie. He knelt down by her side.

My whole body relaxed for the first time in days. There was hope this could be over with in less than a year and she could finally live a normal life.

∽

"I told her I would meet with her because I had no choice."

"No choice?"

Emily's anger seeped right through the phone. "If she wanted them so bad, where was she when their uncle was abusing them?"

"Oh, trust me, Em, I feel the same way. I have no choice. Melanie loves her grandma. Who am I to stand in the way of that if she's good to them? I'm still nervous as hell."

"Is the social worker going to be there when the two of you talk? What are you going to say?"

"I guess I'm going to hear her out, see if what she says is pure. I can only hope for the best."

Did I believe what I was saying? I didn't want to give them up, but the feeling that they really weren't mine was a thought I fought in my head.

"Blood isn't everything. What did Phillip say?"

"He doesn't know. He's with the kids at the Ronald McDonald House."

"You should tell him the truth."

"I don't want to scare him before I know anything. Listen, I gotta go. I'm at Starbucks now."

"Good luck. Call me as soon as you leave."

"I will."

"I love you, Gabbs, and I'm proud of you. This can't be easy."

I hung up the phone and adjusted the mirror. I stared at my puffy eyes and red cheeks and took a deep breath, clearing my mind.

I opened the door to find her sitting in the corner booth staring at me. Here goes nothing.

# LIES, LIES, LIES

I waved and pointed to the counter.

"What can I get for you?"

"Coffee, two cubes of sugar and a teaspoon of cream, please."

I paid for my coffee and focused on slowing down my breathing. She was staring at my back. Sipping my coffee, it burned the roof of my mouth, but I didn't care. For one second I was distracted from thinking about the conversation that was about to take place. As I neared the table, she stood up, and we sat down together.

"Gabriella, right?"

I forced a shy smile. "You can call me Gabby."

"How's Melanie doing today?" she asked, ignoring my words.

"Good. She had so much energy when she woke up this morning. I was worried that was a bad sign, since she's been so sick since the treatments started."

She seemed genuine and caring, and her eyes gentle.

"What did the doctor say?"

"He said there will be good days and bad days."

"It's hard to see her when she's so ill. Thank you so much for taking her in, for taking both of them in."

"They are amazing kids. They won my heart the minute I met them."

"You must be quite scared after everything you heard about what they've had to go through. I wanted to take them in right away, you know."

Her words confused me. Why didn't she take them in? Didn't she know how terrible her daughter's husband was? Why didn't she take them away when she found out what he was doing to them? Why did it take her so long?

She cast her eyes down. "You see, I've been very ill."

"Ill?"

"I was diagnosed with colon cancer before...before my daughter was put in prison. Their mother."

My heart dropped. "I'm sorry. I had no idea."

Colon cancer was very serious, but it mattered how far along she was. Still, how could she not take them in, even if she was sick? "I'm so sorry."

"Don't be. I'm learning to live with it. I have stage four and have had it for over a year and I'm still alive. I'm finally strong enough to visit them. I just had part of my liver removed, but I've had multiple surgeries, including chemo and radiation. It isn't easy seeing Melanie go through what I've been going through. I worry I'm not strong enough to help her and myself."

"I can't imagine."

"I want you to know I'm just sick about what my other daughter's husband did to her. As soon as I found out, I cut them out of my life. Melanie and Ben's mom was badly into drugs. I had no idea Ronnie was, too. They were all selling drugs until Jim stole their supply, and then Ronnie blew up their house and Savannah got burned very badly. Thank goodness Melanie and Ben were with me when it happened."

She looked down at the table, a mixture of sadness and anger in her words.

"And Ronnie is Lizze's husband?"

She nodded.

I was trying to make sense of it all. "So he's the one that blew up their house?"

She nodded again and wiped away tears that were beginning to fall faster than she could catch them.

"The cops didn't believe Savannah when she told them the truth, and Lizze didn't want Ronnie to get in trouble, so she covered for him. Lizze finally got out of his home, and now she's safe, living with me and taking care of me. He won't hurt those children again, I promise. She's done with him."

"That must be so hard for her," I said, hoping she wasn't going to tell me she was taking the kids. I wouldn't feel safe with them being with Lizze, in case Ronnie came looking for her again.

She dabbed at her eyes. "We must seem like a really messed-up family, and I must seem really selfish for letting my grandchildren go into their home and then get put into the system twice. I was so sick, and it was all too much. I was selfish and I didn't know what to do."

"Wow."

She tapped my hand with hers. "I just wanted what is best for them. You seem like a really sweet woman, and I'm so glad you've been there for the kids, but I need to be there for them now. I need to fight for them. Lizze feels that way, too. She can't help but feel at fault for not knowing Ronnie was doing drugs and that he was at fault for her own sister going to prison. Can you understand that?"

"I'm not going to lie to you and tell you I understand, because I don't. Are you sure you can raise them and be there for Melanie with your diagnosis?"

"I'm doing really well right now and feeling great for the first time in a long time. The doctors say I could live for a while or die tomorrow. They don't know. I want to spend the rest of my time with my grandkids. I'm not working, so I can take care of them, and you can return to your life. I feel much stronger now."

"I know I may only be their foster parent, but I love them, and I'd do anything for them."

"I understand that, dear, but they are my grandchildren and Lizze's niece and nephew. She feels like she owes it to Savannah and Jim, and to Melanie and Ben. Lizze and Savannah asked me to come get them."

I swallowed my anger and forced a smile. "I want you to know that I love them, and that I want nothing more than to be there for them. I know I'm not their mother, and I'd never try to take your daughter's place, but they would be safe with me, with me and Phillip. Are you sure Ronnie won't come back into Lizze's life and hurt the kids? Can you promise me that?"

Her eyes were red, and she bit her lip. "I won't let that happen. I need to get my affairs in order and make sure I'm strong enough, so it will be a little bit, if that's okay. I'm coming back to be with them in about a month. Do you think you can protect my babies for another month?"

I could see it in her eyes how bad she was hurting. She wanted to be there for them, but I wasn't sure how she could take care of them when she was so sick herself.

"I know it's a lot to ask, but could I still visit them once in a while?"

She took my hand on the table and squeezed it. "Maybe, with time."

～

"So her daughter left her boyfriend, who was abusing the children, and she doesn't think he will try to find Lizze and hurt those kids again?" Travis said.

"She said that is what Ben and Melanie's parents want."

I held the phone to my ear with my shoulder, coffee in one hand as I opened the hospital door with my other hand, trying not to spill all over my shirt.

"That is so messed up. Do you think she will be able to care for them?"

"I don't know. I'm scared for them since Ronnie is still out there. I mean who's to say he won't try to get Lizze back and hurt them again? I know there is nothing I can do, so I need to make peace with them. I have no rights. I'm only a foster parent."

"That doesn't seem right. How is she going to take care of them when she's sick herself? Aren't you afraid Lizze will take Ronnie back or that he may be around those kids?"

"I really don't have a choice. There is nothing I can do except tell the social worker. She said she will be taking them in a month, so we will at least get to be with them until then."

"This is horrible. What did Phillip say?"

"I haven't told him yet. I am almost back at the hospital with Melanie now."

"Is there anything I can do?"

"I wish there was. I gotta go, but don't let this ruin your trip. We will talk soon."

"Well, if you need anything I'm here for you. I'll be home in a few days. Did you get my gift?"

"No, not yet. I'll talk to you soon, okay?"

"Okay, babe. Don't let this stress you out."

Walking into the hospital room, I saw a doll in Melanie's arms.

"Where'd you get the doll?"

"It came in the mail from Travis. Phillip said it was an American Girl doll."

"Really? Let me see."

I examined its bright aquamarine eyes, blonde hair, and pink dress. "What's her name?"

"It said Caroline on the box, and she even came with a book. Can we read it? Can we?"

"Only if you call Travis and thank him."

After she called Travis, Jill waved goodbye and tiptoed out the door as we laid in the bed, reading chapter after chapter as she snuggled with her doll and I ran her fingers through her hair.

The doctor told us we could go back to The House and Melanie got a twinkle back in her eye.

"Do you think Caroline will ever get cancer, Mom?" she asked as I was tucking her into bed.

Phillip came out of the bathroom with wet hair. "You guys are home. I see Melanie showed you her gift from Travis."

"Yeah, it's adorable."

"Did you open the gift he got you?"

"I didn't know there was more."

Phillip grabbed a small square box off the table and handed it to me. Melanie helped me open it. As we opened the box, we both gasped as I read the title, <u>Annie</u>. How did he know?

∽

The next morning I went for a walk around the block to get some exercise, and when I returned, Matt and Phillip were playing video games with Ben while Melanie was snuggled into my mom's chest watching Emily and Jill as they chatted about the weather.

"How many people can we cram into one room?" I said.

"You're back," Emily said.

Melanie reached out for a hug. "I missed you, Mommy."

I wrapped my arms around her. "How are you feeling, sweetheart?"

"I'm a little dizzy. I ate some crackers and Grandma Dez got me some juice."

I checked out her face and arms. "She did? I'm so glad you're eating."

"I can't wait to sleep in my own bed at our house in Hibbing."

My heart lurched at the way she said her own bed. She was so used to being thrown from bed to bed; that was the only stable bed she knew and considered her own. Her hands were a little clammy and her eyes didn't have the sparkle in them that they had earlier. They were definitely sick eyes.

I whispered in her ear. "Would you like me to ask everyone to leave so you can get some sleep?" She nodded.

"You think they'll be mad at me?"

"No, not at all."

I asked them all to leave because she was feeling tired, and they quickly wrapped up the game. They all waved goodbye, afraid to give her hugs in case they were carrying any sickness. They knew her immune system couldn't handle any germs. Everyone but Ben had a mask on while around her since she started her chemo treatments.

Phillip let me know he was going to take Ben to a movie if that was okay, and I told him that would be wonderful. I took him aside and explained the whole situation with their grandma. Like usual, he tried to be optimistic.

He kissed my cheek and held me close. "We still have thirty days with them. Let's enjoy every minute of it we have left. I have to work tomorrow, but then I get my six days off."

As soon as they all left, I changed into my sweats and crawled into bed next to Melanie. "Would you like me to continue reading your American Girl book?"

She picked the book up. "Please. I love my Caroline, and I want to know more about her, Mommy."

She lifted her head for me to put my arm around her.

"Let me readjust this pillow so we can sit up a little."

As she lifted her head off the pillow, I let out a startled gasp and grabbed the hair lying on top of the pillow and shoved it behind me.

"What's wrong, Mommy?"

I held back my tears and forced a smile. "Nothing, sweetie. I thought there was a bug on your pillow, but it was just lint."

Lies, Lies, Lies.

I began reading, but my mind was not on the story. I managed to hide it tonight, but this was only the beginning. The rest of her hair would soon be gone, and I could do nothing to stop it. The cold cap wasn't working.

After Melanie fell asleep, I grabbed her hair from under the pillow and wrapped it up in toilet paper and threw it in the garbage. It's just hair. Will people look at her differently? Will they stare? How is she going to react? She acts like it's no big deal if it happens, but will her feelings change when she's the one that finds hair on her pillow in clumps in the morning? It's so hard being a mom. How is Sheri going to do this? She just can't.

# A NEW HOME

The next day, Candy Land arrived in a box for Melanie and a small gold chain arrived for me. I took out the antique key from my purse and put it on the chain, then clasped it around my neck. We sat around the table playing Candy Land all day until she was exhausted and wanted to go to sleep.

The next morning morning, she held up a handful of hair left on her pillow and burst into tears. I looked up scarves and bandanas on Amazon while picking out her favorite ones together. The doctor didn't advise we go home yet since she was still pretty ill and had a fever of 102.3.

The next day, a box full of Lindor chocolate truffles arrived. Melanie only ate three before she became nauseous, but the presents gave her something to look forward to every day.

The next morning, she woke up to more hair on her pillow and I suggested we shave her head because it just brought on too much anxiety. Tears streamed down her little face as her hair fell to the floor. Her lack of hair made her big blue eyes stand out and she looked even more beautiful to me.

Ben came back from an outing with my mom and he teased her, but he did it lovingly, in an older brother kind of way. He compared her to Sigourney Weaver in <u>Alien 3</u>. It startled me not only that he saw the movie, but Melanie definitely watched it, too. I was packing up most of our clothes since the doctor thought we would be able to head back home in a day or two as long as her fever went down.

Melanie fell asleep and Phillip ran to the store. I sat on the recliner, thinking about Travis and how sweet it was for him to spoil Melanie when she needed it the most. I couldn't afford to keep buying her gifts like he could. I needed to sign the forms for clothing expenses for her from the state. Melanie was continuing to lose weight, and I didn't want to start getting her clothes when I had no idea what size clothes she was in. When she wore her size 5T pants, they kept falling down on her. Should I buy her a 4T or would she grow out of it too fast? Maybe deep down I just didn't want to deal with running around to buy her clothes when I didn't want to leave her side.

I knew I would need to get her clothes before her grandma stole her from me and I would no longer be able to get them. I didn't know if her grandma would be strong enough to even get to the store. I worried if Lizze went to the store with all that money, she would be too tempted and spend it all on herself.

Ben sat down next to me. I smiled at him gently. I didn't want to scare him away since he made it quite clear he wasn't my biggest fan.

"Do you still have those clippers?" he asked.

I tried to keep a straight face and not smile too much at his words. I took my time answering without looking into his eyes. "Which clippers, buddy?"

"The ones you used to cut off Melanie's hair."

Was this a trick? Was he planning on cutting my hair off in the middle of the night? Who cares? He's talking to me. "Oh, yeah, do you need them for something?"

"I umm...was wondering...if...you would cut my hair?"

"Sure," I said, no questions asked as I went into the bathroom and plugged them into the wall.

"Thank you."

I tried to control my voice. "How short do you want it?"

"Will you shave my head, too?"

Oh, so sweet. He was shaving his head to make Melanie feel better. I just knew it. No way was I going to tell him that. "Sure, sit down on the toilet here."

He did as I said without even talking back to me. I turned on the clippers as I watched his beautiful blonde hair hit the floor in clumps. It reminded me of Melanie's pillow when I first found her hair. I folded the top of his ear to get the hardest spot with the clippers and then I turned it off.

"Thank you," he said, skipping off. "Melanie, oh, Melanie."

I heard a knock at my door and turned just in time to wipe the tear before Ben saw it fall. I opened the door to find another package. Two hearts were on it and it was addressed to me. I snuck it into the bathroom and tore it open.

Inside, a pink lace Babydoll lingerie with a white ribbon on top. I sighed. When would I ever have the chance to wear it? I pulled out the newest Nicholas Sparks book, See Me, with bath beads sprinkled all over. A card beneath the present read: To the love of my life. Two more days until I can wrap you in my arms once again. Give Melanie and Ben hugs for me. Love you, Travis. I pulled out the tiny wrapped gift in the bottom with Melanie's name on it and brought it to her.

She opened it up and smiled as she pulled out a locket. She asked me to help her open it. There were no pictures inside.

"Why isn't there anything inside?"

"I think Travis wants you to decide whose pictures you want in there."

"I can pick anyone?"

I smiled. "Yes."

"Can I put my mom on one side and you on the other?"

"I'll see what I can find."

Nothing could ruin my day. I even asked Emily to watch the kids so I could take a bubble bath and begin reading my new book. Melanie was released from the hospital, but we were told we could stay one more night at The House.

The next day, two packages arrived. One was addressed to me, and one to Melanie and Ben.

Ben ripped it open since Melanie didn't have much strength today. Inside was Mario Kart for the Wii with two steering wheels. He knew we had Phillip's Wii with us. Although Melanie was too weak to play, she snuggled up with Caroline and watched Emily and Ben play.

My box just had one heart on it, so I opened it right there. Inside were black boots with Jimmy Choo on the label and rhinestones on the heels. The very boots I had dreamed about for years. How did he know? I couldn't imagine how much they must have cost him.

My thoughts were distracted by my ring tone. I went into the hallway to answer my phone. "Gabriella, this is Sheri. I'm ready to pick up Melanie and Ben. When is the soonest you can bring them to me?"

⚞⚟

"I'm just putting my luggage in my new vehicle and I will be there to pick you guys up. Phillip took your car back to Hibbing, right?" Travis said, his voice breathless.

"Yeah."

"Well, since they are going with their grandma tomorrow, would you guys like to stay at my house then?"

I thought about the perfect skyline view and the way Ben and Melanie would just love it, and I agreed. I wasn't sure Travis knew what it was like to have kids around, but he would soon find out.

"You okay, Gabriella?"

"No," I said, looking at Melanie as she struggled to put her socks on by herself. She was so vulnerable.

"That was a dumb question. How are the kids with this?"

"They seem excited, so that's good, right?"

"Yes, very good, even though it may not feel that way."

I leaned on the counter. "Travis, should I be fighting harder? Is there something I can do to stop this? She doesn't understand. She doesn't understand they aren't safe there."

"There is always a chance she could give them back."

"I hate this."

"I hate this, too. Is there something I can do?"

"Just come pick us up."

"Be there soon," he said. I made my way to pack the toothbrushes and stood the suitcases next to the door.

We rolled Melanie out the front door in a wheelchair. She gazed at the bright blue sky and a content smile spread across her face. "I can't wait to see my grandma." Her words hit me like a knife to the heart, but I knew I was just being selfish.

"She can't wait to see you, too, sweetie."

Although we took walks outside and only went to The House and the hospital, this time was different.

We sat at the cafe next to The House waiting until Travis pulled up in his SUV. I held Melanie's hand as she got into her booster seat.

"Thanks, Mom," she said.

I kissed her on the top of her head, and tried not to let her see my eyes water up in response to her words. Ben went way in the back to the third-row seats, talking up a storm to Travis. I hopped in the front seat beside Travis, touching the white leather upholstery after I shut the door.

"What kind of vehicle is this?"

"It's a Range Rover Sport."

"You bought this just for us to drive twenty minutes to the hotel where their grandma is staying? Sounds like a waste of money."

His face turned white in response, and I quickly told him I was just kidding, but I wasn't. The amount of money he threw around was ridiculous.

"That's not why I bought it." He leaned toward me, keeping his eyes on the road and in a whisper said, "I want to have it for when Sheri finally decides to give you the kids back."

I shook my head. "That will probably never happen."

I looked over my shoulder at Melanie. Her new pink princess bandana was tightly tied around her head. She looked beautiful with no hair. She loves her many bandanas and tells everyone that she's currently kicking the crap out of cancer and we both laugh.

She caught my glance and smiled back, which sent me digging through my purse to find her the medicated lip balm for her bloody, cracked lips. If I didn't constantly have her putting it on, she would pick the skin off her lips, and then they would burn and bleed so horribly.

I was not ready to give them up yet.

"There is something else," Travis said loudly so Ben and Melanie could hear him, too. "Gabby and I wanted to make sure the two of you have only the best, so I found a home that is only a couple miles from the hospital."

My mouth hung open as I tried to figure out how he could have done this all so fast.

"Yay!" the kids both screamed.

"Is it a big house like a mansion?" Ben asked. Even Ben caught on to how much money Travis had.

"It's not a mansion. That would be too much cleaning for you to do, buddy," Travis said, laughing. I did hire cleaners to come in and sterilize the house, and they will continue to do so twice a week. I know you are probably mad I arranged all this without asking you, but I knew you'd say no," he whispered, so the kids couldn't hear him. "The house is in Bloomington, and I will help pay the bills until Melanie's treatments are over so we don't have to worry about them driving back and forth. I gave Sheri a heads-up, and she is very grateful. What do you think?" he said, trying to look at me and the road at the same time.

"I'm not sure what to say. That...that is amazing. Thank you."

He looked surprised. "Are you sure you aren't mad?"

"Are you kidding me? This is the nicest thing anyone has ever done for me and these kids."

I pulled on his right hand that was on the steering wheel and squeezed it. He opened his hand and interlaced his fingers in mine, pulling my hand to his lips to kiss the top of it.

"I love you," he mumbled. We drove the rest of the way in silence.

The weather was finally warming up, and the hot sun was beating on me through the window. The grass was brown from a long winter of snow suffocation, and puddles and mud were scattered throughout the grass. Although I loved the end of winter and the hope of summer coming, I hated spring. The trees were still naked and bare, and my allergies were at their worst with all the mildew in the air.

Looking at the mess winter left behind made me think of the way I felt having to leave these kids I loved more than life itself. I couldn't imagine my world without them in it. I knew Travis said the house was close, but I just hoped it was in a good neighborhood. Travis pulled off the highway and passed beautiful houses. I hoped their home was just as nice.

"Do Sheri and Lizze know where this house is?"

"I gave them the address. Their moving trucks came this morning, and they should be there any minute now. I told them where the hidden key was, so they shouldn't have a problem getting in as long as the movers left it where I told them to."

The houses kept getting nicer and I wondered where their small house would be in such a mass of big three-story houses.

Travis pulled into a driveway. I hoped he was just lost. "Did you forget where the house was? Why don't you just plug the address into your GPS?"

He smiled and squeezed my hand. "Because we're here."

My mouth dropped open and I covered it as I stepped out of the vehicle to take in the size of the massive house. "You said you found her a small house."

"I didn't say it was small. I said it wasn't a mansion. It looks much bigger on the outside, I promise."

"Wow!" Ben cried out.

"I doubt that," I said to Travis under my breath.

The pillars on the red brick house's entrance was close to three-stories high. The garage had three stalls. I opened up the back door of the car for the kids, while Travis found the key and opened up the front door of the house. I helped Melanie get out of the car.

Her eyes lit up like Christmas morning. "Is this our new home?"

"Yes, I guess it is."

The garage door opened and the kids went running inside when they saw Travis.

"Did Travis seriously get this house for them? He must really love you. I didn't chip in this much, and I'm sure what the rest of us agreed to may only cover the utilities to warm this house," Phillip said as he came up behind me.

"You came?"

"Of course I did. I couldn't miss saying goodbye to the kids with you."

I looked behind him for my car, but it was nowhere to be seen.

"Where's my car?"

"Jill dropped me off. She's driving it back. Now, holy crap about this house, huh?"

"I had no idea, Phillip. He told me it was small," I said, grabbing on to his arm for support. "Or at least he made it seem like it was small."

We made our way inside the three-stall garage and then up the stairs and into the back hallway. We took off our shoes and followed the giggles up the stairs and into the living room. I gasped when I saw the vaulted ceiling and the huge patio spread around the west wall.

I pointed to a room off the living room. "Is this room for Melanie?"

Travis took the bags from Phillip and set them in the bedroom. "It can be."

"I think it's best so she doesn't have to climb stairs, unless there are more rooms on this floor."

"Just one. There are three more upstairs," he said, pointing to the high ceiling and wall, where a doorway was visible from where we were standing. A wall was blocking our view of the stairs that led to it.

Melanie lay down on the bed. "I'm tired, Mommy. Do you mind if I take a nap?"

I pulled the sheets up to her chin and ran the back of my hand over her soft cheeks. "You can take a nap anytime you need to, sweetie. I'm sure you are exhausted from your long day. Do you like it here?"

"I love it. Look there, at the ceiling."

She pointed at a skylight two stories up from her bed. "It reminds me of the hospital."

My stomach turned. "I'm sorry, Melanie."

"No, I loved the hospital, Mommy. I didn't like lying in a bed all the time, but it was like home to me. I loved everyone there and the kids, they looked like me."

She touched her head and chills shot through my body. "Grandma

Sheri and Aunt Lizze should be here when you wake up. Call me anytime, okay?"

She nodded back and rolled over.

"I love you, Melanie."

"Love you, too," she whispered.

Her bedroom was unusual. The walls stopped one story up, but the ceiling for the rest of the house went up two stories, so the view from her bed was open. This might not be the best idea since the lack of sheetrock would keep her up at night if people were talking in the living room, but then again it was beautiful and people would be able to hear her easily if she needed them.

I went into the kitchen and began cutting up an onion from the fully stocked pantry.

Phillip pulled out a stool at the breakfast bar and sat down.

"Where did Ben and Travis go?" I asked.

"There's a playroom downstairs with a ton of toys. Travis is showing Ben around."

"He really overdid it this time."

Phillip watched me chop up the onion. "He said he's renting this place so when they move back up north, he'll make money off the next renter. According to him, this is a great investment," Phillip said, shaking his head. "I wish I had a couple hundred thousand dollars to invest in a home. It is the best thing for Melanie though. She's right by the hospital, and they are far away from Ronnie."

"I'm not really sure what to think. I mean, the kids are so excited, but I worry it's too much for Sheri and Lizze."

The doorbell rang and I quickly wiped off my hands to greet them at the door. I hugged them both. "Welcome to your new home."

Sheri took off her shoes. "Is this for real? This is just too much."

"It was all Travis. He wants the best for the kids, and he worries about Melanie."

"I just can't believe it. This is the nicest house I've ever seen."

They seemed more grateful than upset as we showed them to their rooms, and then I finished making dinner. Lizze was right by my side helping me cook. We chatted about the president and the neighborhood they were living in. She loved the location and said she only dreamed of living in a home like this.

"Thank you for everything you've done for my niece and nephew. You're an angel, you know that?"

"The credit goes to Travis. This is definitely not in my price range."

"If it wasn't for you and your hospitality, we wouldn't be able to live so close to the hospital. I want you to know we will forever be grateful to you and your family. I can't imagine how hard it must be letting them go, but I promise we will take really good care of them. They are blood."

Her words brought tears to my eyes, which made her eyes water in return. She grabbed me in a tight hug and then pulled away saying, "Thank you so much."

Melanie woke up, and we all ate together. I wanted to leave even though we had great conversations throughout dinner. I didn't want to make this goodbye last any longer.

Sheri and Lizze left the room so we could say our goodbyes to the kids in private.

Melanie hugged my leg. "I'm going to miss you so much."

I bent down to hug her.

"I will be back to visit soon," I said. "Get plenty of rest and call me anytime."

Next, I hugged Ben. "I'm gonna miss you, buddy."

For the first time, he jumped into my arms and squeezed me tight. "You aren't as bad as I thought you were. You are the best."

I hugged him tighter.

"You're squeezing me too hard," he said.

I let go of my grip. "I'm sorry. Take care of your sister, okay?"

A smile spread across his face. "I will, Mom."

Travis, Phillip and I As the three of us got into the car. I crawled into the back seat with Phillip so I could cry on his shoulder until I finally passed out. I had nothing left. I just wanted to sleep forever.

# DARKNESS

My neck was cramped as we drove past the Hibbing airport. I sat up straight and rubbed my neck.

Phillip took my hand. "You sure slept a long time. Feeling better?" I saw Travis's worried eyes in the rearview mirror.

"Can you drop me off at my mom's? I just need some time by myself."

"Are you sure? You know you can come home," Phillip said.

"Or I could take you back to Duluth," Travis said.

"I just need some time, please."

"Okay, if that's what you want." Travis put on his blinker and turned onto 19th Avenue. He pulled my stuff out of the back and carried it into my mom's house.

Phillip gave me a hug. "If you need anything, I'm only a phone call away." He got into the passenger seat.

Travis stopped when we got to the door and set my stuff down. "I love you, and I really wish I could help you. Can I come see you tomorrow?"

"You have to work, and I need some time. Those kids were my whole world."

He stared at me, and then kissed me on the lips. "When you're ready to talk, I'm here."

"Thank you."

I pushed open the door and shut and locked it before he could follow. I set my stuff down in front of the door and called out for my mom.

She came running to me, her eyebrows scrunched up and her head tilted at my surprised arrival. "Are you okay? Are they with their grandma now?"

"Yeah, and I really don't want to talk about it. I just want to sleep, okay?"

She nodded, hugged me, and picked up my bag and carried it to the guest room without another word.

"Goodnight, Mom. Please just let me sleep, okay?"

"If you need anything, let me know. If you are hungry, thirsty, or just need to talk."

The exhaustion hit me as I crawled into bed without another word and turned off my phone.

I wasn't sure how long I slept. I woke up a few times, but went back to sleep. I remember my mom coming into my room multiple times and placing water next to my bed, along with crackers and soup I didn't touch. This time she wasn't as quiet.

"I'm sorry, honey, but you need to wake up. Travis is here, and you've been in bed for forty-eight hours. You've only had a couple sips of water and a few crackers, and you really need to shower. I get that you're depressed, but you need to see someone."

"I don't want to see anyone."

I put the pillow over my head and rolled on my side, away from her.

"Can Travis come up to see you? He's called at least five times, and he drove a long way."

I groaned. "I don't want to see anyone."

"Well, that's fine, but I'm not leaving until you eat this sandwich and drink some water. I'm really worried about you."

"I will eat as long as you kick him out."

"What happened with the two of you? You were so happy. Did he say something to upset you? I know you are hurting after losing Melanie and Ben, but you need to move on. You knew this was a possible outcome."

"I just need some time. I can't just move on, Mom."

She nodded, as if that explained it all, and left. A few minutes later she returned to watch me eat.

"Will you talk to me?"

"There is nothing to talk about. They are gone, and I just want to sleep."

"You're depressed, Honey. If I make you an appointment to see a therapist, would you go? It would help a lot, I promise. I understand where you are at right now. This is how I looked and acted after your father died, and one time my mom had to pull me out of bed, too. Therapy is what helped me survive."

She knew mentioning my dad would give me no choice but to say yes, and I reluctantly agreed.

I got up once the sun finally went down. I didn't want to be awake during the day, and my routine became sleeping during the day and up at night when my mom went to bed. I started focusing on my homework, and I quit my job, although Denise promised me the job was waiting for me when I was ready. One more month of school and I'd graduate. My professors understood my situation and gave me time to make up my missed assignments as long as they were all done by May 1st.

My mom woke me up a couple hours after I went to sleep one morning to tell me that I needed to get ready for my therapy appointment. I didn't argue as I got out of bed, even though I dreaded going.

I mainly filled out paperwork that first appointment, and we touched base on my situation, but it felt good to talk. The therapist asked me what made me happy other than Melanie and Ben, and I told her writing. She suggested writing a book, and I felt excitement for the first time in a long time. I had time to do it when I was taking a break from my schoolwork. I was glad I decided to finish college online.

When I got to my mom's, I began writing a children's book on child cancer. I drew pictures of Melanie and changed her name to Melissa in the book. I spent hours in the bedroom on my computer, making the story come to life with dreams of helping other children that had to go through what Melanie did.

April turned to May and I was finally ready to talk to Travis. I'd be graduating in two weeks and I wanted him to be there. "Hi Travis."

"Gabby?" His voice was filled with excitement. "How are you? I've been so worried about you."

"I'm doing okay. I'm sorry I wouldn't call or see you. I just needed some time to myself."

He cleared his throat. "Well, I'm sorry you had to go through this alone. How are you?"

"I've been focusing on me. I have my thesis to turn in next week, and then I graduate."

"Wow, that's amazing."

"Can I come see you? Where are you? Duluth or Minneapolis now?"

His voice suddenly cracked, and I could feel his nerves over the phone. "I'm heading to Duluth in a couple hours. I need to talk to you about some stuff. It's been a long time and so much has changed."

My stomach was suddenly in my chest. "Is everything okay?"

He went silent. "We'll talk soon. See you around four?"

"Okay."

I took a cold shower and couldn't quit thinking about how nervous he sounded. Something was wrong. Did something change with him? Did he meet someone else and move on? I couldn't blame him if he did.

I charged my phone and called Phillip on my way to Duluth. He sounded happy to hear from me, but also upset that it took this long for me to call him. I could tell he was hurting just as much as I was. I promised him I'd call soon.

I called Emily next.

"Oh, Gabby, I'm so glad you are okay. How is everything? Have you talked to Travis or Phillip yet? I've been keeping in touch with your mom. She prayed you'd get up."

"Actually, I'm on my way to Duluth now to see Travis. He seems upset, and I don't blame him. I was just so depressed, you know? I didn't realize how much I hurt everyone."

"It's not like you meant to. You were going through a lot. Please tell me if there is anything I can do to help you."

I know she wanted me to let her in, but I just didn't know how. Getting out of bed was still tough for me.

"Sorry, Em, I just don't know right now. Give me some time."

"Let me know if you feel up to helping me prepare for the fundraiser."

"At this point I'm just hoping I make it to the fundraiser."

"You have time to think about it. Promise me you won't make up your mind yet."

"I promise I'm still thinking about it."

"And Gabby, everything is going to be okay, I promise."

"Thank you."

"Call me when you get back from Duluth, and good luck with Travis."

"Thanks for understanding. I thought you were going to be mad."

"I'm trying to understand. Irene misses you, too. Plus, there is still three months until the fundraiser."

He answered the door in his suit and tie, looking more handsome than ever. I tried to kiss him, but he pulled away. I followed him into the living room, nervous to hear him talk. I felt the awkwardness between us that I never felt before with him. He seemed cold and sad, guilty even.

He paced back and forth in front of me without making eye contact. "Can I get you something to drink?"

I chewed on my nails. "No thanks. I'm not thirsty."

"Missy had her baby," he blurted out.

My mouth involuntarily opened and I stared without a word.

"Well, my baby, too. The paternity test came back with a ninety-nine percent chance it's mine. You were right the whole time."

He stood there waiting for me to talk, but I did not know what to say. I always knew there was a chance, but he was so certain the baby wasn't his, and I believed him without a doubt.

"I wanted to talk to you about it, but you wouldn't talk to me. I have to try to make it work with her. I'm sorry."

Disbelief overtook me, and I went numb trying to take it all in. "You're a dad."

"She's beautiful, Gabby, just beautiful. I never knew what it felt like to be a father."

"I'm happy for you," I said with absolutely no emotion.

He ran his fingers through his hair. "I didn't know what to do; you wouldn't talk to me."

"I was depressed, Travis. Do you even understand what I've been through? You're a father, and I'm no longer a mother. You don't get it at all. What if someone ripped that all away from you?"

"What am I supposed to do, abandon my own child because you finally decided to get out of bed?" He closed his eyes and sighed. "I'm sorry. I didn't mean that."

"You never loved me. You wanted me to move in, you told me you loved me, but this whole time you didn't love me at all."

He made his way over to me and took my hands firmly in his. "I loved you more than I have ever loved any woman in my life, Gabby. I wanted to marry you. I bought a home and paid for Melanie and Ben to live there so they would be safe. I was there for you, and I fell in love with them, too. You were my world, but when times got tough, you cut me out. I'm sorry, but I have to do this for my baby. I have to try."

I stood up. I had to get away before I said terrible things I couldn't take back.

"Wait, talk to me," he called after me.

I walked out the door, looked back at him, then slammed the door with all my might. As I put my mom's car into reverse, he stood out front watching me pull away, and I flicked him off.

# BLINDFOLDED

"Gabby, what are you doing here? I thought you were in Duluth with Travis?"

"I was, but I came back because Missy's baby is actually Travis's and now they are back together. He chose her. He chose her," I said, kicking the stairs and screaming out in pain because I was pretty sure I broke my big toe. I went to grab my throbbing foot and I started falling, Phillip catching me right in his arms.

"I'm so sorry. I can't believe it. I can't believe he did this to you."

"It just keeps getting worse. My life is a mess. How can this keep happening to me?"

"Would you like a glass of wine? Maybe it will help calm you down a little bit. Look at you, you're shaking," he said, holding up my hand.

I nodded and followed him into the kitchen. One glass turned into three. He had me laughing when he told me about Lucy's broken nose again.

"Are you two back together now?"

He shook his head, and an odd sense of relief washed over me. I forgot how good-looking he was, and his blue shirt brought out his tan skin and bright eyes. I touched his face, and he leaned into my hand.

"Is there any way I could move back in with you?"

"You know my door is always open for you. I didn't want you to move out in the first place. What did Travis say when you got there?"

I told him the story, including flipping Travis the bird as I left, and he couldn't help but laugh.

He held up his wine glass and clinked it with mine. "I wish I could have been there to see you give him the middle finger. You brought out your sassy side. I like it."

"Can you believe he was jealous of us? Why does everyone think there is something going on between us?"

He examined his glass. "I don't know."

"Maybe we're missing something."

He turned and looked at me, our noses almost touching as we stared into each other's eyes. He slipped his hand around the back of my neck and pulled me in. Our kiss was deep, open-mouthed, and eager. I stood up and began walking in the other direction.

"Where are you going?"

I turned around and motioned for him to follow. I pulled off my clothes and remained in my bra and underwear. He watched with his mouth open. I threw my shirt his way, then my pants. It was obvious he was unsure of what to do next.

Hands on my hips, I tapped my toe on the carpet. "Well?"

He pulled off his shirt. "Are you sure you want to go there? We can't turn back once we do this."

I moved closer and unzipped his pants. "It's time to feel the chemistry."

He swiped everything off his desk and onto the floor. I pressed my hands hard against his chest, which knocked him off balance. He steadied himself with his hands on the desk and grinned at me.

He reached around to unsnap my bra. "I had no idea how dominant you can be."

I looked down and saw his excitement as he stared at my naked body.

"You are so beautiful, Gabriella."

A touch of fear flooded my body. He was right, there was no turning back.

I found myself on top of his desk with a burst of pleasure I hadn't felt in so long, but I couldn't shake away the thought that Travis was probably having sex with Missy.

We had sex every night for the next two weeks. It became impulsive and eager. It took the pain away, and I couldn't get enough. The day of my graduation, Phillip asked me if I was going. I said no. He tried to talk me into it all day and finally gave up.

"Let's go for a drive," Phillip said.

"I don't want to go for a drive. Let's have sex."

"Gabby, you are going to break me. The bed will be waiting when we get back. I want to take you somewhere. Please come with me."

I took his hand and gave in. "This is scary, you know. I have no idea what's going on."

"Just trust me, okay?"

He put a blindfold on me and I fought to take it off, but he convinced me to keep it on. It wasn't easy to talk to him when I couldn't see anything, but we talked about the book I was working on.

"It's almost finished," I said with more certainty than I felt.

He stopped the car, and I begged him to let me take off the blindfold.

"Not yet. I'm coming to get you, okay?"

I waited until he came around, and I held on to his arms as we walked on uneven ground.

"Careful, there's a step. Okay, another step, just one more. Now stop."

He pulled off the blindfold.

I stared ahead, taking in the lake, and then the panic swept over me. My knees collapsed, and I stumbled.

"Are you okay? Are you okay? Gabby, I'm sorry. I thought this would help."

I shooed him away as I sat up, waiting for the dizziness to fade. "Why would you take me here? You know I haven't been here since my father died."

The familiar lake and cabin increased my anxiety. I pictured my father walking down the path with me, my hand in his. His tackle box and fishing pole in one hand while we sang all the way to the boat. He was always making jokes and never happier than when he was in the boat. I saw the boat on the dock, and I couldn't believe my mom still had it. Did it even run anymore?

"Let's go for a ride," he said, looking toward the boat.

"I can't. I just can't."

I found myself getting up and making my way down the path. I stopped because I could see my dad in the boat, waving for me to join him, and so I did. He disappeared and Phillip sat where he had just been. I told him to start the boat.

"There are no keys."

"Then just sit here with me."

And he did. By the time I finally got to my feet, darkness was settling in.

"Want to go in the cabin?" Phillip asked.

"No, that's just too much for me in one day."

"Are you still mad at me for bringing you out here?"

I shook my head. "I think you're the only one I would let get away with such a scheme. Thank you."

"You missed graduation."

"So."

"Graduation used to mean the world to you."

"I lost Melanie. I lost Ben and Travis and my dad."

"I know."

We sat on the deck, hand in hand, staring at the calm water.

"Are you sad you missed your graduation?"

"No. I didn't need to walk across the stage to graduate."

"I know, but you've worked so hard. I'm sad you didn't get to feel the sense of pride as you hear your name called."

"It's fine."

He brushed the hair out of my eyes. "I'm worried about you."

"I know you are, but I'm okay."

"Do you regret what we're doing?"

"No. You're my best friend, and I'm having fun," I said, walking toward the lake to get a closer view.

"Do you miss him?"

"Who, Travis?"

"I was talking about your dad."

"Oh," I said, looking away.

"Do you miss Travis?" he asked, brushing his hand against my leg.

"Sometimes, but he made a choice and it wasn't me."

"Was I just your backup this whole time?"

"No, we're just screwing, right?" That sounded terrible once I said it aloud.

"That hurts."

"I did not mean it like that. I love you. You are my best friend. I meant at first and now we..."

"Now we what?"

"Phillip, I want to have a baby."

He hissed and glanced at me. "A baby?"

"Yes. What do you think about having a baby together?"

"Gabby, we just started this new relationship. Are you sure you're ready for that?"

"Why not?"

"I can think of a few reasons, but if that's really what you want. You think you can handle that? Do you really feel that way about me?"

"I don't know, but even if we don't end up together, we will always be friends."

He pulled on my arm and began kissing my hand.

I pushed him onto his back. "Let's start now."

"Not here, Gabby. Let's finish this at home," he said, kissing the top of my head.

We kept trying for the next few weeks. I took pregnancy tests, and they kept coming up negative. I began to feel like our sex life was no longer an exciting, impulsive time of the day anymore. I loved Phillip and he loved me, and that, I hoped, would bring back the passion.

Right after the fourth of July we received a card from Ben and Melanie standing in front of their house. The card read, "In Remission!" Her hair was short, spiky, and dark brown instead of the light blonde color it once was. She looked so happy, yet skinny and frail. I cried out in happiness as the battle was finally over. I hoped she was doing okay.

Phillip looked at the picture over my shoulder, and hugged me as we sat there crying and telling stories from our time with the kids.

"You don't think Ronnie came around, do you?"

"I have faith that Sheri would call us."

"That's true."

"Look how cute she is," he said again, pointing at her hair.

I placed the photo on the fridge with a magnet. "I miss them so much. I tried calling them again yesterday, but Sheri won't answer her phone. Do you think the kids forgot about us?"

He kissed my neck. "No way. I think Sheri just wants to do this on her own. We just can't give up trying. Just like we can't give up trying to get pregnant."

I pulled away.

"What's wrong?"

"There has to be something wrong with me. Why can't I get pregnant?"

"Sometimes it just takes time. Be patient. People try for years sometimes."

I looked away. "Maybe it just isn't meant to be."

"You've been under a lot of stress. Just give it some time, okay?"

I nodded. He gently kissed me on the lips and made his way down my chest.

He always knew exactly what I needed. I fell back on the couch and let him make love to me.

# THE MONSTER

Throughout July, I continued to try to call the kids, but Lizze and Sheri wouldn't pick up our calls. I was starting to wonder if they changed their numbers. Melanie's and Ben's rooms remained untouched because we held out hope that they would come home one day. I talked to the social worker multiple times about seeing Melanie and Ben, but she said Sheri wasn't ready for us to see them yet. She'd give me little updates and tell me they were doing fine, but weeks ago she let me know she was closing their case, and that had me nervous.

I was finishing the last page in my children's book and working on the last touches of my sketch when I received a call from an unknown number. I don't usually answer calls when the number is unknown, but on this day I didn't think twice as I answered the phone call that would forever change my life.

"Hello."

I waited for a computerized solicitor to tell me I had won a trip or credit services offering me a low-interest loan, but to my dismay I heard a familiar voice on the other line.

"Gabby, it's Lizze."

Her nasally voice sounded like she had a cold.

"Lizze?"

For a second I was excited to hear from her, but it quickly turned to worry.

"Is it Melanie? Is Melanie okay?"

"Melanie is fine. It's my mother. The cancer took her in her sleep last night."

"Oh, I'm so sorry, Lizze."

I chewed on my nails. I wasn't sure what else to say. I know people say things like, I'm sorry for your loss, or if there is anything I can do, just let me know, but that didn't apply, especially since they never wanted to communicate.

"I can't raise these kids without her, Gabby. They're just so upset, and they've been crying for you and Phillip. Can you please come take them? I just can't do this right now."

"Call the social worker. I'm on my way."

I didn't take the time to pack a toothbrush or even a hairbrush. I grabbed Phillip and we ran out the door in just the clothes on our backs. Melanie and Ben needed us.

The drive to the house in Minneapolis was filled with silence, but Phillip held my hand the entire drive. We never even stopped to eat or even go to the bathroom.

I tried but failed to remember the sound of their voices. Why hadn't I fought harder to visit them? Would they even want to come with us?

My joy was bittersweet. Yes, we were taking them home, but their hearts had to be broken over losing their beloved grandmother. Once again they were dealing with another loss of someone they loved.

"To just cut us off from being able to see the children altogether and then calling us and saying come get them months later," I said, staring out the window at the green grass and pine trees flying past. "I just don't understand."

"She knows they are better off with you."

Me? Did he still not see he was needed? Would he ever be ready to be a parent?

Phillip and I arrived at the house in Minneapolis a speedy three hours later. As we walked up that driveway to the door, memories of the pain from leaving the children we loved circled in my head.

"I don't know if I should be happy or sad," Phillip said.

I turned around and looked him in the eyes, then grasped his hands. "This isn't going to be easy. They're going through so much, but we can do this together."

He smiled at me. "I can't wait to finally see them."

"Since she's in remission, we may actually be able to take them home."

We rang the doorbell and waited for what felt like hours. The door opened and there stood Ben. His blond hair was short and spiky, and he must have grown a foot since we last saw him. His chubby cheeks were thin, but he looked healthy.

I wrapped my arms around him. "Oh, Ben."

Phillip joined in the hug and I didn't want to let go. I dreamed of this moment for so many months.

Melanie pushed past Ben and joined our group hug. "Mommy."

I promised myself I wouldn't cry, but I couldn't keep my promise as my eyes filled with tears of joy.

I kissed the tops of both their heads. "I'm so sorry to hear about Grandma Sheri." I took Melanie's face in my hands and stared at her short brown hair, kissing her right in the middle of her forehead, then on each cheek.

She sobbed. "I can't believe you came back. I've missed you so much. Why did you leave us?"

"We never meant to leave you. We love you both so much."

Lizze waved to us. "Come in, come in. The neighbors brought over enchiladas and an apple pie. They loved my mother. I don't want to waste this. Let's eat."

We followed her into the kitchen, and I hugged her. She showed no trace of sadness as I sat down across the table from her. She had to be in shock.

Melanie climbed on my lap, her arms tightly wrapped around my neck, as if she was afraid I would leave her again, and Ben sat down next to Phillip. His bottom lip quivered as he crossed his arms, looking down.

"You okay, Ben?"

"You left us, and you never even called. Are you going to leave us again like everyone else?"

His words pierced my heart, and everyone stopped what they were doing and stared at him.

Phillip turned Ben toward him by the shoulders. "Oh, Ben, it's not like that at all. We love you, buddy."

Ben pulled away and stomped up the stairs. "Liar! You left us, just like everyone else."

Phillip and I both started to get up, but Lizze made us sit back down. "Melanie, I know you're excited to see Gabby and Phillip, but we need some adult time. Why don't you go check on your brother?"

Melanie wrinkled her nose and clung to me. "I don't want to check on my brother. I want to stay with them."

"Go play with your Barbies, please, sweetheart. We need to have an adult conversation, okay?"

Melanie looked to me for help, but I didn't want to go against Lizze. I wasn't ready for her to leave yet, but we needed to talk about things that children shouldn't hear.

"Listen, you go play with your Barbies, and when we are done having an adult talk, I'll come up so you can show me your room. I can't wait to hear all about what you have been doing since we've last seen you."

She stared at me for what felt like forever. Then I heard, "O-kay." She stuck her lip out and sauntered up the stairs at a considerably slower pace than her brother.

I let out a deep exhale and waited for Lizze as she dished up our plates. Maybe she should have sent them away after they filled up their bellies, but I was not about to make any suggestions.

"You know she lived a lot longer than the doctors expected."

I shook my head.

Phillip reached for my hand under the table and my heart slowed down a little bit.

"First of all, I want to apologize for not inviting you to see the kids and not letting you talk to them when you called. We needed some time to sort through Melanie and my mom as they both went through so much these last few months. This morning I woke up and she was gone. I knew it was any day now, but to feel her so cold and not breathing sent me into shock. I called you without even thinking."

I shot Phillip a worried glance as her words no longer sounded the same as the conversation we had earlier. Was she not going to let us take the kids anymore?

"After I got off the phone with you, we talked, and we don't think it is a good idea for you to take the kids."

We? Who is we? No way was she talking about Grandma Sheri because she passed before she called me.

"We?" Phillip said, taking the words right out of my mouth.

"Me and Ronnie."

My heart stopped and I dropped my spoon loudly on the plate. I was pretty sure all the blood was now in my head. I wanted to scream at her. How did she not care about what he did to those kids? Was he living here in this home my family was paying for to keep the kids safe? The house that belonged to Travis? How dare she let him back into her life and back into Melanie's and Ben's lives?

Phillip stood up. "Is he living here?"

I yanked on his arm to pull him back down.

He glared at me, but listened. His muscles tightened around his jaw. "Continue."

She squinted her eyes at us. "He's changed. You may not believe me, but people can change."

I watched Phillip's hands turn into fists, but he refrained from saying a word.

"Now, as I was saying, we don't think it's a good idea for you to take the kids. I should have never told you to come without discussing it with him first. Melanie is still cancer-free, but we need to continue to live here while she gets her monthly checkups. Unless you disagree?"

I struggled to keep my voice from shaking. "Although we understand where you are coming from, we are not the ones for you to talk to. Travis is the one who owns this house, so you will have to talk to him. His conditions were that when Melanie's treatments were over, he was going to rent out this house. I don't think he will be very happy to know that

Ronnie is living here. He is, isn't he?"

"Yes, he is. Like I said, he's changed and he's getting help. He found God. The kids love him. Just ask them."

I highly doubted that. I saw Melanie's head peeking out from the top of the stairs, but I pretended not to see her.

Phillip lost control. He stood up. "If he hurt those kids, I swear--"

"You obviously don't care very much about those kids if you are kicking us out when they have nowhere else to go."

I heard the door open behind me. As I turned around I saw a huge man with a red and black flannel shirt and dirty jeans walk toward us with a look of anger that terrified me. I felt the negativity and the fear in Lizze's face as he bunched his hands in fists.

"Who the hell is this," he said in a demanding, emotionless tone.

Lizze was no longer breathing as the fear replaced her anger. "They were just leaving, weren't you?"

"Can we say goodbye to the kids first?" I said with as much kindness as I could muster. I didn't want this man to think he could scare me.

"No!"

Melanie came running at us, but was stopped by Ronnie's giant hands. "No, no! I want my mommy! Mommy," she cried, reaching out for me. "Don't let him hurt me, please. Take us with you," she squealed.

I heard little footsteps coming down the stairs as Ben tried to reach us. "Help us, please help us. Don't leave us here. Don't leave us here again."

"You are gonna get it, you little shit. Go upstairs, now! You will never see them again. They don't care about you. Only your family cares, and we are your family," Ronnie said through a clenched jaw.

His straight arm came up by his neck and with an enormous amount of power, his hand collided with Ben's face, sending him flying into the wall.

"See what you made me do? Now get out! The only one hurting these kids is you."

I screamed, "No, please, no!"

Lizze pushed me toward the door. I reached out as if I could grab the kids from across the room, but Ronnie picked them both up and shut them in the back room and locked the door.

Phillip went running at him, red-faced, his fists at his side, but I knew he was no match for this monster.

I screamed again. "Phillip!" Phillip turned around to look at me, and Ronnie pushed him down and kicked him in the stomach over and over. Phillip started coughing up blood all over the white carpet.

I pushed past Lizze and jumped on Ronnie's back to try to stop him, but he had me on the floor, too.

Lizze screamed. "Stop it! Just stop it!" The kids were banging on the door as hard as they could, crying and screaming for us.

Lizze tried to grab Ronnie's arm. "Let them go, please."

My arm was on fire as I struggled to get up. Ronnie turned his back. I knew this was my chance to get away. I helped Phillip make his way to the door. He was heavy, leaning on my shoulder, hunched over in pain.

Ronnie tried to come after us, but Lizze begged for him to let us go.

"Hide, Ben and Melanie, hide! We will be back, I promise," I screamed as loud as I could.

Once we were safely in the car, I dialed nine-one-one and we headed to the hospital. There was no way for the two of us to go up against this monster.

# VISITATION

"Stop the car," Phillip said.

As soon as the car came to a complete halt, he opened the door and began coughing. At first I thought he was going to puke, but when I leaned over to see outside the door, I realized it was still blood.

"Are you okay?"

He nodded and coughed again. "Don't worry about me. It's just a little blood."

"Should we go back and help them?"

He cleared his throat and wiped blood off his chin. "I don't think it would help if we did. I want to go back just as much as you do, but we're no match for him. Maybe they are still locked up in that room, and if we go back he might hurt them even more."

I accelerated with my left arm resting in my lap. I could no longer feel the burning pain. "I'm so worried about them, Phillip."

"I know, me too, but the police are on their way. We could try to sneak in the window, but we don't even know which window would lead us to that room. We just need to pray they are going to be okay. Something wrong with your arm?" he asked.

I tried to focus on the road, but it was so hard to see through my tears. "It's fine. It's just bruised. I'm crying because we weren't there for them when they needed us. I'm a terrible person to think everything was okay. We should have fought harder to make sure they were okay."

"Gabbs, you had no choice. Social services had to close your case. This is not on you."

"I promised them no one would ever hurt them again, and I lied."

⚮

The doctor said I had some mild bruising on my arm and wrist, just as I thought. He gave me six stitches right above my elbow. Phillip was going to be okay, but he needed to stay in the hospital overnight. I sat there with my phone in my hand after calling law enforcement for an update, but they couldn't tell me anything. What would happen to the kids? The system was the safest route right now.

I hesitated, but I had to do it. I searched the T's in my contacts, found his name, and pushed call.

His phone went straight to voicemail, and it was hard to listen to his voice. I thought about hanging up, but I had to do this for Ben and Melanie.

"Hi Travis, it's me, Gabby. Grandma Sheri passed away and Lizze called us to get the kids, but when Phillip and I got there, she no longer wanted us to take them, and then Ronnie showed up. I guess he has been living in your house with them. The kids were just terrified of him. He threw me and Phillip around and locked the kids in one of the rooms, and now I'm at the hospital and the police won't tell me anything. It's your house, so maybe there is something you can do. I'm really sorry to bother you, but I didn't know who else to call. Anyway, I wanted to let you know what's going on. I know how much you loved those kids. I hope you are doing well."

Just as quickly as I hung up the phone, the phone rang from an unknown number. Travis?

"Hello," I said, my voice a little shaky.

"It's Lizze. Before you hang up, I just want you to know I'm so sorry for what happened. Ronnie has been out of control, and I couldn't get him to leave. The police took him to jail, and he's finally gone."

I cleared my throat. "That was horrible. Why did you let him back in?"

"You don't get it. He loves me. He just gets so angry sometimes. I never should have called you. I knew without my mom around he would get so much worse. I'm afraid he's going to get out, and we both know the kids would be better off with you and Phillip."

"I'd say--"

"Just listen, okay. If you visit Jim at the Iron Range Correctional Institution, he will let you have custody of his kids. I'll get you on the visitors' list, but you need to talk to him. Go alone, okay? It's the only way."

"I can call Renee. She will help us."

She groaned into the phone. "Listen, do what you want, but I will put you on the visitor list, and if you want to adopt them, this is your chance."

"What about their mom?"

"She is a little harder to reach. They have her in treatment for her mental health. She is schizophrenic, you know."

"I had no idea. You think he will approve for us to adopt them?"

"I think you have a shot."

I thought about that. Melanie and Ben finally with us for good. But I'd have to run this by Phillip. What if he said no? I fought to catch my breath.

"I want you to know I called Travis, so you really need to get your stuff out of there before he locks the doors. You know Ronnie wasn't supposed to be there. We let you live there for free and even paid the bills for you."

"I know, I know. I'm so sorry. I'm going to make this right for the kids."

"Lizze, I need to know, did he hurt the kids? I mean, did he touch Melanie? I've seen the kids' scars from him."

The line went quiet, but I could hear her heavy breathing. "I don't know. I just don't know."

I closed my eyes and dropped the phone to my knees. I breathed deeply, then picked it up again. "Would you tell me if he did?"

"Yes, I would. Listen, I gotta go. I need to get away before he gets out. He always gets out."

The line went dead.

I put my hands over my eyes and called NERCC to find out their visiting hours. I got up to go to the bathroom, but stood there, frozen, as I watched Travis walking toward me. He hadn't changed one bit. I struggled to breathe as he crossed the room, and my body tingled from head to toe. The closer he got to me, the more nervous I became. I had to clasp my hands behind my back to hide the shaking.

I did not notice the carrier he was carting around until it was right in front of me. I looked at the pink blanket wrapped around the carrier, then back at his lean, powerful body, then back to the baby. His eyes studied me, and I hoped my face didn't betray the hurt I felt inside. Although he showed up, this did not make up for what he did.

He put the carrier down, and then with a swift movement, his arms were wrapped around me before I could react.

"Gabby, I'm so sorry."

I pushed his arms down and took a step back. His face paled. I fought to maintain my composure when his hard, handsome face I dreamed about touching again was just out of my reach. I wasn't going to let him seduce me with those deep azure eyes again. I was with Phillip now. Phillip was amazing, and Travis was with Missy now. I shook away the overpowering thoughts. Focus.

"Gabby, please talk to me."

He reached out to touch me. This time I couldn't move. I stood there closing my eyes as he stepped forward. I felt the gentle and fluid motion of his hand on my face, making my stomach dance with butterflies. Softly he rubbed his hand across my cheek. I grasped his hand and held it there a moment. And then without thinking, it came out. "I'm seeing someone."

This time he backed up, nearly tripping over his baby carrier. "I understand."

"You left me, remember? Anyway, I'm taking it you are here because of my message." I couldn't help the anger that came through my words.

"Yes. I've sent someone over to change the locks and make sure Lizze gets out okay. Thank you for calling me. I'm so sorry about the kids."

I rolled my eyes. "Thanks."

"Are you okay? How's Phillip?"

"Ronnie hit him pretty hard. He was even coughing up blood."

Travis touched my bad arm, leaving me wincing in pain.

"He hurt you?" His eyes were filled with concern and love, which pissed me off more.

"I'm fine."

He put his hands up in the air as if surrendering. "Well, since I'm here, I'd like you to meet someone."

I wanted to run away. I didn't want to see his baby's face, ever.

Too late. He lifted the blanket, her big blue eyes opening wide. She kicked her feet and shook her hands, and I fell in love. I was on the floor, my face so close to hers, unable to keep my hands off those tiny little feet.

A deep sorrow filled me, and I stood up. "I can't do this, Travis. I can't. Just please keep an eye on the house. If you hear anything, let me know."

I walked away from him before he could seduce me anymore with those ridiculously sexy dimples and that beautiful golden skin tone. And his perfect baby.

"Gabriella!"

He caught me off guard. I turned around.

"It was nice seeing you. I've missed you."

I insolently turned up my nose at him, and stomped away, almost running into a man with balloons in his hands.

"Excuse me."

I walked around him and hoped Travis didn't see it.

"I'm here to see Jim Howser."

"License, please," the tiny, red-haired woman behind the glass window said.

I opened up the slot and placed my license in it, then pushed it shut.

The woman picked it up and looked at it. She shoved a form through the slot. "Fill this out. Visitation will begin in twenty minutes. Someone will come out and get you. You can give a quick hug and kiss, but no contact at all during the visit or we will have to end it. Do you understand?"

"Yes."

I headed to the adjoining room to fill out the form. The room reminded me of the hospital waiting room I was in yesterday while waiting for Phillip.

Once finished, I gave the form to the lady. Her red hair glowed on top of her head. How could she control the residents at the prison when she was so tiny?

A stocky, six-foot-tall man let me in the visitation room. He escorted me to a long table and called for Jim Howser over the mic on his shoulder.

"He'll be just a couple of minutes," he said.

He made his way back to the wall and watched the residents interact with their families.

I waited impatiently. I didn't even know what Jim looked like, and I knew he had no idea what I looked like.

A man resembling Neil Patrick Harris came into the room and scanned it twice before giving me a questioning look. I stood up to greet him and shook his hand. This had to be him.

"Jim?"

He was wearing a blue shirt and baggy pants. I expected them all to be in orange jumpsuits like on television and was surprised he looked so normal.

He sat across the table from me and folded his hands together in front of him. "Yep."

"I take it Lizze called you?"

He shot me another questionable look. "Yes, she did."

"So you know why I'm here."

"She may have mentioned it."

"I have to tell you, your children are absolutely adorable."

"Thank you."

He winked, which made me feel quite uncomfortable. Was he hitting on me? Showing his dominance? I couldn't be sure.

"As you know, I was their foster mom a few months ago. I took care of them at the shelter and helped Melanie through the beginning stages of her cancer."

"So I heard. Do you want a medal?"

He looked around and checked out a woman in a low-cut shirt across the room.

I couldn't hide my disgust. I rolled my eyes and debated getting up and leaving. It was obvious he didn't really care that I was here, and there was little chance he was going to let me adopt his children.

"I'm here to see if you would be willing for me and my...boyfriend to adopt them."

"Over my dead body. They is my kids."

"Mr. Howser, if I don't adopt them, they will probably go back into the system."

"You ain't touching them. Over my dead body is some black-haired rich bitch gonna raise them kids."

"I really hope you'd reconsider. If you could just give me some time to explain."

"You really want em?"

"Yes, more than you know."

"What's in it for me?"

I shook my head and looked around nervously. "I'm not sure what you mean."

"What do I get out of it?"

"A safe place with a loving family to help raise your children."

"Oh, and you think you's the best thing that ev'r happened to them, huh? You look like a rich bimbo to me."

"Excuse me, sir, but that's not what I'm saying at all."

He leaned forward and whispered. "I'll tell you what. Y' all can have em' for a small price."

"Excuse me?" I really hoped I didn't hear him right.

"You heard me, little lady."

"I'm sorry. It's illegal to sell your kids, you know."

He laughed. "Not that. I have money, bitch. I want a conjugal visit with you."

I sneered at him and stood up. "You pig."

His high-pitched laugh made me even more nervous.

"Do you really think a minimum security prison would have conjugal visits? What is this, your first time outta the mall? That was so worth your reaction. Now sit down. My only request is that you keep them away from that child molester uncle of theirs, got it?"

"Yes, sir."

"Don't 'yes, sir' me. If you don't, I'll find you. Got it?"

"Loud and clear. What about your wife?"

"What about her?"

"Do you think she will sign the paperwork, too?"

He stood up to leave. "She'll sign whatever I tell her to sign."

"Is that a yes?"

He shook his head and laughed as if I somehow missed his joke. I was thinking that was a yes.

I got out of there as quickly as I could, the creepy way he talked stayed with me. He was disgusting and crude, and if I never saw his face again, it would be too soon. I grabbed my phone out of my car and called Renee to let her know the good news. I could finally keep them safe for good.

# PUBLISHED

Renee worked quickly with the social worker from Minneapolis. I was a little worried that Jim wasn't going to sign the paperwork, but he did, and the kids were on their way home. I hadn't seen them since the incident, and I worried they were upset we left that night without saving them. Renee told us they were in a shelter in Minneapolis, and they were just happy to be safe.

August had arrived with warmer weather and more humidity. I dreamed of going back to my cabin and having family days swimming in the lake and tubing like I did as a child. My happy days with my dad. I told myself I may try to go back next summer with the kids.

Mom sat beside me on my couch as we waited for the kids to finally come home. "Are you excited?"

I bit my nails. "More than you can imagine."

"Are you going to show her the book you wrote about her?"

"Not right away. I think it may be too much for her right off the bat, and what if she's upset?"

"I don't think she'll be upset. She'll love it."

"I hope so."

"You wrote a beautiful book about a little girl that resembles Melanie, struggling with cancer. Trust me, she'll be honored."

"Hope so."

"So, has Travis tried calling you since you saw him at the hospital?"

"A few times, but I just can't get myself to answer the phone or call him back."

More like ten times, but if he wanted to know about the kids or something important, he'd leave a message, and he never did.

"So, did he and Missy get married?"

"I don't think so. He wasn't wearing a ring. It doesn't matter, Mom. I'm with Phillip now, and we are happy." An image of Travis's little baby and her big, beautiful blue eyes flashed in front of me. I was angry I couldn't get pregnant. I shook myself. I was more than happy to have Melanie and Ben back in my life, and that would definitely complete our family.

I heard a car door and ran to the window. Renee's car was parked out front. I watched Melanie run for the door, Ben close behind her.

I wrapped my arms around them both and kissed the top of their heads.

"I've missed you both so much."

They clung to me. Even Ben didn't pull away.

"Come in, come in. I'll go help Renee with your bags."

They ran to my mom and gave her the same greeting.

I went out to meet Renee. The back door was open, and her head poked out with two backpacks in her hand.

"Can I help you with their things?"

She shook her head and lifted the two backpacks. "Sadly, this is it."

I nodded and took the bags from her. "I can't thank you enough for all you've done. How are they?"

She closed her door and stood by my side, staring through the window at the kids hugging my mom. "Not so good, but all they talked about was how excited they were to finally be with you. Their grandma was bedridden for a long time, and I am not sure how long Ronnie was there, but it's been quite a while."

She pulled out a card. "Listen, I have a name and number for a great therapist, and I think it would be a good idea for them to have someone to talk to. Someone outside your family. There is an open investigation with CPS, and they both have been interviewed, but I can't really talk about the open case. All I can say is that they have been through a lot and trauma can be very emotional. Their worker's name is Jillian Hannon, and she may be trying to get ahold of you."

I took her card from her. "Thank you."

"You take care, and call me if you need anything. It's okay to ask them questions. You know they've been through a lot."

I smiled. "Thank you. I can't believe this is finally happening."

"Jim and Savannah still have time to change their mind, as we talked about. A year actually."

"I know. I'm just trying not to think about that. Were they at a good shelter in The Cities?"

"They were in a great shelter in Bloomington. I wouldn't worry too much about that. They were well taken care of. Now, understand they have had a lot of trauma in the last few months, so they may act a little out of the ordinary."

"I understand."

I watched her car drive off. It wasn't over for them yet, but I was willing to do whatever it took to help them understand they were safe and no one would hurt them again.

The kids were delighted to see their new rooms. I was sitting on Melanie's new bed with her while Phillip and Ben were playing video games in Ben's room.

"We fixed them up a long time ago for you guys. I hope your rooms aren't too dusty."

"I love my new room. It's almost as nice as my other..." Melanie put her head down.

"What's wrong, sweetie?"

"I don't ever wanna go back there. Promise me you won't let them take me again. Promise."

"I will do everything in my power to make sure that doesn't happen again. Social Services won't let that happen either."

"That's what you said last time," Ben yelled angrily from the door.

"Come here, buddy," I said, getting up. He crossed his arms and turned his back to me.

"Oh, buddy, we didn't mean for any of this to happen. We had no idea he was living there," Phillip said.

"You never called," Ben yelled.

"Yes we did. We tried everything. We didn't know," I said.

"C'mon Ben, we are home now, right, Mom?" Melanie said.

"Yes, sweetie. We love you both very much, and if you want to talk to us about anything, we are always here to listen."

We put the kids to bed. Ben wasn't really talking to Phillip or myself since the incident in the bedroom, which had me worried about what happened. We read a book, and although Ben pretended not to listen to the story, I knew he was enjoying it. We said goodnight and headed to bed ourselves.

A blood-curdling scream woke us up in the middle of the night. I went running down the hall to find Ben screaming and crying.

"Are you okay, buddy? It was just a dream, just a bad dream," I said, hugging him tightly. "Do you wanna talk about it?"

"No!"

"Would you like me to sit here with you for a little while until you fall back to sleep? Get you a glass of water or something?"

He shook his head.

I heard the door squeak behind me and found Phillip and Melanie at the door.

"Hello there, kind of looks like a slumber party now."

Melanie nodded her head, clinging on to her teddy bear.

I looked back and forth between the two kids. "Would you two like to have a sleepover in our bed tonight?"

They both screamed in unison, "Yeah," and jumped up and down as they raced each other to our king-size bed.

"Are you sure this is a good idea?" Phillip said, shaking his head at me.

"What could it hurt? We can try putting them back in their beds tomorrow. Phillip, they've been through enough. They need this."

"I guess."

"And we need this."

Although they were sleeping in our bed with us, Ben still woke up again with a terrifying blood-curdling scream. In the morning there was a stain on the bed sheet from his night sweats and urine.

Melanie was back to hoarding food and crying for her mom. I felt so bad for them and I didn't know what I could do to help.

Phillip took me aside. "We need to get him some help. That is not normal for him to be screaming that much in the night. Did you feel his hands and face? He was burning up."

"I know. Renee gave me the name of a good therapist in town. I'll call this afternoon."

"That would be a good idea."

"What about Melanie? Do you think she should go to therapy too?"

"I don't think it would be a bad idea. She's been through so much," Phillip said.

"She's been hoarding food again," I admitted.

"I know. I didn't want to say anything."

"It's so hard when she cries for her mom. She doesn't understand why she can't be here."

Phillip grabbed my hands. "I know. It's going to take time."

I nodded. "I just don't know what to do."

He squeezed my hands. "You are doing everything right. You just need to keep doing what you are doing. It's going to take a lot of time to heal."

I blinked away the tears. "I don't think they will ever heal from this."

We went to the hospital for Melanie's monthly checkup. The doctor said everything looked great after the tests. She was still cancer-free.

On the drive home, Phillip started singing "Bingo" and we all chimed in.

Phillip looked at Ben in the review mirror after the singing stopped. "You know what a clean bill of health means, Ben?"

"What?"

"You both can start school in the fall. No more home schooling."

They both erupted with cheers.

"I'm so glad everything is going so well for you two and the kids," Emily said.

I looked at Phillip, and he smiled back at me.

"Have you changed your mind about the fundraiser?"

"I don't know--"

"Yes, we are going. I already cleared it with your mom to watch the kids," Phillip interrupted.

I turned to him. "You can't just ask her without talking to me. I can't leave them yet. Look what they've been through."

"It's your mother. They will be fine. It would be a waste of that red satin dress that's been hanging in your room for how long. You're going to look so hot."

"He's right," Emily said.

Phillip ran his fingers through my dark brown curls.

"I guess."

"You have a speech, right?" Emily asked while sending a text from her phone.

My chest dropped into my stomach. "I haven't had any time to write it. I've been so busy."

"You can do this; it doesn't have to be long."

"I guess. By the way, I have something to show you guys."

I held up my children's book with my drawing of Melanie on the cover.

Emily snatched the book right out of my hand. "You published it? I can't believe you published it."

Phillip leaned over her shoulder. "I want to see."

Emily decided it was time to celebrate and opened a bottle of Merlot. She handed each of us a glass. "To family."

"To family," we said in unison.

"And to the fundraiser," she added. My heart felt like it was going to pop out of my chest.

∽∞∾

The next morning I went upstairs to wake Melanie with my book behind my back. I had to get her approval before I showed it to the world.

"Wake up, Melanie. I have something to show you."

She sat up and rubbed her eyes. "Is it a surprise?"

I sat down on her bed beside her. "Yes, but first I want to say you have been through so much these last few months fighting cancer. No matter how hard times got, you never gave up, and I'm so proud of you. Although I didn't get to be by your side the whole time, I never stopped thinking about you."

"It was scary."

"I know it was, and you did so good. I got to thinking that your story could help other children that are fighting cancer or know someone fighting cancer, so I brought your story to life."

She wrinkled up her eyebrows. "What do you mean, Mommy?"

I pulled out the book. "While you were away, I wrote this book about your cancer story."

I put it in her hand, and she squealed with excitement. "Is this me, Mommy? Is this me?"

"Yes, and can you read her name?"

"Melanie?"

"Yes. I was going to name her Melissa, but it wouldn't be your book without your name."

She jumped up and hugged me. "I love it."

"Tonight I'm going to a fundraiser with Aunt Emily and Phillip, so would you like to have a sleepover with Grandma Destiny at our house?"

"And Auntie Jill, too?"

"We can call her. I'm sure she will if she doesn't already have plans."

She bounced on the bed. "Thank you, thank you. Can I read this book tonight?"

"Honey, this book is just for you. You can keep it."

It felt so good to see her so happy and healthy. All those days in the hospital, wondering if she would even make it through the night, and now here she was, just a normal little girl now.

We left the kids with my mom, Jill, and Uncle Mike. When we left, Melanie was trying to put makeup on Ben, but Mike volunteered to be her guinea pig. I'm pretty sure he couldn't stand to see her sad after all she'd been through. I loved how my family treated them like blood.

"So, Matt's home with Irene, huh? They should have come over to my house and hung out with everyone."

"Irene is still a little sick, so I didn't want her to get your kids sick."

"I appreciate that. Melanie's immune system is much better, but I'd hate to see her sick again after everything she's been through."

Emily and I went to Duluth to get our hair and makeup done. She had to go to a certain salon because she never let anyone but them touch her hair. I had a feeling it wasn't going to be cheap.

"I can't believe you guys finally have the kids back. You and Phillip look so happy. I always knew the two of you would end up together."

"Yeah, it's been a heck of a year."

"I'd say. But if it weren't for everything you've been through, you wouldn't have everything you ever dreamed of."

I stared out the window at the green grass and tall trees as we turned onto highway 53. I loved the way everything looked so green and healthy after such a long, cold winter. Maybe a run in the morning would be just what I'd need after a long night of drinking and chatting. We had reservations at the Sheraton Duluth Hotel, which Emily assured me was right next to the Greysolon Ballroom. She said it was actually connected by a skywalk. Emily raved about the ballroom most of the drive, telling me how exquisite it was and how radiant I was going to look in my red dress.

"So, when's Phillip coming?"

"Around five. He had to work until two."

"Must be nice to climb into a tux and they're ready to go. But then again, nothing beats pampering."

"I don't know. It's a lot of work and a lot of time."

She looked at me out of the corner of her eye, hands perfectly placed on ten and two. "You're going to love being pampered."

"I just miss the kids."

"I miss Irene, too, but you need this. How is everything with you and Phillip anyway?"

"It's good."

"Good?"

"Yeah. He's my best friend. It's always been good."

"So what's wrong then? I was just going on about the two of you being the perfect couple."

"Sometimes I just feel like we are pushing this relationship. We were better friends, you know."

"Does this have something to do with seeing Travis?"

"No, not at all. I love Phillip, and Travis left me for Missy, remember? They had a kid together, and I would never get in the way of that."

"But you want to."

"No, not at all. I'm over him."

"Girl, you can't lie. You are still madly in love with him, aren't you?"

"No way. I hate him. Em, he left me for a crazy ex-girlfriend he lied about knocking up. How can you even think I'd still have feelings for that man? It's ridiculous."

"Well, if you hate him that much, you must have feelings for him."

"No, I don't. Can we quit talking about him now?"

"What are you going to do if he shows up tonight?"

I raised an eyebrow and my heart beat increased. "What? Why would you think he would show up tonight?"

"Because he bought tickets from me."

I flopped back on the seat. "He's not coming."

"You never know."

"Oh stop. Missy would never let him go, and why would he even want to?"

"I don't know, maybe because he loves you, too."

"Please stop. Promise you won't mention his name tonight. It hurts too much."

"I'm sorry. I promise."

# PROPOSAL

As we made our way down the big, steep hill that overlooked Lake Superior, I thought about Travis's huge house. I looked out at the lake and the beautiful lift bridge that reminded me of the view off the rooftop at his house.

As we hit Superior Street, I took in the streets made out of brick and realized how beautiful the city of Duluth really was: the lift bridge, the water, and the hills that surrounded the area. I wondered how often people went through brakes on their cars around here.

We arrived at the ballroom around five, an hour before the fundraiser began. The outside of the building reminded me of a theater in New York City. The marble bricks covered the front of the building, surrounding the marquee sign, which was lit up by dozens of lights that read Greysolon Plaza. The arched windows on the front of the building and the hanging lanterns added an old-fashioned vibe. This was the first year our fundraiser would be held at such an elegant venue.

We walked in the front doors together, and I gasped when I saw the elegant water fountain right in front of us. My eyes were wide with admiration as I tried to take in the exquisite building, mahogany walls, and hand-painted ceilings. I felt like I was living in an old movie from the nineteen hundreds and at any minute a king or a queen would be coming out.

"When was this ballroom built?"

"It was built in nineteen twenty-five and named one of the finest hotels on the whole continent back then. Black Woods has restored it to what it is today."

"I never knew a place like this existed in Duluth. I feel like I've just stepped into a high-class hotel in New York City."

"Oh, I know. Wait until you see the ballroom. This is nothing. The ceilings in there are so much higher."

I followed her into the ballroom.

"It reminds me so much of the historic Hibbing High School auditorium, but even more beautiful." Sparkling crystal chandeliers hung from the high ceilings. The many tables were decorated with elegant white tablecloths sprinkled with gold, along with beautiful bone china and antique crystal glasses set to perfection in each place. The polished silverware shined in the light of the chandeliers. Gold satin wrapped around the back of each chair, leaving it almost too perfect to sit down on.

"How many tickets did we sell?"

"Three hundred and seventy-five this year. We sold out every seat in this place, and at two hundred dollars a chair, we made a killing for the children. Did you bring your book?"

I looked down at my huge black purse. "Yes, I did."

"Good, are you using it in your speech? If not, you should."

We checked to make sure all the donations for the fundraiser were laid out the way we wanted them. People started showing up about fifteen minutes early and were shown to their assigned seats, which were labeled by gold place cards.

"I can't believe how much work you put into this, Emily," I said in between greeting guests at the door.

Emily squeezed my hand. "Thank you. I can't take all the credit. I had a lot of help. We're going to raise so much money this year."

"The children deserve it."

Phillip showed up looking as handsome as ever in his black tux. He gave me a hug and leaned in to whisper to me. "You look absolutely stunning tonight. You just about knocked me right out of these expensive shoes Emily made me wear."

I laughed and showed him to his seat.

"Kick some butt out there."

"I'll do my best," I said.

As soon as everyone had taken their seats, Emily began her presentation. The raffles were definitely a success and everyone seemed to enjoy themselves. There were a few empty seats from guests who bought tickets but couldn't make it for one reason or another.

When the fundraising was finally over, Emily returned to the podium.

"I hope everyone is enjoying this delicious meal."

Enthusiastic applause broke out.

"None of this would have been possible without my partner, Gabriella Fredrickson. Gabriella, would you like to come up and say a few words?"

I wanted to say no, but that was no longer an option. I gave her a hug as I stepped into my spot at the podium.

"As many of you may know, I'm Emily's sister-in-law. For years I've had a dream to put together a fundraiser for children in need. North Star Children's Project came about one day when I told Emily my dream of raising money for the shelter I worked at on The Range, specifically for children who are abused. Did you know that one in three girls and one in four boys will be sexually abused before they are an adult? A lot of people don't know this. We tend to turn a blind eye to the things that make us uncomfortable and pretend they aren't happening in our backyards."

I looked up to see every eye on me. I paused and for a brief moment enjoyed the feeling of power from having the crowd's attention. No one could interrupt, no one could say a word, they had to listen to me, and they had to hear the truth through my words, even though my hands were shaking.

"I used to be one of those people until I started working with children who were sexually and physically abused and I could no longer ignore the truth. This charity is about raising money for shelters in Duluth and all the way up to The Range. I've seen children with deep scars, not only on the outside, but the inside. The scars we see are the only ones we believe happened, but what about the scars we can't see? They aren't visible and can't be found on the outside, but they are there and they run deep. We need to put a stop to this horrible cycle and be the voice for the children that can't speak.

"This year I am honored and thrilled to tell you that I adopted two beautiful children who were in the system. They were both victims of abuse and neglect, but every child has a story and their story has become mine."

An image of Melanie and Ben popped into my head. I took a deep breath. Here it goes.

"I fell in love with a little girl named Melanie, and sadly, not only did she have a very abusive childhood, but while she was in the shelter, she was diagnosed with acute lymphocytic leukemia, also known as ALL. It is a type of cancer where the bone marrow makes too many immature lymphocytes, which is a type of white blood cell. At the age of five, she endured months of radiation and chemo. I watched her lose her hair and a lot of weight. It was hard to watch. I can't imagine how hard it was for her to endure.

"At first we were lucky enough to be placed at a Ronald McDonald House--and let me tell you, it was amazing there--but she needed a more permanent home. Her grandmother wanted to take care of her and her brother, but she had stage four colon cancer and didn't get to be around as much as she would have liked. After she passed, her father signed the papers in prison for me to adopt them so they would have a better life."

I looked down at my papers. How much should I say? "My kids were abused by their uncle, a trusted family member that no one suspected. The wounds run deep, and after losing their grandmother, Melanie surviving cancer herself, their dad being in prison, and mom being in a long-term mental health facility, this is the first time they can breathe. It still isn't easy for them, and more than ever, they finally have the stability of a family and no longer have to endure abuse or neglect. They have changed my life more than they will ever know and they have changed me and the way I look at life in the system."

I tried to fight the tears, but they began falling as I spoke. I didn't want to wipe them away. I wanted them all to feel what I had felt during that time, feel the way Melanie and Ben felt as they endured the pain and suffering by someone they loved and trusted.

"Today I stand before you, and for the first time I am showing you what I did to get through the pain of when they were taken from me. I wrote this children's book about childhood cancer. It's called Melanie's Story."

I lifted up the book to show everyone the cover that I drew and colored. I heard a few wow's from the audience.

"This book is for sale on Amazon, and all the proceeds will go to Melanie and Ben's college fund. Thank you all so much for coming, and I hope you stay to enjoy the music. Don't ignore what's going on in this world. Fight to make a difference and help to end child abuse. I know foster care isn't for everyone, but there is no better feeling in the world than being able to let in a child that just wants to be loved. Thank you."

I stepped away from the podium and everyone stood up in their seats and clapped. The standing ovation caught me by surprise and my face grew warm with pride. I smiled as I continued to walk to my seat.

Phillip placed his hand on my shoulder, and I turned around and smiled back at him.

The band fired up. People started to move from their seats and began to dance. Phillip held his hand out in front of me. I took it and began dancing with him. We whirled around the dance floor, spinning and even dipping. A few times I thought I might be showing my back end to everyone, because the dress went right down to my tailbone, but no one seemed to notice.

"You know, if I didn't know any better, I would think you actually enjoyed giving that speech."

I smiled. "I really did."

The song ended, but Phillip reached into his pocket and got down on one knee. I'm pretty sure I stopped breathing as he said the words.

"Gabriella Fredrickson, you have been my best friend, role model, and truly the most giving person I have ever met. You pushed me to become a better person, and for that I will be forever grateful. I love you as a best friend, a lover, and hopefully you will accept my proposal and make me the happiest man in the world."

The room went quiet and everyone circled around us to hear my reply.

I stood there, frozen, with everyone in the room staring at me. I grabbed his arm and helped him up. "You know I don't like this kind of attention."

I clenched my teeth and smiled at everyone, and nodded at the band to start up. Thankfully, they did.

Phillip's face glowed red as we walked toward the doorway, but I had to be honest for both our sakes.

"You're my best friend, and I never want anything to get in the way of that, but you and I both know we aren't meant to be together. I will always love you, and I love raising the kids with you, but I'm not in love with you."

I expected him to be broken and hurt after putting himself out there in front of all those people, but instead he said, "I wanted to do what I thought was right for our family. I love you more than anything in this whole world, and I thought this was what I--you wanted, but I think I was more nervous you would say yes. Don't take this the wrong way. I think I'm relieved."

We burst out laughing and rested our foreheads together.

"Best friends?" I said, taking a step back.

"Best friends it is," he agreed.

My body went limp as Travis punched Phillip in the face. It all seemed to happen in slow motion. Phillip fell to the floor holding his jaw.

"What are you doing, Travis?"

"You told me you were just friends. You promised me."

I helped Phillip up. "We'll talk, I promise." I turned to Phillip. "I'm going to handle him, if that's all right."

He nodded and held his jaw. He glared at Travis, but did not say a word.

Travis and I walked into the back to the ladies room. A white antique dresser and a red sofa were pushed against the wall. The room was empty.

"What the hell are you doing here, Travis? Don't you have a wife and child to be with?"

"Missy and I aren't together anymore, and we were never married. We broke up a few months ago. When you said you were seeing someone, I didn't think it was Phillip. How could you? Anyone but Phillip," he said, hands on his hips in anger.

"How could I? You left me, Travis, remember? After you promised me the baby couldn't be yours, and I didn't doubt you for one second."

"I know," he said. "I'm so sorry I hurt you."

"Hurt me? You left me right after I lost the children. You didn't care about me."

He moved closer to me, and tried but failed to take my arm as I stepped back.

"I do. I care. I love you more than anything. You are all I can think about. Missy went crazy and left one day. We had nothing between us; we tried, but it just wasn't there. She knew where my heart was. She knew it was with you."

"You punched my best friend, Travis. How could you do that at my fundraiser for abuse? That was abuse. You'll be lucky if no one called the cops."

"I'm sorry I ruined your night. I wasn't thinking. I was just so angry. How could you marry him?"

I clenched my jaw and talked through my teeth. "Because he would never hurt me like you did. He was there for me when you ran away. He's a good person, unlike you."

He reached out and pulled me into his chest. He took my breath away as he kissed me with fire and passion. I knew I should pull away, but in this moment his seductive kiss had me weak in the knees. I couldn't think straight as the anger and hatred turned into passion as I took it all out on him in this heated kiss. I pulled him in tighter, pushing harder. I clasped his face with my hands, and as our lips finally parted, I slapped him and turned away.

He caught me by the arm and slipped me a key, and whispered in my ear, prolonging each letter as it came out of his perfect mouth. "If you love me, here is my key. I'm in the wedding suite, room four-o-five."

His words not only made my heart flutter, but my body feel warm and tingly. I looked him in the eye, took the key, and ran out the door.

# THE KEY TO HAPPINESS

I ran out the door, down the stairs, trying to get outside into the fresh air so I could breathe again. I had to hold on to my dress as I ran in my high heels, almost stumbling, unable to catch my breath. Once outside, I hunched forward, hands on my knees as I collapsed in tears.

The door behind me opened as I tried to stand up.

"Are you okay?" Phillip said.

"He kissed me. He kissed me."

"Yeah, and he may have broken my jaw. That man truly loves you, you know that?"

The key card burned my hand, which made me realize I was squeezing it too hard. "What should I do?"

"I don't think you should let this man go," Phillip said, holding me up by the arm.

"I slapped him."

"You what?"

"He kissed me and I slapped him." I began to laugh at myself for what I did.

Phillip laughed, letting go of my arm. "Look at me. If you love this guy, follow your heart."

I nodded. "It really doesn't bother you?"

"I just want you to be happy. That guy can sure punch, you know that? Now go get him."

I grabbed his face and gave him a quick kiss on the lips, leaving him with a sisterly smile.

"Go," he demanded.

I nodded and hurried to the hotel next door.

Once at his room, I stared at the card for a moment before swiping it. No turning back now.

The light turned green and I opened the door. Travis did not hear me enter. His back was to the door. He was staring out the window, holding the curtains open as he stood there in his white dress shirt and red bow tie.

"Hi," I said.

He jumped and turned around when he heard my voice. "You came. I didn't think you would."

I walked over to him, sparing a glance for the hot tub, full kitchen, and king-size bed in the huge suite. "Is this a normal hotel room for you?"

He laughed and moved closer to me. "Still the same old Gabriella. You haven't changed a bit, have you?"

He touched my collarbone and gently ran his finger along it.

Goosebumps enveloped my whole body.

"You have to be the most beautiful woman I have ever set eyes on. Inside and out. When I saw Phillip on one knee proposing to you, I was so damn angry. But I was more angry at myself than the two of you. How did it happen? Are you going to marry him?"

I ran my fingers through my hair, unsure of what to do with them. "We tried to have a relationship, but we don't love each other like that. He's my best friend, not my lover."

"Do you still have feelings for me?"

His voice was so tender, I found it hard not to jump into his arms. "I'm here, aren't I? I thought I was over you. I mean, I had myself convinced I hated you, but now I know I can't live without you in my life."

"Do you still have that key I gave you?"

I nodded, showing him the card for the hotel room.

"Not that key. The key I gave you that day at the park."

I slipped my fingers between my breasts and pulled out the key that was on a small chain around my neck. I never went anywhere without it on me. I knew it would keep Travis close to my heart, no matter how far away he was or how much I hated him.

He put his hands around my neck and I couldn't fight the warmness I felt between my legs with his touch. He pulled the necklace out and took the key off the chain and handed it to me.

"What do you want me to do with it?"

He reached into the drawer next to his bed and pulled out a box with a key hole. He dropped to one knee in front of me and brought my hand up to his mouth and kissed it tenderly.

"Marry me, Gabriella June Fredrickson, marry me."

I didn't reply as I put the key in the hole and turned it. Inside was a huge princess-cut diamond ring. It looked very old-fashioned and must have cost more than I made in a year.

"What...how?"

"I knew I'd marry you one day. Will you marry me?"

"You knew? Yes, yes, I'll marry you."

I grabbed his hand and pulled him up, my lips desperate to explore his again.

He leaned in and kissed me on the forehead. I grabbed his arms and pulled him in tight for another hard, passionate kiss. He didn't disappoint me. My body quivered with desire I never felt before.

His hands reached around my neck and undid the strap that held up my dress. In one quick movement, it dropped to the floor, leaving me in just my red underwear.

"Hey, that's not fair." I grinned. "Your turn."

I wrapped my hands around his neck, trying to remove his red bow tie, then I stopped. "Nah, I'm leaving that on."

He laughed, watching me as I unbuttoned every button on his white shirt, slow and seductive, pulling it off his shoulders. His arms were much bigger than the last time I saw him. I pressed my hands against his chest and pushed him on the bed.

He didn't fight me. He let out an excited laugh instead.

Kneeling down on the bed, I undid his belt and pulled off his pants. He put his hands behind his head to support his neck so he could watch me. His stomach contracted and his abs looked chiseled and perfect, too perfect.

Heat flooded my entire body. I kept my eyes open as I kissed his stomach and slowly climbed my way up to his neck with my tongue, then to his chin, his jaw, and then he hungrily grabbed my hips and threw me on my back.

"I forgot how amazing it was with you."

"I could never forget," he said.

A small breathless whisper escaped my lips, and his delicate touch made me inhale sharply.

We shared a passion that was so desperately missing for far too long as we made love over and over until we were too exhausted to continue.

I didn't sleep much that night as I snuggled up in his chest, wondering if I was dreaming or if this was really happening. I watched him sleep, the streetlight outside his hotel room shining in, enough to see his chiseled cheekbones and strong jaw. A smile spread across my face. My life was finally complete.

His eyes opened, looking startled until he saw me. He brushed his lips against my forehead. "I thought I was dreaming, but you're really here with me."

"Do you think Missy will be angry when she finds out we're back together?"

"Missy's gone, Gabby. It never clicked between us. After she had the baby, we tried, then we split up, and she disappeared."

"She just left and didn't say anything to you?"

"Well, she left a note saying that she was depressed and that she just couldn't handle being a mom. That she needed to take care of herself. I think it was very big of her to admit she was sick."

"Yeah, I guess."

He stroked my hair. "And Phillip?"

"Phillip proposed to me because he thought that should be the next step. We never got past being best friends. There wasn't any chemistry. I think I was still in love with you."

Was Travis jealous or hurt? Maybe both?

"He must hate me. I hit him in front of all those people."

"He doesn't hate you."

"Oh really? And how do you know that?"

I popped my head up and gazed at him. "Because he told me you must love me to hit him like that after a proposal. He told me to go find you."

His eyes widened. "Are you kidding me? Why would he tell you to chase me after I sent him flying across the floor? I don't know if I could have said the same thing if I were him." He shook his head. "He is a much better person than I am."

"I'm not saying he's going to give you a big hug and kiss the next time he sees you, but he wants me to be happy and he knows it's with you."

"He's a great friend to you, you know that?"

"I do."

He hesitated. "Gabby, I have to ask. Did you sleep with him?"

I wasn't sure if I should answer that. "Do you really want to know the answer to that?"

"You just answered my question. I'm not going to lie, it bothers me that his lips brushed against these sweet lips, his lips kissed this beautiful shoulder."

I closed my eyes as he kissed the places on my body as he named them.

He sighed. "It might be more awkward for him than it is for us."

I laughed. "You're probably right, but he'll get over it. Phillip is like a brother to me."

"So you'd screw your brother? Does Matt know that?"

I threw a pillow at him and began dressing. "You jerk."

He laughed and watched me as I tried to put my dress on. Putting on a dress from the night before was never easy the next morning. I felt like I was doing the walk of shame. Come to think about it, I was doing the walk of shame. I laughed at my thoughts.

"What's so funny?"

"Nothing. It's just that I feel like a teenager doing the walk of shame."

"Oh, a teenager. I bet you were a hot teenager. Probably a cheerleader."

I jumped up and down to pull the dress up. "Wrong. I was a swimmer. I tried out for cheer and failed miserably. It was quite embarrassing, actually."

"I doubt that."

"You have no idea. I tried to do a split and broke my leg."

"That's some devotion. Well, their loss. I think that shows commitment."

"After a lot of therapy, I'm working through it."

I sat down on the bed, my hand on his cheek. "I have to find Emily. I'm so glad you came last night."

He grinned. "Me, too."

"Oh, shush."

"Wait, wait, I need a kiss." I bent over to kiss him.

"You know I can see down your dress."

I rolled my eyes and grinned.

"But seriously, when do I get the honor of seeing you again?"

"I'm not sure."

"Do you still live with Phillip?" he asked.

"Yes. Do you have a problem with that?" I said, putting my shoes on.

"I should. I'm your fiancé."

I shook my head at him and disappeared out the door without a goodbye. What the hell was I thinking saying yes to him? I got into the elevator and took the ring off and slipped it into the front pocket of my purse.

I looked at my phone. Four text messages and seven missed calls from Phillip and one from my mom. I had to call Emily first. Did my mom already know?

"Hello, you slut," Emily yelled into the phone.

# FACING PHILLIP

"How did it go last night? I want to hear every detail."

"Where are you?"

"I'm driving back to Hibbing, of course," she said.

"Then how the hell am I getting home?"

"I thought you went home with Travis?"

"No, we stayed at the hotel."

She started laughing. "I'm just kidding. Phillip told me to go. He wanted to talk to you. Maybe clear the air."

I exhaled. "Uh, I don't want to do this right now."

"Sorry, he didn't exactly give me a choice. I'm meeting your brother in Canyon for lunch. Call me and let me know how it goes. Better yet, can you record it for me?"

"Seriously, Em?"

"Well, I had to try. Oh, your brother said hello and that he hopes you are coming to dinner tonight at Jill's. We just walked into the restaurant."

"Yeah, I'll be there."

"Later."

‿‿‿

"Mom, it's me. Sorry I didn't answer last night. My phone was on vibrate from the fundraiser and--"

"Sweetie, last night Melanie had a fever of one hundred and two, and I was trying to reach you to find out if you wanted me to take her in to the hospital or give her Tylenol."

"Oh, my gosh. Is she okay?"

"Yeah, she's fine. After the whole cancer thing, I didn't want to chance it, but the doctor said she's fine and that her tonsils were a little swollen. Just a little cold, that's all, and she's feeling great now. I told her she has to stay in bed until you get home."

"Oh, Mom, thank you so much for taking care of her."

"This isn't my first rodeo, Gabriella. You have nothing to worry about. I've got this."

"Thanks, Mom. How's Ben doing?"

"Well, he was a little worried last night, but he's okay now. No nightmares. I think they are missing you guys. Are you on your way?"

"Uh...Phillip and I will be leaving in just a few minutes."

"Funny, I just talked to him and he was trying to find you."

I panicked. I couldn't talk my way out of this, so I told her I had to go. I felt like a sixteen-year-old kid sneaking around.

I got off the phone and knocked at 102. The door was open.

"Phillip?"

Phillip's eyes lit up. "Gabby! I've been so worried about you! I checked everywhere for you, and the guy at the front desk told me Travis didn't have a room here, that no one reserved a room by that name."

I took his suitcase as he put on his shoes.

"How are you?"

"I'm okay. How's your face?" It was purple and swollen.

"About as good as it looks, I guess."

"I'm so sorry about last night."

He grabbed my face with his hands and pulled me close. "Gabriella, you will always be the love of my life, and I never want to lose you, but you and I both know we pushed this relationship because it was convenient and easy. Best friends are supposed to be just that, best friends."

I grabbed his hands and pulled them off my face and squeezed them. "Thank you."

"Now, let's go." He stopped mid-stride and turned around to face me. "Oh, and we're listening to Prince the whole car ride home, just an FYI."

"You think so, huh? How about we compromise and shuffle your songs and see what happens instead?"

"You turned down my engagement in front of a couple hundred people. I think the embarrassment alone should leave you owing me favors for at least the next month."

"Are you kidding me? I'm sure all the single women will be hunting you down because they feel so sorry for you. If anything, I helped you get laid."

"Too soon."

"I'm sorry."

He laughed. "I'm so good at this."

I punched him in the shoulder.

"What's that for?"

I growled and followed him to the car.

"You seemed a little upset when you left this morning," Travis said.

"It's just a lot, that's all," I said.

"Do you regret promising to marry me?"

"I don't regret it. I just need some time to think about it before I tell everyone."

"Who is everyone?" he said.

"My mom, my family, everyone. Melanie was sick last night and my mom had to bring her to the hospital, so I guess I've just been focusing on her this morning."

"Oh, no. Is she okay? How's she feeling? What happened?"

The sound of Travis's voice gave me chills over the phone. Why did he make me feel so nervous?

"She's doing well. It was just a fever, but it broke and she's sleeping now."

"And Ben?"

"Ben's just fine."

"And Phillip?"

"He's at work. Why?"

"Just curious," he said.."

"Why?"

"I'm just getting into town. I'm driving by the Thirsty Moose right now."

I ran my fingers through my messy hair. He never said he decided to come into town tonight, and I didn't want him to see me like this. I looked down at my green Grinch pajama pants. I needed to change, quick.

"Why didn't you tell me you were coming into town today?" I said, a little anxious but excited he was coming.

"I wanted to surprise you."

"You sure surprised me."

"I'm sorry. So, what did you guys do today?"

"Since Melanie wasn't feeling well, the three of us watched <u>Despicable Me</u> and took a lazy day. Phillip had to work for a few hours."

I wasn't going to tell him I was glad Phillip had to work because when I got home, things were a bit awkward between us. We were so used to kissing on the lips hello and sleeping in the same bed. I wasn't sure how we were going to break it to the kids or make our living arrangement work anymore. Would moving out be for the best?

I ran upstairs after we got off the phone to put a bra on and clean up. As I was putting on deodorant, I heard a car door slam. I looked out my window to see Travis and Phillip both getting out of their cars at the same time.

"Oh, shit."

Travis walked over to Phillip and shook his hand. I thought about going out there to make sure everything was okay between them, but they were grown men, they could do this on their own. Even thinking about it made me uncomfortable.

I watched them for close to ten minutes, and then I couldn't take it anymore. I slid open the bathroom window as quietly as I could to hear what was going on.

"We should go to a Vikings game sometime. I bet the kids would love that," Phillip said. "About Missy, you need to talk to Gabby. It's better that she knows all of it."

"Do you think she's ready? I mean, we just got back together."

"She can handle it. If it makes you feel any better, I know she couldn't stop thinking about you. I tried so hard to brighten her days, but with you and the kids gone, she was just so sad. I'd do anything for her and that includes finding you and beating the crap out of you if you break her heart again."

"I won't lose her again."

"Yep, I got that when you punched me in the face."

He looked away. "Yeah, sorry about that, man. Gabriella told me right after that you told her to chase after me, that I was a keeper."

"Did I say that? Well, she's my best friend. I don't want it to be weird. I don't think of her that way anymore. You know that, right?"

Travis put his arm on Phillip's shoulder and squeezed it. Even from way up in the bathroom, I could see he was squeezing it a little too hard, but playfully.

"Yeah, I'm not worried about it. You did what you had to do. Hey, should we go in there and I'll hold my eye and say you punched me and see what she does?"

Phillip looked over his shoulder. "If I know Gabby, she's hiding in a window listening to every word we are saying."

Oh, crap.

Travis scanned the front windows, so I ducked down just in time. I turned on the shower and hopped in. Putting my hair up in a bun, I decided to forgo the tedious task of putting on my makeup. He saw me many times without it on.

Wrapped in a towel, I headed to my bedroom to get dressed and then, after checking to make sure the kids were asleep, I snuck to the stairs to eavesdrop. Phillip and Travis both stood up when they heard the stairs creak beneath my feet. Stupid old house.

I hugged Phillip and then Travis. "Hey there. Looks like the two of you are bonding." Travis put his arm around me. "Yep, Phillip here slapped me around a little bit, but we're good."

"I'm glad."

Travis and I sat down on the couch. The Twins were down two to four, and both Phillip and Travis had a beer in their hands already.

Travis turned to me. "I have to work in The Cities this week, but on Friday would you and the kids like to come to Duluth and spend the weekend with us? I invited Phillip here to come, but he said he has to work all weekend."

"I think that's a great idea. I'd love to get to know your baby, too."

He smiled and squeezed my hand. "I'd love for you to get to know Erica. She is the sweetest little baby."

Melanie cried from the top of the stairs. "Mommy, Mommy."

I jumped off the couch. "What's going on, honey? Are you feeling okay?"

"Will you sleep with me? I had a bad dream."

"Be right there," I said.

I turned to Travis. "I'm sorry, but I need to be with her right now. Will you two be okay? You can sleep in my bed if you want."

"Can I say hello?"

"I'd rather you didn't right before bed. She'll be too excited to sleep."

"Okay, I understand. Yeah, I'm going to hang out for a little bit, then I'll probably head back to Duluth tonight or early in the morning. I have a long drive ahead of me if I'm going to get to Minneapolis for my noon appointment."

I kissed him on the cheek and ran up the stairs to my impatient daughter. "Goodnight."

# ADVENTURE ZONE

We played laser tag for the third time before Travis and I decided to sit this round out.

Missy's mom had Erica, and we needed a rest so we took Melanie and Ben to the Adventure Zone. The air conditioning kept everyone cool as we watched children run around with tickets, their parents trying but failing to keep up with them as they trailed behind.

"I need to tell you something."

Here it comes. This must be whatever he told Phillip about.

"It's about Missy."

He really knew how to get my full attention. "Okay?"

"I didn't tell you everything. Missy is gone and we did try to make it work, but I ended up kicking her out, she didn't just leave."

"You what--"

"Sit down. Let me explain. Missy was against nursing the baby, and I was okay with that. I believe it should be the mother's choice. Anyway, then she started drinking every night. She never wanted to hold our baby, and she started going out late at night and not coming home until early morning. Pretty soon it was days at a time. I thought she was suffering from a little postpartum depression, you know, like Brook Shields, just in her own way. Then one day she was lifting our daughter into a swing and she pulled up her sleeve. That's when I saw the needle marks."

"Oh, my, Travis. What did you say?"

"I told her to get out until she cleaned up her act. I told her it was over, to go to her mother's house."

"And did she?"

"No. Her mom hasn't seen her."

I covered my eyes. "That's scary, like, really scary. Is it heroin?"

"I'm not sure, probably, maybe meth. I'm not sure."

"What are you going to do?"

"What do you mean what am I going to do? She's gone. There is nothing I can do."

"And what if she wants to see your daughter?"

"Then she can see her, as long as she gets tested for drugs first."

"That's smart."

Our conversation ended when the kids came running out of the room, Ben first with Melanie trailing behind him, crying.

I got down on my knees and took her in my arms. "Are you okay? What happened?"

"Ben ran into me and my gun hit my nose."

"You'll be okay. Don't worry, it's not even red,." I said, examining her nose and then planting a kiss on it.

"Benjamin, did you apologize?" Travis yelled out.

He hung his head. "Yes."

"No, he didn't. He didn't apologize, liar!"

"Mom," Ben whined. "You heard me apologize, right?"

I had to change the subject because I couldn't keep a straight face after he just called me mom. He warmed my hearts with his words as I repeated them in my head.

"Why don't we walk back to Travis's house now and take a little break from all the excitement. Maybe jump in the hot tub?" I said.

"Yeah!" They both screamed.

When we got close to Travis's house, the kids decided to race. I had to stop them as soon as I saw someone standing in front of the house.

"Do you see that person? In front of your house?"

Travis squinted his eyes and studied the figure. "Oh, no. It can't be."

"What, what, who is it?"

And then I saw her dark brown hair. "Missy?"

He sprinted over to Missy. I took off behind him, calling out the kids' names.

Both kids turned around and waited for me with worried expressions. "Let's go back down to the bike trail for a little bit."

Although it took a little convincing, we sat down on the huge rocks off the shore and threw pebbles. Waves splashed against the shore and reminded me of Big Sturgeon after boats would go by. My dad and I would climb onto a tube and ride the waves. Sometimes he would even get on the knee board and pretend to surf.

Ben tried jumping rocks. He almost took a tumble, so I made him get off the rocks. We headed up the path in the direction of Canal Park. The wind was a bit chilly, even though it was summer. The lake effect kept it cool by the lake in the summer and much warmer in the winter.

My phone vibrated. Travis told me we could head back to his house now. The kids were curious about what was going on. I told them not to worry, it was an old friend of Travis's. We sent them to the hot tub without us when we got there. Ben promised to keep a close eye on his sister, and we watched them from the window through the closed door so they couldn't hear us.

"How did that go? Was she on drugs?"

He began to pace, his hand rubbing the stubble on his cheek. "Oh, she was high all right. She admitted to using heroin. She asked me for money, and I told her not until she's clean. She continued to argue with me that she was clean and then threatened to take our child."

"What did you say?"

"I told her over my dead body, and I asked her where she was living. She really had no answers for me and kept circling around my questions without answering anything at all. She wasn't happy about you being around, and I didn't tell her my daughter was with her mother. Her mom doesn't want her there, not like this."

"I'm so sorry, Travis. What can I do?"

"I don't know right now."

"Why don't you put on your suit and get in the hot tub with us? It will be relaxing."

He brought out his little plastic boats that were identical to the ones he used to have in his grandparent's Jacuzzi tub growing up. His mom's parents lived in Florida and he would go there to see them every other year. Ben was a little more excited than Melanie about the boats, and he even convinced Travis to let him keep one.

We ended the night playing Monopoly, and although I warned Travis I never lost a good game of Monopoly, he still challenged me.

Melanie asked if Travis could read to her tonight. It wasn't easy to let him take my place, but I agreed. We all snuggled in Travis's king-size bed to listen to him read a few of the books they brought with them until they finally fell asleep, so we snuck out of the room.

I sprawled on the couch, and Travis sat down and picked up my feet. He pulled off my socks and rubbed them while we watched <u>Friends</u>.

I never had a man pick up my feet and start rubbing them without me asking. It was so relaxing. I closed my eyes and moaned.

"Now this I could get used to."

"I'm pretty sure you already agreed to that for life. Speaking of, where is the ring I gave you?"

"It's in my purse."

"Are you having second thoughts?"

"No, no, not at all. I just haven't really told anyone yet."

"Because you aren't sure?"

I got up and sat close to him on the couch, grabbing his hand in mine. "That's not it at all. I'm scared."

"Scared of what?" His eyebrows raised and his lower lip swelled up.

"Scared of losing you again."

He put his arm around me and pulled me in close, our mouths just a whisper away. Our eyes locked and his mouth opened. "You will never lose me."

I jerked my head back. "But Missy is the mother of your child."

"Yes, she's the mother of my child, but she has some things she needs to work through, and one of those things is not me. I never loved her that way. I told you all of this. You just need to trust me."

I looked away, holding my eyes open so the tears wouldn't fall. "I guess I'm just scared."

"Of what?"

"Of losing you again."

He cupped my chin with his thumb and gently turned my head toward him. Our eyes locked. "Gabriella, I love you, and what I did was stupid. I can't force myself to love someone out of convenience."

"I know the feeling."

"Yeah, you do. Take a leap of faith and marry me."

My mouth gravitated to his. Opened-mouthed, he pushed me onto the couch, and I wrapped my legs around him. His lips were warm and wet against mine. My desire grew as the image of him in the hotel that night ran through my head.

"We can't," I whispered. "What if the kids come down?"

"You are absolutely right," he said, jumping off the couch. He picked me up and carried me in his arms. "It's time to use my Jacuzzi tub. You're gonna love the jets."

I giggled and wrapped my arms around him. "Who has a hot tub and a Jacuzzi tub?"

He gave me the stink eye, challenging me.

"You have no idea how much I've missed this."

"Oh, I know. I've never stopped thinking about you. I promise this time is going to be different."

I put my thumb to his lips and ran my fingers around them, taking in every curve before I kissed him.

He stumbled a little bit as he tried and failed to open up the door.

"Let me," I said, reaching out to open it.

"Have you ever made love in a Jacuzzi tub?"

"I refuse to answer that," I said, smiling at the jealous look on his face. "You'll never know."

"You are horrible, you know that?"

I pulled off my clothes while his back was to me as he ran the water in the tub and added bubbles. He turned around and stood there, frozen, exploring every inch of my body with just his eyes.

"Well, aren't you going to get naked? You're making me feel a little shy here."

He pulled his shirt over his head. I stepped into the tub, not taking my eyes off him as he stepped out of his pants.

"Is that better?" he said, pointing to his bare legs.

"You're getting closer, but you still aren't naked yet."

He pulled his pants down past his hip bone, where I could see the indents and treasure trail.

I cleared my throat loudly in response.

"More?" he asked.

"More."

He slowly slid his underwear down, an inch at a time, and then he'd look back up at me with a questioning look.

"Will you just rip the Band-Aid off already and get in here? You are driving me insane."

He turned around, dropped his pants, and flexed one side of his butt, then the other. I turned around and ignored him.

He jumped into the tub with me, splashing me in the face.

"You're no fun, you know that? I think you need a back rub."

"I think you're right," I said as he began rubbing my shoulders.

I started moaning softly.

His kisses started on my neck, gradually working his way up my face and to my lips. His hands explored my body in the water.

"Should we stop just in case the kids--"

"No, don't stop. The door is locked," I pleaded. "I don't want this moment to end."

And he listened.

# NEW BEGINNINGS

"Emily, thank you so much for driving my car all the way to Duluth. I just think it's better for the kids to start school here."

"It's no problem. I hate that you are an hour away from me now, but it gives me a reason to shop in Duluth more, too."

I put the plate in the cupboard while reaching for another clean one out of the dishwasher.

"What are you doing? It's so loud."

"Unloading the dishwasher. Are Matthew and Irene with you?"

"Nope, just me and Irene. Matthew has been putting in a lot of hours at the prison lately."

"I'm so glad he got on there."

"Is that Emily?" Travis asked, slapping my butt from behind as I jumped and hit him in the shoulder.

"Yes, it's Emily," I giggled, shaking my head at him.

"Hi Emily!" he yelled into the phone.

"Sounds like you guys are up to trouble. I'll see you soon. I'm just a couple blocks away."

I hung up the phone and kissed Travis again, biting his lip playfully.

"You be good," I warned him.

"I'm always good. It's just Emily." My ring caught his eye and he reached over to twist it so he could see the diamond. "You are finally wearing it."

"I finally told everyone, so now I can finally wear it."

I heard Erica crying through the baby monitor that was on the counter. "Want me to get her?"

"I got her. You need to watch for Emily."

I went out on the front deck of the mansion, finally feeling deserving of everything this life with Travis was bringing me. I waited and waited until finally Travis came outside.

"Where's Emily?"

"I don't know. She said she was almost here. She probably turned around and went to the mall, knowing her."

I tried calling her three times and there was no answer. Not out of character for Emily.

We put the kids to bed after reading two stories and singing, "Goodnight Sweetheart," to them. Ever since we moved into Travis's home, Ben was finally sleeping through the night without nightmares, and all the kids were sleeping in their own beds.

I became worried after not hearing from Emily at ten. "I'm going to call Matthew," I told Travis, reaching for my phone on the floor in front of me. After he didn't answer either, I left a message. I didn't want to worry my mom, but figured Emily must have gotten distracted and Matthew was probably still working.

"I think Emily is knocking at the door right now," Travis yelled to me from the kitchen.

I breathed a sigh of relief as I answered the door with a smile. My demeanor quickly changed as I saw Missy standing there instead.

"Hi, Gabriella, right? I'm Missy. We met briefly a long time ago."

"Do you want me to get Travis?"

"No...I was wondering if you would talk to me."

I shut the door behind me, standing outside with her. "Are you going to hurt me?" I asked.

"No, no. Listen, I know Travis loves you and you love him. I don't want any trouble. I just want you to know that I love my baby girl, and I'm putting myself into treatment."

I looked behind me. "Why are you telling me this? You hardly know me."

"I know Travis won't listen to me or believe me right now and I just want him to know I'm not disappearing. I'm going to get help. Our daughter deserves better than this, and I want to be a good mom. You see, I didn't have the best upbringing. I ran into your sister-in-law, Emily, at the gas station."

"Emily? I've been worried sick about her."

"Yeah, I stopped to get gas and she opened the door for me, recognizing me from Facebook. She actually told me she stalked me after you and Travis broke up," she said laughing, as she put her hand on my shoulder. "She took me to coffee and one thing led to another, and now she is meeting me here to bring me to treatment tonight."

From behind Missy, I saw headlights as my car pulled up in front of my house. Missy turned around and waved as Emily stepped out of the car.

"Anyway, I have to get going, but I just want you to know how lucky Travis is to be with someone who loves him and our daughter so much. Please, just take care of her, and all I ask is when I get better and you think I'm ready, that you will not let Travis keep her from me."

I crossed my arms as the cold wind off the lake chilled me. "I would never want to take a child away from her mother. You get the help and I know Travis would love for your daughter to see her mother. I can't promise you anything, but I can tell you we both know he only wants what's best for her."

"You're right. Thank you," she said, stepping forward to give me a warm hug. "I'm so sorry about all of this."

"Don't be," I said, smiling back at her. "Get healthy for you and for your baby."

I turned to look at Emily and she waved back at me. I turned around and walked back into the house with a little skip in my step.

It was just like Emily to help another person get help with their chemical dependency issues.

"Was that Emily?" Travis asked, walking toward me as I shut the door.

"And Missy."

"Missy?" he repeated, staring at me with a very confused look."

"Yeah, it surprised me too. Emily ran into her and talked her into going to treatment."

"Really? How'd she do that?"

"I don't know. She did the same for Matthew. All I know is her parent had problems with drugs and alcohol and Emily has a way of helping people understand they need help."

"It's crazy that she never got hooked on drugs, growing up in that kind of household."

"I know. She's made it her life's mission to stop others from going through what she had to go through. I know there are many more she's helped."

"Have I told you I love your family?" he said, kissing my neck.

"I'm not sure you have."

"Well, I do. If she gets help and stays sober, Erica may actually be able to have a healthy relationship with her mother."

I clasped my hands around his neck. "Is this what life with you is going to be like?"

He gazed into my eyes and playfully bit my lip. "Fate brought us together three times now.

I grinned at him. "Well, there's no fighting fate."

#

# CHRISTMAS MORNING

"Mommy, Mommy, wake up, wake up. It's Christmas morning," Melanie said, jumping on top of Travis and me in bed.

I jumped up, with Travis close behind.

"Where's Ben?" I asked, looking around as we came down the stairs. I turned on the light at the bottom of the stairs to find Ben under the Christmas tree, a brand-new blue hat on his head, multiple toys in his lap.

"Santa didn't even wrap them. Look at all of these new toys," Ben said to Melanie.

Melanie made her way to the Barbies, hair bows, Baby Alive doll, board games, and suckers. She just stared at them and didn't say one word.

"Is everything okay?" I asked her, kneeling beside her. I realized she was crying.

"What's wrong, Melanie? Didn't Santa bring you what you asked for?" Travis said.

She nodded. "He brought me everything I could ever ask for."

Travis came closer. "Then why are you so sad?"

She wrapped her arms around him. "Because I wish my mommy could see all the presents I got. I think Santa brought me all the presents he made me since I was little. I think he just couldn't find me before."

"You think so?" I asked, exchanging glances with Travis.

"Oh, I know so."

I pulled her off of Travis and looked into her sweet innocent eyes. I ran my hands through her short hair, thinking about her long blonde hair she had before the cancer treatments.

"I'll tell you what. Why don't we write your mommy and daddy a letter and send it in the mail to wish them a Merry Christmas."

Ben stood up, dropping the toys that were in his arms and making his way to us. "You wouldn't mind?"

"We wouldn't mind at all," I said, smiling at Travis. He nodded in return. "Maybe when Mommy and Daddy get better, we can go visit them."

"Yeah," they both yelled out with smiles.

"We do need to make them a card before New Year's," Travis said, trying to keep a straight face.

"Why is that?" Ben asked.

Travis got up and went into the kitchen. We heard rattling of the cupboards and then he came back with a big gift with their names on it. "This present is for our three children," he said, putting it in between Melanie and Ben to open. I looked at him curiously, unsure of what was inside.

Ben lifted the top and Melanie squealed with excitement as she put the Minnie Mouse ears on. Ben put on the Mickey ears too as they continued to dig for more.

"What's this?" Melanie asked, pulling out paper pamphlets.

I grabbed them from her and read them. "They are plane tickets out of the Duluth airport to Orlando. We are going to Disney World!" I yelled, picking up Melanie and squeezing her.

"Disney World? Is it true?" Ben cried out. He pulled out multiple plastic bracelets from the box. "What are these for, Travis?"

"They are wristbands to get into the gates at Disney. We are leaving on New Year's Eve," Travis said.

"The five of us?" Ben asked.

"Not just the five of us. Grandma Destiny is coming and so is Emily, Matthew, Irene, Uncle Mike and Aunt Jillian, Uncle Phillip, and Missy."

We all screamed while Travis covered his ears. We started piling up on him, tackling him to the ground. Travis started tickling anyone he came in contact with. We were all red-faced and excited at the news.

Melanie turned to Ben, her finger inches from his face. "I told you Santa was real. I told you."

The kids ran upstairs to play, leaving a big mess on the floor I was not going to pay attention to right now. Travis put his arms around me.

"Wow, you are good at gift giving," I said. "How did you plan all of this with my family without me finding out?"

"You'll never know my tricks," he said, kissing me on the nose.

"And for you to invite Missy after everything she's been through. I'm so proud of you."

"I did make sure her room was on the other side of the hotel."

I shook my head. "I still can't believe they are all coming. This is going to be so amazing."

"Well, they had no choice when I told them that it was also our surprise wedding."

I covered my face with both hands, jumping up and down as if I was on a pogo sticklike a child who ate a whole plate of Christmas cookies. "You have to be kidding me!"

"How do you feel about a Cinderella-themed wedding on New Year's Day?"

"I feel like I have less than a week to get a dress!"

"You can call Emily and see if she wants to go looking tomorrow with you."

"It sounds like I'm missing time by not calling her yet. I just need you to do one thing before I call her. "

"What's that?" hHe asked, looking a little skeptical.

"Promise me you'll invite your mom and dad. It's time to forgive them. It doesn't mean you have to forget what they did, but do it for Erica--the kids. Do it for you."

"I think you're right. You truly are selfless and bring out the best in me, you know that?"

"Well, our kids need to get to know all of their grandparents, and we need to teach them to forgive. As my mom always says, you need to forgive to let go of the anger."

"Let's celebrate tonight, after the kids go to bed. How about a hot bubble bath, a back rub, and some champagne?"

Perfect timing. "I'd love to, but I'm not supposed to drink while I'm pregnant."

This time he was the one to scream. "What--how long have you known? Since when?"

"I found out last night before bed. I was waiting until tonight to tell you. I think I'm six weeks pregnant."

Travis picked me up and spun me around, stopping in mid-air and setting me down. "Oh, no, did I just crush the baby?"

I laughed, "No, you didn't crush the baby. I didn't think I was able to have kids and here I am having your baby. It was almost like it couldn't happen until it was meant to be."

"I love the way you think."

I picked up the Mickey Mouse ears and placed them on his head. He then reached down and picked up the Minnie Mouse ears and put them on mine.

"How about we announce our baby right after our wedding?"

"I think it's going to be hard for you to keep a secret that long," he teased.

"You're right. I will at least have to tell my mom."

Travis dimmed the lights and turned on "Tomorrow" from his iPhone and it blared through his Bluetooth speaker. We began to sing as loud as we could to get the children's attention. Melanie came running down the stairs dancing, and Ben came down with Erica in his arms. We smiled and danced most of the morning. All I could think about was that coincidence and fate brought every one of us together as a family.

Travis spun me around and then dipped me. He looked into my eyes and said, "Anyone who doesn't believe in miracles hasn't heard our story." And then he kissed me.

www.ingramcontent.com/pod-product-compliance
Lightning Source LLC
Chambersburg PA
CBHW072235170626
46813CB00003B/1230